ONCE UPON A TIME IN LA

A ROCK AND ROLL NOIR NOVEL

HOWARD PAAR

First Edition

MUSIC MILITANT NOIR BOOKS

Printed in the United States of America

ISBN 978-0578882949

cover photos © Mona Kuhn
photo of the author by Christiana D'Amore

To all the Los Angeles record men and women who were
lucky enough to work here in these times.
It was fun; right?

in memory of Sam

find the soundtrack to this book
by going to bit.ly/oncesnd

PLAY LOUD

CHAPTER 1
1998

Jacqueline Harper blazed out the front door of her family home, kids Amy and George—eight and ten years old respectively—followed in her wake, not unused to sudden dramatic changes of plan with their mother. She drove her white Volvo station wagon erratically, west into the middle of Hollywood frequently glancing down at the ten grand in hundred dollar bills she'd dropped in her lap. She turned off Franklin south on Cahuenga towards the drop spot. She was already more scared than at any point in her life but somehow seeing the sleazy old Greyhound bus station almost petrified her. She got out of the car locking the kids in and forced herself through the chrome and glass double doors into the Grape Vine Bar. The Raspberries "Rose Coloured Glasses" came softly out of the jukebox for the afternoon drinkers. Although she knew she just had to find the locker number that bitch had given her and this could all go away again, the overwhelming sense and stench of the 1970s was too much. She steadied herself against the grimy nicotine ravaged wall trying not to throw up and cursed James Dual. Then she ran for her life.

James Dual was becoming increasingly absorbed—some might say obsessed—with avoiding the clichés that seemed to riddle his life. It was one of those February days in Los Angeles, Malibu to be specific, that anyone who'd grown up with real winters should cherish. In this respect, James, who was born and raised in London, was no different. The hot, dry Santa Ana winds blew across the Pacific Coast Highway and through the window of his clichéd black BMW.

He glanced down at the flashing call sign on the inevitable car phone and ignored it. To most people, this would be insignificant, but to James, whose obsession with the phone had led his last girlfriend to offer to have one surgically implanted for a Christmas present, it was worthy of note. Instead of answering, he pushed in a cassette and felt a twinge of guilt as "Cheat" rang out at earsplitting volume because he liked to pride himself on a relentless resistance to nostalgia, but some days only The Clash would do.

He continued down the highway at a fairly measured speed, only slightly above the limit. As on any day of the week, he'd already passed two drivers who were contributing new funds to the California Highway Patrol's burgeoning cottage industry: speed traps. Traffic slowed as he neared Topanga Canyon, which was dense with the influx of commuters from the Valley who used the winding old canyon road as a shortcut to the west side and Santa Monica area whenever the 101 Freeway was backed up, which was virtually always. He looked across at the 1930s Hearst-built Topanga Ranch Motel, its dilapidated orange and white-walled tin roof shacks so inviting somehow.

Despite only having lived in Malibu for a few years, James had already adopted an exclusionary "locals only" attitude, which was irked by Valley people who clogged his highway with their crap SUVs. Instead of continuing on to his Ocean Avenue office in Santa Monica, he turned left onto the beginning of Sunset Boulevard. He was on the winding, well-banked venerable old road, headed for record producer Don Was's Benedict Canyon home, due to a call from an old friend who was working for author Elmore Leonard. Leonard was in Los Angeles to research a new novel to be set among the music industry. Leonard had expressed an interest in being at a recording session and who in their right minds wouldn't want to see him formulate? So James had arranged for him to visit Bon Jovi guitarist Richie Sambora, who was working on a new record with Was. Combining the odd cast of characters had appealed to James.

He found his way onto the garden patio that led into the studio part of Was's home and settled into one of the nicely baking blue and white striped deck chairs alongside the producer and guitarist. Richie was a rarity in that he was entirely happy and comfortable with his success and acknowledged the luck involved in the process. He wore a near constant smile. Leonard arrived, and the conversation covered the modern realities of major record companies shrinking from six to five corporate owners who reported to shareholders quarterly resulting in quick, throwaway hits, no artist development, etc. James laughing opined that the music industry had historically been its own worst enemy by not controlling the biggest promotional vehicles from MTV all the way back to the early days of radio. Leonard asked about the Internet mentioning that the first MP3 player was coming out next month. There were rueful smiles all round, the consensus being that lack of trust between the majors would ensure things would get fucked up somehow. They were interrupted several times by Was's assistant telling him that Mick Jagger was on the phone. It was open to conjecture whether this was done for effect or not, but the producer refused to take the call each time. The afternoon drifted away, with everyone getting a little bit of what they wanted. Except, apparently, Mick Jagger.

James offered Leonard a ride back to his hotel, more out of the hope of getting further career anecdotes than any thought that he really needed a lift. As it was, Leonard and Richie had both limo'd to the studio, so the three left in James's four-door, with the guitar player riding shotgun. He and James gave each other these looks as every time they tried to turn the conversation to Leonard's novel, he answered with more music queries. Richie obliged with good tales. The most defining one to James was Richie's reflection on waking up in bed, rolling over, and realizing he was in Malibu with Cher lying next to him, and figured his life was pretty much made. James was basically appalled by Cher, but he did understand most aspects of the dream when he heard or saw it. It was on the knife-edge of these clichés that he was all too concerned he existed. It had been a few years since he had lived in Hollywood, just long enough that he had started to forget the reasons he left.

With Mulholland now behind them, they turned onto Coldwater Canyon. James glanced out the window as the street numbers descended like years going by—1990, 1980, 1972, 1970—and reflected how much he liked losing all sense of time, not to mention reality, this way. Richie was meeting his manager for a drink and Leonard seemed happy enough to be talked into joining them. They ended up at Dominick's, this old joint at Beverly and Robertson, on the edge of Beverly Hills and West Hollywood. It had been around in various incarnations since 1948. James had seen Swifty Lazar there, the legendary agent, and Bob Hope, in the last days of their lives, and whatever reinventions it went through, had always liked its survival instincts. These days you'd get a variety of diners and drinkers who would be appreciative of the history and keen to emulate the exploits and attitudes of the past.

Leonard was conversational but clearly observed more than talked to his companions. It was almost a perfect evening when James spotted Terry Harper. No big surprise to see him, but definitely a decision whether to go to the bar. Old habits ruled, and they greeted each other warmly. Now, these two had known each other twenty years or so, going back to when James, only three months off the boat, had been hired by Terry to an A&R staff position at Real Records. James wanted to keep it brief, mainly to make the most of his time with the author, but he also realized Terry's presence might lead to reflections he didn't want to look at.

Terry, obviously surprised, said, "You're a bit far east, eh?"

"You're right. You know what though? It's a nice change. Even though I'm virtually a tourist here these days," James replied.

Terry nodded.

"You out to see a few bands tonight?" James knew the answer already and figured they might well have a girl vocalist among them, if history was any judge.

"Of course."

Now this wasn't to demean Terry in any way, as he was actually a rarity in many respects and fairly fearless in his beliefs, but James was aware of his clichés, too. The record industry was one that, from certain perspectives, was always in trouble. On top of that, a lot of people in it were overly nostalgic about the good old days, forgetting that most companies, including the golden era of Warner Records, always dealt with some corporate parent who thought it worked like selling Coke, or for that matter, shoes. So when you threw people who just loved music, naively and passionately, into those companies, a lot of bad things could happen.

On the other hand, as James had always been keenly aware, there was a disproportionate amount of self-serving shoe salesmen. So anyway, they slipped into easy common ground, and talked about the Raiders and their fondness for when LA had had a football team. James was way more happy with this, although he sensed that Terry was pretty drunk, and perhaps felt a need to go a little deeper into their history. James steered the conversation towards Bill King and Rich Marottas's classic commentaries, reminisced about Howie Long getting into it on the field against the New England Patriots and then going after their GM on the sidelines afterwards. They had both moved to Los Angeles from England before the Raiders' early days in town and had felt an immigrant's connection when the team arrived on the lam from Oakland. Not to mention, that for James, having grown up standing on the terraces at the Stretford End in Manchester watching United, walking down the streets to the Coliseum with the Raiders fans made him feel very much at home. The potential for mayhem with visiting supporters, be they from Pittsburgh or from Liverpool, was very, very similar.

The bar filled up as the crowd moved from diners to drinkers. James glanced across the room to Leonard, Richie, and his manager, who'd been joined by a couple of barfly girls. He couldn't see whether that was being welcomed, but he felt he could comfortably leave them for a while.

Terry shook the ice in his glass. "So are you happy living in Malibu?"

"Yeah," said James. "You know, I was down in Hollywood on Formosa at Warner's lot the other day and the neighborhood hadn't changed so much, which was reassuring, given how for a minute it looked like all Hollywood was gonna get remodeled. Mini-malls a specialty, right?"

"Yeah." Terry grinned but the truth was he still spent more time than he cared to around Hollywood streets, from one club to another, so he didn't quite have the fondness James appeared to have for their old haunts.

"So you want to actually come see a band?" Terry expected a

no, but James agreed, figuring Leonard would come for homework's sake, though he was probably done for the night and too gracious to push for an early exit. James wandered over and found the author amused, but ready to leave. He agreed to come. They bid goodbye to Richie and left in Terry's car. Scarily to James, he had an SUV, but given he had two kids, he got a semi-pass from James's obsessive hatred of the vehicles. Certainly, not a full pass, because he didn't live in a canyon or really need a four-wheel drive. Just to be clear, in reality James had more issue with the way they blocked his driver's view than he did with the pollution aspects.

Leonard was now asking about new bands that would no doubt get sprinkled into his next book. James had always been impressed with that aspect of his writing, being caught off guard years ago when Iggy Pop was casually mentioned in one. The only thing he mused on when he first read Leonard was how stupid many of his protagonists were. James would be lured into thinking they were smarter than they were for two hundred pages and then be shown that a lot of crooks are dumb.

Terry had taken Beverly Boulevard east, headed past the upmarket boutiques, antiques shops, and an increasing number of dog joints. Now a lot of people might use these dog parlors as a basis for another LA joke, but James found them endearing in a crazy-old-lady kind of way. He was definitely a believer in the man's best friend and all that, but somehow would have been unlikely to bring Highsmith, the Springer Spaniel puppy he had recently rescued, to any of them.

They cut up La Brea and went east on Santa Monica Boulevard, a dingy, semi-sleazy stretch. They all peered out, and tried to spot the Dragonfly entrance on the poorly lit block, which was made easier by the incongruous sight of valet parkers. There was a sprinkling of glam rockers who waited to get in—young, not 80s left overs; they'd mostly let their hair be mercifully straight. Apart from the lack of actual glitter, they looked closer to original 70s glam rock kids, James noted happily. Leonard skipped out, astutely pushing some high-tech, form-fitting earplugs in as he did so. Not for the first time, James hoped that he could be anything like as sharp at seventy or so as this guy evidently was.

The usual fat, surly doormen—think any rock club, anytime, anywhere—begrudgingly acknowledged that Terry was on some list or other and they advanced into the gloom. "Personality Crisis" by the New York Dolls blasted out of the PA at live band-like levels and reduced their alcohol decisions to sign language. Terry got stuck into another Scotch, James a Rolling Rock, and Leonard a ginger ale. The bar ran along the right-hand wall of the club and was pretty busy for a weeknight. A band was setting up on the smallish stage in the center of the room. Terry led the way through the club to an outdoor patio that was already full, mainly because you could smoke out there, James figured.

Lou Reed's "Vicious" played as the author told his drinking companions he was going to visit Ron Deutch and Gary Kalusian, a pair of the most sleazy, corrupt, and successful radio promotion men of the modern era.

"Well, if they're even halfway honest, they'll give you some incredible quotes. Good character study stuff." James didn't like the faraway look on Terry's face that appeared at the mention of these guys from both of their pasts.

"How's Jacqueline?" He hoped to get his old friend away from reflections of the past that would do neither of them any good to revisit.

"Uh, not so great, actually," Terry slurred. "She and the kids have gone away for a break."

That didn't sound good to James, considering it was the middle of the school term. He wished he hadn't gone there, but not easily able to change the subject again, he asked what was the trouble.

"Her nerves have been really bad and she's just sick of being anywhere near the record business. She'd been okay. Having George and Amy has been so great for her—well, for both of us—but they are at school fulltime now, and for the last few months, she's been really morose."

Fortunately, Terry saw a black leather-clad girl stride by him. She looked almost a dead ringer for Joan Jett, but was about twenty, had a softer expression, although the glimpse James caught of her eyes meant she could be a thousand years old. Some staggeringly loud punchy guitar riffs reverberated from within and it was obvious this was who they were here to see.

Terry snapped to. "Look, why don't you come over to the house later and stay? You can drink and I'll take you back to get your car from Dominick's in the morning. It would really help."

James semi-reluctantly agreed and then all conversation ended for forty-five minutes of truly cathartic rock. The room was shoulder to shoulder now and it felt like the beginnings of a scene, something LA hadn't had for a long time. The crowd was unabashedly into it. James was amazed how instantly he connected to the songs. The four-piece was solid; the classic long black hair death head's guitar player was obviously tempted to guitar solo every other minute but kept himself reined in. He hit Mick Ronson-like guitar riffs that were timeless but fresh sounding. The singer didn't move much but James bet that somehow everyone in the audience thought she sang directly to them. She sounded somewhere between

Axl Rose and Angus, if they had been girls. She looked happy to be there, no bad girl affectations, but those eyes and that wrecked-from-hell voice made her somehow soulful but cold and dangerous too. They finished with an anthemic song called "Cool As Fuck."

James saw a few junior A&R guys beelining towards the side of the stage. Terry slipped through the crowd with James and Leonard in tow and introduced them to the band. James thought the singer said her name was Katrina. Hard to tell 'cause her voice was almost gone. He figured she had never taken singing lessons and was probably raw after each show. A quick exchange of cards and scrawled numbers on bar paper—apparently they didn't have a manager—and the three headed out, while Bowie's "Rock 'n Roll Suicide" lowered the volume over the sound system.

The valet took forever, as usual, and James was conscious of that pervasive, bad aftershave smell most cars had post-valet, as he got in the back.

"So, Terry, would you sign them?" asked Elmore.

"Mmmm, perhaps. They have good songs but there's not much radio for them in this day and age, so it would have to be the right kind of deal."

Meaning horrible, and next to no up-front for the band, James thought.

"What about all your junior competitors? Worried someone'll convince their boss and swoop in quick?" asked the author.

"No, they're all scared of losing their jobs, so they don't want to push for an offer until someone else has. That way, if the band tanks they have an excuse." Terry was more animated now, energized by the performance. "Besides, they may not have a manager, but I bet there's a lawyer somewhere in the mix. If someone makes an offer, I'll hear from them 'cause they'll want to see if they can get a little bidding war going."

They had gone north to Sunset and headed west to drop Leonard at the Chateau Marmont, a little tatty but iconic 1920s hotel.

"So, Elmore, it's been genius getting to see you in action," said James.

Leonard smiled. "Thanks for taking some time with me. Terry, can I come to your office and get your take on the modern business realities from the record label side one day before I head back to Detroit?"

"Yes, of course." Terry agreed but sounded miles away again.

They let the author out at the low slung garage entrance where he could take the elevator directly up to the lobby. Terry reversed back out at the side of the hotel and ill-advisedly U-turned back east onto Sunset. James flinched, but didn't say anything. Traffic was light and they soon passed through Silver Lake, which appeared semi-gentrified since James had last seen it—probably a decade ago, he realized with surprise. A few minutes later, they pulled into a carriage sweep driveway at the decent-sized 1940s Los Feliz home that Terry and Jacqueline shared with their kids.

Inside, the rooms had high ceilings, and were smartly appointed, but the detritus of two kids scattered everywhere offset what might otherwise have been a slightly sterile feel. They walked through the living room and down a corridor and turned in to the kitchen which had a big, cozy, wooden country-style, benched breakfast nook littered with coloring books and other art paraphernalia. He pulled a bottle of Scotch from one of the wooden cupboards that surrounded the room and pointed to the fridge. "You still on beer?"

"Yeah. Thanks." James grabbed a Red Stripe.

"Let's go through here." Terry motioned to a door on the far side of the kitchen that led them to an office/den that was covered on two walls with CD shelves. Otherwise it was fairly sparse, other than a desk and a nicely worn-in black leather couch that faced a large TV. Terry put an old Graham Parker and the Rumour CD on and they flopped down on opposite ends of the couch. "James, I don't know what the odds were of running into you tonight and I'm not a big believer in signs and all that bollocks, but I am for once going to take something as an omen."

"Look, Terry, if you're leading up to something, let's leave the past we don't want where it is, okay?"

Terry shook his head gently. "Everything I told you about Jacqueline earlier is true, but there's something else. She got a phone call here at the house the other day. I was at the office. She called me, hysterical, screaming she knew something like this would happen one day, that she should never have married me with the history we share. That she still hated your guts for being such a stupid punk and ruining everything. She was terrified. Said someone was demanding money but she was too unhinged to get much else out of her except that she was taking the kids, maybe to Mexico, but it would be better if I didn't know where. That I'd better sort this shit out, and she was gone by the time I raced home."

James sat and nervously waited for him to finish.

"I found she'd taken $20K out of our account but so far nothing's showing up on our credit cards. James, I know she's shunned you for a long time but she had a reason for that and you were friends once. She—we—need your help now."

"Why don't you go to the law?" said James.

"I can't risk the authorities' involvement. Her bouts of depression have had her close to being institutionalized more than once. Running off with the kids during school term could be the end for her. Help me find her. You know what it must be about if she's blaming you."

"If that's true and some blackmailers opened that Pandora's box, finding her won't be the end of it," said James grimly.

"More reason why it's in your interest to help try to get to the bottom of this."

"I'm no private eye, Terry."

"Maybe not, but I know you got involved with that murder and missing person case back in your club days, so you have some experience."

"Fuck, that was a long time ago and I had no choice."

"You really think you can just walk away from this now? Besides, do you want someone else poking around that part of your history?" asked Terry morosely.

James took his cue. "Let me sleep on it."

Terry led him to a bedroom that he guessed was the kids' empty room. A scattering of toys and books lay on the floor between the twin beds. A small chest of drawers sat against the far wall, TV on top, and a connected bathroom.

"Oh, James, thanks. I know this is fucked up for you, too."

"Yeah, yeah. G'night."

As he pulled back the duvet on the bed nearest the window, he uncovered a well-worn bear that he guessed would never have been left behind if someone wasn't in a blinding rush.

James took a last gulp of the Red Stripe and reflected that he'd begun the day dreaming of breaking free from the constant clichés of his life. Yet here he was, thrust into something mystifying and potentially dangerous, and he wanted no part of it. Be extremely careful what you wish for, huh?

He had always loved those sequences in noir films where

the private eye gets drugged or coshed and you got that fall into the pit of darkness and confusion with echoing voices and nightmarish, distorted visuals. He got his version in dreams tonight, starting outside a big house, its 1978 sign pointing down Coldwater Canyon to arrive at the last of the sunny, happy-face 70s, bringing an amphetamine sulphate-and-Scotch attitude to a Quaalude-and-white wine city. It was always going to lead to trouble.

He saw fragments of street life: Two-drink minimums at Dino's. Telling the old-time mob guys who worked the door for aging lush Dean Martin it was insulting to think he would want only two drinks. Then into trendy faux Mexican Carlos N Charlie's for his first margarita, which in the dream was as big as he was. Stepping out onto what he thought was grass but was actually Astroturf. Stumbling off the Sunset Strip, frustrated there really was no number 77, the TV address where the private eye firm of Bailey & Spenser had left its indelible mark on his five-year-old mind. He heard an echoed version of the *77 Sunset Strip* theme, with its cool finger snaps, as he drifted down Holloway and into beer joint Barney's Beanery. The ex-cop owner, voluminous gut hanging over his belt and hateful visage reflected through a fun house mirror behind the bar, was yelling something unintelligible at bartender Eddie Money. Along the bar Jim Morrison had once pissed on, hundreds of different beers were hurtling towards James but none was the one he wanted. He threw the huge container of red matchbooks at the ex-pig and yelled, "Get some Kronenbourg beer before I come back, you cunt."

As he turned on his heel and left, he was sure he was going to get shot in the back. He took refuge a few doors down at the hallucinogenic Yellow Submarine Café, which was shaped like one. Punching in Kraftwerk's "The Model" ten times on the jukebox to fuck with the bikers who'd been doing the same with the Doobie Brothers.

Skating a lot because no one knew what to make of this skinny, spiky-haired little fucker with a big mouth. Didn't hurt that English accents were still a bit of a novelty, of course. He felt blind drunk in the dream, as if he couldn't see straight or where he was going.

CHAPTER 2

James woke from a fitful night, flashback dreams surprisingly intact, given that he rarely remembered them. The lingering image was of Jacqueline soon after she became an assistant at Real Records, still dressing like the prim and proper Illinois-raised girl that she was. Her brown eyes, blonde hair, and farm girl figure must have been Terry's idea of the American dream, he mused. Couldn't have been her love of cheesy rock bands like Foreigner, that's for sure.

He dragged himself into the shower for a while, and then dressed in yesterday's Levi's and found a plain black T-shirt among Terry's drawer full of primarily band promo shirts. They were both still pretty skinny, so small worked. He found a note from Terry in the kitchen with the number of his car service. Forty-five minutes later, James was in his BMW just in time to avoid a ticket from the weekly street cleaners. As he turned the ignition, he was reminded of his inner war against clichés as the car symbolized the exact kind of person he didn't want to be perceived as. He'd also decided he had to learn to cook after travels to Jamaica and Italy had inspired him to give up the eating out every night in LA cliché.

It was 11:00 a.m., about the only time of day you could get across the city easily, so he was soon in Santa Monica, headed to 1333 Ocean Avenue, the small converted house where he had kept his office for the past eight years. The tiny parking lot was in the alley behind the building. The building itself was two stories, historically preserved and Victorian to boot, a source of some concern to James, who had a deep-seated dislike of all things Victorian. He pretended to find the surprising fact that anything was being preserved in LA encouraging and left the minor detail of its origin aside.

The ground floor, whose entrance faced the street, was occupied by an old-school law practice. James's second-floor offices were reached by a white wooden staircase at the back of the house. The garden, which was surrounded by an ornate but unkempt swimming pool area, also held half a dozen or so white one- or two-room cabin/ bungalows that were occupied on an ever-changing basis by artists, hustling film producers on their way up or down, and the occasional masseuse. His latest assistant, Lainey, sat at the white L-shaped desk that half faced the door. Blonde, aquiline-faced, usually with a fairly quizzical, amused expression on her face, she was from the Pacific Northwest. James could never remember whether it was Portland or Seattle. What stuck in his mind was that she preferred the weather up there, which was so far the only serious philosophical disagreement they'd had in the nine months she'd worked for him. Although a little offhand with people indiscriminately, James had so far let it pass, for it somewhat reminded him of how diplomatic he had become in recent years—something he felt he needed to do something about.

She gave him a list of the disparate calls he'd missed yesterday that reflected the various ways he made money: music supervising for films and representing music licensing to film and TV, a growing business that he thoroughly enjoyed. He nodded thanks and went through to his pool-facing office and its goofy turquoise Jetsons-ish desk. He ignored the call sheets, and pulled cards from an old Rolodex to look for anyone who might still be in touch with Jacqueline. No one he reached had heard from her in a long while, though.

He made a few more calls to deal with the most pressing business. He worked with mostly independent filmmakers, helped them find and license cool songs for their films for the money they didn't have which had been the best fun he'd had in years. Oddly, for all of its mirrors with the music industry, most of the film people he now dealt with actually still loved music, and the discovery of new artists excited them instead of scared them.

Trying to refocus on Jacquie, he walked to the front of the house which had high, vaulted, white wooden ceilings and a huge bay window that looked out at the Pacific Ocean across the road. A couple of Deco-ish stuffed, blue couches faced each other. The right wall had a big monitor and a rack of audio-visual equipment James used to try music to picture. It was a perfect room to meet, but its one drawback was that it was often tough to get visitors to leave, especially when the sun was about to drop a perfect sunset across their line of vision—which was about to occur now, and he'd gotten nowhere. He decided he'd have time for dinner in Malibu and then would be back in order to let his Springer Spaniel sidekick out later that night. The cliché that Englishmen showed more love and affection to their dogs than anyone else was the only one he embraced and saw no reason to change.

He called Granita, booked a table with the longtime host Loretta, and asked whether Denny Golden was booked in.

James would usually have gone out of his way not to see his old boss at Real, but a day of getting nowhere with finding Jacqueline had made him curious to check the label mogul's temperature. She came back on.

"He has a reservation at eight for six people. Do you still want your table?" She chuckled. James and Denny's mutual distaste was well known.

There were several "non-tourist" restaurants in Malibu, but Denny kept a high profile so it was an even bet that if he was in town, he'd either have been at Granita or Bambu. Allegria was just great for Italian cuisine, but not showy enough, and the beachside restaurants were mostly about paying for the view and an oversized and overpriced slab of fish.

Nonetheless, James felt a slight surge of adrenaline that he'd one decent deduction today. He called Terry, who sounded calm enough. "I've made a few calls but gotten nowhere. The thing is, if this really has anything to do with our illustrious past, Denny and old Real people are really the key, right? Obviously, this thing with Jacquie doesn't seem like his style, but it could be interesting to see how he reacts to seeing us together."

"Oh, James, it seems pointless. He's too shrewd to tell us a damn thing and, like you said, it's not his style."

"There is a chance he's been approached. Look, what do we have to lose? We'll have a good dinner, right? Just keep it together and we'll see what happens."

"Me keep it together, James? You are joking, right?"

James laughed. "Whatever. Just be there, okay?" He hung up.

After going over some of tomorrow's business with Lainey, he retrieved his car and headed north a couple of blocks and turned down the California Incline onto PCH once again. The drive was easy. He turned onto Webb Way. The huge lot had once housed a lot of dirt and the Colony Coffee Shop, a long-gone local diner. Now it was an outdoor mall of sorts with a handful of high-priced boutiques, but also the more mundane Sav-On Drugs and a large Ralphs supermarket. Just before all this was Wolfgang Puck's Granita, incongruously located off a parking lot. Designed and run by the master chef's wife, it had been dubbed an aquatic nightmare in one early review. However, James had always had a kind of fondness for the wacky décor, feeling somewhat like he was in a Sub-Mariner comic or an episode of the old Supermarionation show, *Stingray*.

He walked into the expensive space and gave Loretta a quick hug, who was already stationed just inside the door at her reservation table.

"You're early, James. Do you want to sit or wait at the bar?"

"Bar sounds good, thanks." He glanced over to the right side of the restaurant. The bar was raised slightly and had a good vantage point to see the whole space, other than the open kitchen located against the back wall. Two Malibu mother types sat at the near end of the bar. He hated the expression "soccer moms" but in their super-expensive, Malibu casual way, that was as good a description as any. He drifted past them to the far end of the bar. He ordered a bottle of St. Emilion, as he wasn't as keen on the California reds (that were available by the glass) as everyone else seemed to be these days.

He felt a presence behind him and turned to see a tall blonde grinning down at him. At first glance, she looked rather like Cate Blanchett, but on closer inspection, and James was definitely doing that, he realized she was toned in a much more athletic way and her green eyes had a playful glint to them. She eyed the bottle. "Drinking alone? Don't you know that's the first sign of a problem?"

"Actually, I'm way past the first sign."

"Mmmm. Maybe you are a lost cause. It had crossed my mind for a second that I might be able to help."

"Would you have a glass while you evaluate me?"

"Yes, I think that could be helpful."

James motioned to the bartender for a second glass. She swung her long legs onto the bar stool. She wore skate punk clothes, which were definitely incongruous for Granita, but there was an elegant air about her that transcended any mode of dress. She took a drink from the quickly provided glass and looked James long and hard in the eyes. "So where do you think this all started?"

James was happy to play along. "Well, I grew up in England and we tend to start a lot of things early there."

"So gulping sherry, port, or whatever out of the bottle at twelve or thirteen when your parents weren't looking?"

James leaned back, only partly feigning surprise. "Close. You English too?"

"No, Canadian. Toronto. But my mother's Scottish."

"Oh, Scotch in your case then?"

"Close enough. So what other early things do you English do?"

James, not taking the obvious bait for now, said, "Uh, leave school at sixteen."

She laughed huskily at this. "You know, I wasn't far behind you. Was it your choice?"

James paused. "Somewhat mutual. I'd been suspended for punching my math teacher. The headmaster had got it into his head I was a drug dealer, which was not true although I can sort of see where he got the notion. It felt like time to start working. You?"

"Oh stuff. I loved the sports, swimming, climbing, but I didn't have friends, really. All the girls thought I wanted to steal their pathetic boyfriends…a million things. I ended up an outsider without even trying."

James sensed there was more. Her mouth had hardened slightly, as if she put a tough exterior in place, the way she probably had as she walked the school yard every day. She smiled ruefully. "Then the cliché, unfortunately. Acting. First Canada, now here."

James was slightly disappointed. "You know, maybe I'm the one who needs to help you. I've got a big head start on clichés. In fact, I've been devoting quite a bit of thought to the problem."

She smiled broadly at this. She had a really big mouth, but somehow it was perfect for her.

At that moment, the unmistakable, whiny, nasal voice of Denny Golden echoed across the still half-empty restaurant. "Loretta, there'll be more of us than I thought. Figure it out, sweetheart." He was quite tall, probably six two, but the pear-shaped body and the fact that he was very out of shape made him look shorter. He tended to wear pastels: a pink business shirt tonight under what looked like a Savile Row tweed jacket. His pants were brown corduroy and the shoes scuffed, but very expensive. In his wake were what James supposed were a couple of Olympian execs who flanked the rock band from last night's Dragonfly show. Coming at the rear were the promotion king Ron Deutch and Eric Brody, lawyer and one of Denny's best friends. James shook his head ruefully, thinking that this probably very excited band was being set up with a lawyer whose conflict of interest would be enormous. Not that that didn't happen pretty much all the time in this town. The blonde slipped off the stool with a quick, "There's my party. See you later, Doctor. Good luck with your clichés."

"Yeah, you too, Doctor." James realized with a sinking, sad feeling that surprised him that she was joining Denny's party. She sat down next to one of the execs, a woman about the same age who wore a sharp Prada-looking suit. James guessed publicity. The marketing people tended to look a little more conservative these days. If Denny was in sign-the-band mode, a good vocal publicist was always a help to start the dreams. He wanted to watch, but couldn't hear the conversation from where he was, so he turned disgustedly back to face the bar and poured another drink.

Terry arrived half an hour late, blamed the traffic on the 101 and then complained about rocks lying on Malibu Canyon, and how can you live out here, etc. Truth was, James remembered, he was always late. The hostess came and brought them to a booth a discreet distance from but within earshot of Denny's round table. It quickly occurred to them that this also meant that should anyone at Denny's table take an interest, they could also eavesdrop.

"Jesus, James, some private eye you'd make." Terry gently mocked his old friend.

"Look, we'll just keep the conversation light and maybe, just maybe, hear something useful. In the meantime, are you doing all right?"

Terry nodded. "Yeah, I'm hanging in. I hate to admit it but I'm glad I talked to you, and I appreciate your trying to help me even though you don't know what you're doing."

The menus arrived and they ordered another bottle of St. Emilion while they decided. "I have to get the bouillabaisse," James enthused. "Do you remember that scene in *Our Man Flint* when James Coburn traces the villains to a specific restaurant in Marseilles by the amount of garlic he detects on a guy's necktie, which was precisely the amount used for bouillabaisse? Genius. I've wanted to have this dish all my life."

Terry rolled his eyes, but ended up ordering the same. Meantime, Denny, who had his back half turned away from them, held court and didn't appear to have noticed them.

"Peter, here, has been to all your shows, you know." He smiled and patted the scruffy young guy next to him, who James recognized now from last night's show. "I trust Pete's ear completely. He'll fight for his artists through thick and thin, and protect their integrity. I'm not so thrilled he introduced you to a lawyer like this guy, though." He nodded at the portly Brooks Brothers suit wearing Eric. "He always rapes me over every damn deal we do."

Eric smiled thinly. "Oh, Denny…"

Denny headed into bullshit overdrive now. "I better make sure you pay for dinner. It'll be the last I benefit, eh?"

James looked at the singer and death head's guitar player for their reaction. The bass and drums weren't invited along in the first stage of divide and conquer. She smiled politely, not saying much. The guitar player was cool but had a harder time keeping a big smile off his face. He had to be thinking this was it—the big time.

James looked at Terry. "You liking the bouillabaisse and the bonus floor show? Think they're buying this?"

Terry said, "I'll still have a crack at it if I decide to. Denny's never done a deal without seeing the act."

Sure enough, once the cocktails had been flowing for another course—the guitar player was probably on his fourth Scotch and Coke—Denny said, "So I'm excited to see you play. When's your next show, Katrina?"

"We're doing a one a.m. set back at Dragonfly, two weeks on Thursday, right, Davey?" The guitar player nodded.

"Oh, that'll never do. Two weeks is far too long away and besides, one a.m. is way past my bedtime." Denny smiled happily at his self-mocking. James thought everyone else squirmed in their seat, but maybe he was just wishing. Denny turned to the A&R guy. "Pete, do you think you could get us a nice room at SIR rehearsal, say around five o'clock Wednesday? Get the department heads down. It'll be fun. Olympian will pay, of course." He smiled indulgently at the artists. "Anyway, Katrina, you'll be able to hear yourself too, for once. The monitors at Dragonfly suck."

"Denny, if I can ever hear myself, it'll mean Davey's not playing. Besides, we don't do showcases and our friends aren't up at five in the afternoon."

James grinned at Terry, who had stopped eating. Pete looked panicked and quickly said, "Don't worry, Katrina, Davey—we'll work it out."

Denny looked as if he were going to explode, but remembered they weren't his property yet, and forced a smile. "Rock and roll, ha, ha." James wished he could see the blonde's face, but she had her back to them. Denny switched gears and ignored Katrina for now, although no doubt he filed the moment away for revenge in the not-too-distant future. "So, Davey, who were your favorite guitar players, growing up?"

James dug a tiny clam from its shell. "Well, looks like dear Denny is his usual sweet self."

"Yeah, he's always been a right asshole—unless he's dealing with the media, of course," Terry said ruefully.

"Maybe we should go over and wind him up a bit on the way out, Terry. What do you think?"

"Yeah, all right. Better let me do it. You're liable to go too far."

James took that as a compliment, although he feared he'd be too out of practice to live up to the billing.

The requested check arrived, which Terry dropped his AmEx corporate card on, and they finished the remnants of the wine.

"Just think James Fox as Chas outside the courthouse in *Performance*, Terry. You do remember that scene, don't you? 'Apply a bit of pressure. Give 'em a bit of stick.'"

Terry shook his head. "Who do you think you are? The Lone Ranger? Jack the Lad? You're an out of date boy," His response proved he remembered the perfect film. They got up and took the two or three steps to the table, where the group picked over an array of shared desserts. Terry leaned between the singer and guitar player. "Davey, nice surprise to see you, although you have to be careful of the company you keep in the wilds of Malibu."

They grinned back at him. "I'm starting to think you're right," Katrina said.

James said nothing but raised an eyebrow at the blonde, who wore an amused expression, perhaps sensing the tension and enjoying it.

"To what do we owe the dubious pleasure?" asked Denny acidly.

"Couldn't resist a hello to such a fascinating group," said Terry. "Is this your lawyer, guys?" He looked at Eric but addressed Katrina and Davey, who nodded. "Wonder if anyone thought to tell you he and Denny are best friends, which is so sweet unless, of course, dear Eric's negotiating a deal on behalf of Olympian. What fun it will be when they pretend to get angry with each other while they decide how shitty a deal you'll swallow."

"I'll thank you and your lunatic companion to take your leave," seethed Denny.

"And I'll thank you to stay away from my family, Denny."

James thought he could only detect puzzlement on Denny's face. Terry, on the other hand, looked like he might dive in on Denny any second, so he gave him a gentle steering hand on the elbow and they headed for the door.

"Let's get out of here. I like this place and I want to be able to come back. Besides, Deutch looked ready to relive his mob youth on you any second. I swear his hand went inside his jacket. Why don't you head home and we'll talk in the morning. That Springer

Spaniel's waiting on me."

"Jesus, you and that dog."

"Fuck off, Terry. You just worry about not driving off Malibu Canyon and I'll start thinking about what to do next. My gut says Denny was so angry that it would have been hard for him to fake surprise when you mentioned your family. Go home, check your answering machine. Maybe she's called."

Terry walked out to his wagon and left. James took a minute to find his car in the unlit lot. As he unlocked the door, he felt a hand on his shoulder and was turned around firmly.

The blonde put her hands on his shoulders. Her green eyes again looked long and hard at him, but this time she leaned into him so that he was pressed back against the body of the car. That beautifully wide mouth was on his. His arms moved around her back. They explored each other for a while and then her tongue probed him in the most erotic way imaginable. He truly lost track of time. He felt her long, slightly coarse hair through his hands, their cheeks against each other's shoulders now. Slowly, she leaned back and again looked at him, straight in the eyes.

"I hear you're trouble, James Dual, but I always like to judge for myself."

"How am I doing so far?"

"Holding your own." She pulled a cassette tape out of her pocket. "Listen to this. I'll be in touch."

CHAPTER 3

He stared at the tape. *Tell me this isn't a demo*, he thought. She was away in the shadows now. He got in the car, pushed the cassette in and headed out of the parking lot back by Granita, turned down past the now-closed news stand and made the Malibu PD-enforced series of lefts that put him back on Pacific Coast Highway, headed north to Point Dume. There were minimal man-made lights on this stretch of road and it was a clear night with a lot of stars visible.

The scratchy tape started. Voices and scraping noises that could be chairs. Then Jacqueline's voice. "Shall I take meeting notes again this month?"

Then Denny's unmistakable tones: "Make sure the tape player's going too that you can transcribe from later. You missed a number of commitments last month. I want everyone held accountable to what they commit to here. Besides, it'll be fun to play back promotion's promises at radio if they fail to deliver." His voice raised now. "All right, are we all here? Great. So I know our marketing meetings are usually just for you geniuses who are department heads, but as Terry and I recently brought in a new A&R guy, he's sitting in this month. He's still learning how we work here at Real and conversely I'm sure you'll find him a breath of fresh air. If you can understand a fucking word he's saying, because I can't. Just kidding, James."

James, with a tightening gut, floated back twenty years into the wood-paneled fifth-floor conference room in Burbank. There they were, all the players at Real Records: Charlie Major, consummate bullshit artist, promo king, probably around thirty-five at the time but already with a shock of silver hair. Played his "aw-shucks" Southern twang to the hilt, mostly to disguise a very fucking smart, cunning, and ruthless mind. Fawn Hill, late twenties, publicity head. Good-looking in a very straight sort of way. Managed to feign a passion for music which she did not possess, heralding the beginning of the new breed of corporate publicists. Cockroach survival skills well developed, even at this young age. She acted just flirty enough that most of the powerful, tastemaking journalists would take her call and expense account meals, even if they didn't quite buy her. She doled out the access to the tough-to-get interviews in just the right measures to make sure no one bad-mouthed her too much. Jeff Stanley, head of sales. Such a cliché—where to start? Mostly bald on top, black curly hair—what was left of it—tied in a ponytail. Fat enough; his age was tough to call. Actually wore a gold chain from which a coke spoon dangled just out of sight, buried under his very visible chest hair. Shirt unbuttoned only a discreet three buttons that day. As you might imagine, he sweat despite the air conditioning. He could just as easily have been a shoe salesman. Finally, Ann Landry, artist development. Sounded like a cool job until you realized it was really just about setting up tour support and doling out money to road managers, which was what she'd been. One of the first women to land that kind of gig. She was tough because she had to be. Bands loved her and she had great instincts.

Denny continued. "Let's cover our priorities, starting with our biggest. Charlie, how's our Southern rock heroes the Confederacy doing at radio?"

"Well, the regional staff's all over this, Denny. Big adds in

Miami, Ft. Lauderdale, and some major stations right across the South. We're hanging in on the West Coast. KMET, which is of course the number-one rock station in our fair city, added this week in medium rotation. Even the highly selective Jim Ladd is giving us some love. So to use the station's catchphrase: A little bit of heaven on 94.7. East Coast is not reacting to the track well, though."

"Charlie, you know we put a lot of dollars out there on this one. The South should be automatic and in heavy rotation. You lay the pressure on the staff heavy. I do not want to come back and hear bullshit next month. You better rock me. All right, Fawn, what about press?"

"Pushing for *Rolling Stone* feature, Denny. If not, it's pretty certain we'll get a review. *Creem* very resistant. Regional reviews, though. *LA Times* will review the album but not willing to do a feature at this time. I'm taking Hilburn out to dinner next week, but you know how he is."

"Fawn, I don't really care how he, the almighty dean of LA rock critics, is. In case you haven't noticed, this company is not selling enough records right now. We need this act to be seen as credible. Do what you have to do."

"Of course, Denny, but you know I can't provide him the, uh, 'incentives' that Charlie can for his people."

"I want results. That's what you're paid for."

Charlie's voice now: "Honey, don't you be inferring nothing about ol' Charlie's business practices, ya hear?" James could still see that shit-eating, untouchable grin on his face. He could induce airplay via any combination of cash, drugs, and women he instinctively chose.

Denny now: "Enough. What's the retail story? Jeff?"

"Well, we shipped platinum. I jammed that million records

30

out on everyone, just like you told me to. We have major displays in the Tower stores, Licorice Pizza. We need everyone to deliver radio, though, otherwise in sixty days the returns could come back in an avalanche. Is the tour set yet? That's what could really push this through. We need to remind everyone they're great live."

Denny again: "Make sure you hold that placement. Pump as much co-op advertising as you have to, within reason. So, Ann, that brings us to your tour realities."

"Right, Denny. I've got an unusual request from Billy, their tour manager. He has a tour more or less in place that could start in three weeks. But with this kind of notice, the routing's not great. They'd have to start in Florida, head east, hit New York and then a lot of jumping around before ending up on the West Coast, down from Vancouver, Seattle, San Francisco, LA on to Arizona. They want to send the band out on a small plane. Billy, if you can believe it, has a pilot's license."

Denny interrupted: "That'll cost a fucking fortune. Are you high?"

"Wait, Denny," she said firmly. "I've seen the budget. Some redneck fan is lending the plane for next to nothing. Fuel's expensive but once you look at what they'd save in hotels, bus, etc., it looks pretty good. Plus, we can get their road crew on a hellacious driving schedule to make that nutty routing work in a way the band would never survive. Hit a lot of towns fast."

"Send me the budget by the end of the day. Maybe it could work."

James became lost in memories. The tape wound on through updates on half a dozen more artists, none of whom were selling, until he was jolted by his own voice from the past—a much harsher London accent then fully intact.

"You lot are so fucking out of touch it makes me sick. I thought the music business was about discovering the new, not perpetuating the past. Have you ever heard of The Clash or the Sex Pistols? What is it with these disgusting clichéd crap bands with city and state names—Boston, Kansas. You can't get enough of it, can you? So import another one. Foreigner. Disgusting! I'd always heard American FM radio was brilliant, but every other song's some old Led Zeppelin song. 'Stairway to Heaven'—give me a fucking break! What the hell is the deal with reviving the dead, rotting corpse of Fleetwood Mac? Coming here is like getting in a fucking time machine. Do you think kids are going to keep sucking up the tired crap like Styx and Steely Dan they've had to suffer hearing from their older brothers for the past God knows how long? They want their own music. That's why your shit's not selling.

"I'll sign some bands to wake things up around here. In the meantime, I'll tell you something. There's only one way you're going to sell records by your tired old Southern rock heroes. Get them that plane, let me put on a case of Jack Daniels and Southern Comfort, Jim Beam, and plenty of beer to chase it with. Then you wait for those ignorant hillbillies to fly it into the first obstacle they come across. Bang—instant rock mythology. They'd be timeless icons frozen in a moment, Confederate rebels forever. You'll sell millions of this record and their back catalog. Give me a day or two and I'll come up with suitable demises for some more of this sorry roster of shit you've got. They're all dead already—the only people who don't know that are you and them."

Terry's voice then: "James, what the fuck?"

Shouting from everyone, but Denny's voice the loudest. "Get this arrogant little prick out of here right now..."

The tape stopped. He ejected it. "Drive Blind" by Ride was

playing on college station KXLU, the only good radio in LA, even now. He'd been so lost in the past that he hadn't been aware of the turn off PCH onto Point Dume at Heathercliff or his ride down to the end of Grayfox.

He put the tape in his pocket and walked through the easement down the steep dirt path until he got to the tiny cottage. Highsmith, the aforementioned black-and-white English Springer Spaniel, ran out. James felt the lift in spirits that always occurred when they were together. They walked the short distance from front to back door by the low-ceilinged, wooden-floored 1940s guest cottage. There was a sharp drop thirty or forty feet down to the beach below. Simple slatted wooden steps led the way. There was a lowish tide and the moon, although not more than three-quarters full, was bright enough to see to walk by. Highsmith had brought his tennis ball, but sensing James's reflective mood, seemed content to keep it in his mouth rather than play throw-and-catch, his usual obsession.

They headed south towards Paradise Cove. James loved this stretch of beach, as it encapsulated the blur of fact and fiction that was LA for him. This was the beach where not so long ago, in Ross Thomas's *Chinaman's Chance*, the immortal character Artie Woo had fallen over the dead pigeon. Of course, even in the end of that story, the dead pigeon had been one more tall tale.

He was having trouble distinguishing fact from fiction right about now. One thing was for damn sure, though: six weeks after that boardroom meeting twenty years ago, those good ol' boys' plane had gone down in flames over Phoenix, just like he'd wanted it to, and life had never been the same for him again.

James and Highsmith arrived at the Sandcastle, the beachfront bar and restaurant that still retained the old Malibu spirit. They'd made a series of new Rockford Files TV movies in recent years, and

James Garner's original 70s mobile home had been put back in its old spot in the parking lot. Highsmith sadly knew he wasn't allowed inside and agreed reluctantly to wait while James went in to get a beer to go.

He walked through the heavy double doors into the gloom. Even though he'd just eaten, he couldn't resist grabbing a handful of peanuts from the huge wooden barrel that sat in the entranceway. No one was at the hostess booth, and only a handful of diners scattered along the ocean view window booths ahead. He turned right and into the bar. Ray, the night manager, sat at a stool on the customer side of the counter and gazed up at ESPN news on the decrepit TV that hung from the ceiling.

"Oy, oy, Ray, all right?"

"Yeah, good, James. Nice and slow this time of year—just a few locals. Lucky I ain't paid on commission, though."

"Yeah, really. Listen, I want a beer to go. Highsmith's outside so I should be quick—unless you want one more for dinner?"

"Sorry, James. He's a smart critter that one, and I'd love to, but odds are there'll be sheriffs in here for a shot or two. Shifts switch about now and there's a couple of officious pricks I could name who'd be all over me."

"Yeah, got you. Just a Rolling Rock then."

Ray disappeared into the kitchen for a minute and reappeared with a healthy-looking lamb bone in one hand and grabbed a beer from the fridge with the other.

"Nice one. Thanks, Ray."

He left a bill on the bar and headed out. He traded the tennis ball for the bone, and he and Highsmith walked back onto the beach and onto the old wooden pier that stretched out from Paradise Cove into the Pacific. They sat down at the end.

Where the fuck did that tape come from, and why now, James wondered. And did this connect to Jacquie's disappearing act?

CHAPTER 4
DENNY GOLDEN

Denny Golden's eyes opened and his mind instantly whirred. Given his continuing propensity for rich food, vodka, and cocaine, it was quite impressive how sharp he was first thing in the morning. He rolled over in bed. Oddly enough, staring down at his extremely large belly didn't bother him in the slightest. He was master of his own world. Like James, he lived a lot of the time in Malibu but on a much grander scale, it should be noted. He'd bought Dick Clark's estate a few years ago, which was at least the ten thousand square feet of property with a massive expanse of ocean view. He also owned a penthouse on the 32nd floor of the Sierra Towers, a 1964 building out on Doheny Drive, just north of Sunset, with a three hundred sixty degree view on the border of West Hollywood and Beverly Hills, along with properties in several cities where his business as chairman of Olympian Records took him, including New York, London, Paris, Tokyo, and Sydney.

This being a Tuesday, he planned on conducting his business from his bed. Every Tuesday for a number of years, he'd adopted this practice. Make no mistake about it, this wasn't because he was lazy or hung over. Denny used it the way he did everyone or everything he could—for power. Imagine it this way: You are a young manager of a band and you are pissed about the label's performance on behalf of your artist. You are actually granted a meeting with Denny—at his home. Sounds promising, right? Until you arrive and are walked into his bedroom, which, by the way, has no chairs. There's Denny, resplendent in silk pajamas, which match the wall decorations. Perhaps under the covers, perhaps not.

First off, there's no way you're going to sit on the bed uninvited, right? And even if you were, who'd want to literally get in bed with this voluminous man who, as he ages, looks more and more like a modern-day Sydney Greenstreet? So you stand there, almost like a servant, and are most definitely in one big hurry to get out of there. Denny probably explains that your record's run its course—at the end of the day, it's all about him—and that he knows best about everything. Unlike most label people, he doesn't even begin to lie or bullshit you. It's all about him and his power, and you are dismissed. Funny thing is, most people are too embarrassed or humiliated to even recount their stories.

This being a Tuesday, which is the day radio station program directors announce which songs have been added to their ever-shrinking playlists, his first call is to the independent promotion firm of Kalusian & Deutch. Radio promotion, in essence, hasn't changed all that much since the 50s payola scandals when some DJs like Alan Freed got caught for taking money, etc., and had their careers ruined, while others like Dick Clark skated and prospered. At least DJs then seemed to love music, too, but that's another story for another time.

Periodically, over the years, the Justice Department turned up the heat and in doing so, forced the record industry to create different structures to fork over money, women, drugs, etc. Such heat occurred most recently in the mid-80s and forced the record companies to have the heads of radio promotion pay for the services of independent promotion men who, in turn, would "promote" the records to radio stations by whatever means they thought expeditious.

When Denny left Real to start his own label Olympian, one

way for him to protect himself was to hire far less expensive promo persons than Charlie Major and use an independent company whose practices he could not be held accountable for.

Perhaps you'd think as chairman, Denny should have better things to do than find exactly what songs were added to which radio stations every week, but involvement with what was still the single most important element of selling records was common sense, not to mention what gave him an iron grip of control over his own label's destiny. You might be surprised at how many label presidents had lost their jobs over the years because they couldn't understand the workings or keep control of their promotion departments, especially in an era when record producers had been given the reins of various labels.

As his phone rang with Denny's call, Ron Deutch was behind his uncluttered glass desk. As a careful man, very little of his business involved paperwork or documents that might tend to incriminate him. He and Gary Kalusian had a three-story building just down the block and across the street from Tower Records on the Sunset Strip. He could, in fact, see the latest records that adorned the walls of Tower Records from his window. Although he was a very bad man, coming up through the ranks of a minor Philadelphia mob family, he genuinely loved the record business and the glamorous life it afforded him. He always wore very tasteful tailor-made suits that didn't accentuate his rock-like body and shape. He kept his wiry black hair cut old-school short, which somehow helped him look younger than his fiftyish age.

After they covered the almost exclusively good news, Denny addressed last night. "I don't like seeing Harper and Dual together. They haven't been close for a long time. Why don't you quietly see what you can find out? Obviously, make sure no one knows it's on our behalf. Whoever you use, let them think it's primarily about Damaged. I'll deal with that situation myself but I do want to know if Harper actually intends to try to sign them."

"Yeah, I got you, Denny. Consider it done."

"Hey, Ron. I had those rough demos sent over on Damaged. If I put them with the right producer, think we could put it across at radio?"

"Shit, Denny, that's a big ask. Maybe there's gonna be a burnout on all this rap/rock hybrid shit sooner or later, so maybe something like this could work," he said.

"All right. Play it for Gary too, okay?" said Denny.

"Sure. He's meeting with that crime author, Elmore Leonard. I'm going in to join them once we finish up."

"What the fuck for?" Denny asked.

"He's researching a book on the music business out here. I love his shit, but I gotta put him square on some stuff. Not all wiseguys are stupid, for instance."

"Jesus Christ, Ron. Do you really want to advertise your history?"

"Relax, Denny. Gary and I'll be smart, but I gotta admit it would be great to be immortalized by a guy like that."

"Be careful what you wish for." Denny hung up.

His morning continued with a call to his head of business affairs, Margery Cunningham, who was somewhat of an anomaly in his world: a fair-haired, somewhat matronly lawyer from New Hampshire. Happily married, mother of several, she unquestioningly did his bidding, somehow remaining unsullied by his innumerable devious maneuvers.

"Let's see if we can nail this Damaged band quick and cheap. Make Eric this offer: I want an afternoon showcase this week. Fuck their late-night show bullshit. I know they have a local following, but I want them to know who's in charge from the get-go. If we put them on the road, they'll need to deliver night after night to people who've never seen them before. I want to see if they can handle that. If they agree, prepare a demo deal memo with a first option for a full deal. Make it good for forty-eight hours, take it or leave it. I'm not going to get into a bidding war with Harper or anyone else. Keep the royalty points low and don't agree to an advance of more than $100K. Anything urgent we need to talk about, Margaret?"

"Well, Denny, Tommy Keene's threatening to audit for back royalties and Warrior is trying to invoke the seven-year contractual limitations based on California law."

"Jesus Christ, makes you nostalgic for simpler times," said Denny in an almost wistful tone.

CHAPTER 5
ELMORE LEONARD

Ron walked down the hall to Gary's slightly larger office, where Elmore Leonard had just sat down. Like his junior partner, Gary favored handmade suits, but his way of making a living was a little more evident in his dress. He favored a fair amount of gold and sad to say, his slicked-back graying hair was tied at the back in a ponytail. He eased his slender, six-foot frame into the black-and-chrome swivel chair behind his desk.

"Perfect timing, Ron. This is Elmore Leonard."

"An honor to meet you, Mr. Leonard."

"Likewise, I'm sure," replied the affable author, happily anticipating the conversation. "So Gary, how did you get your start in the business?"

"Two words. Morris Levy. One of the great record men was my mentor. I was a kid in the Bronx and I wanted to be a DJ, you know? Alan Freed was my hero, and Morris was his manager. So I managed to hustle an audience with him through a guy in the neighborhood. Morris had two clubs at the time and owned his own label, Roulette. So when I walk in the door wanting him to make me a DJ, I walk out the door with a job delivering the envelopes. Morris said that's the best way to get to be friends with DJs."

"The envelopes?" asked Leonard.

"Yeah, when you promote a new 45, you bring an envelope with cash in it to make sure it got played, right? So I'm having a ball when the payola hearings come down. Freed doesn't make it out of this; he's dead in Palm Springs by '65 Tragic. Meantime, another DJ, Joe Smith, plays it a bit smarter and he ends up running Elektra for Warner Brothers. Can you fuckin' believe it? He gets this gig and I get a call to come out to the coast. And the rest, as they say, is history.

"I went the independent route in the late 70s. Things got a little rough in the mid-80s, when we were still building this company, but we weren't really on the feds' radar yet. They go after Morris in a big fucking way. Really disgusting, as he's pretty much an old man by now. But that's a whole other story. Me, I brought in Ron here, as my protégé, and teach him the business. He knows how the game is played and he definitely knows how to close."

Leonard glanced across at the smiling, carved-from-granite Ron Deutch and imagined there would be few radio programmers who would refuse to see him in this or any other era.

CHAPTER 6

James woke up late, but surprisingly rested, perhaps helped by the Springer Spaniel's sleeping presence next to him. He rolled out of bed and fixed some coffee in the small, low-ceilinged kitchen.

It had been a long time since he had allowed himself any reflection on the times that had blasted back into his life last night. This morning, all he could think about was the aftermath.

The Confederacy plane crash killed everyone on board. Along with the band and tour manager were Ann Landry's assistant Nora Westlake, junior publicist Dana Jones, and retail assistant Veronica Salazar, who also happened to be Jacqueline's best friend. Grief stricken, Ann and Jacquie turned on him. Ann, in her hippie way, believed he'd called down the wrath of the gods, tempted fate by advocating the crash at the boardroom meeting. Jacquie had been a bit like a kid sister before. He'd teased her mercilessly about her taste in cheesy rock bands warning her what lay behind their façade but they'd been friends. That ended. It was if something had broken inside her. All innocence stripped away.

A month later, just after the Arizona authorities' investigation announced they weren't ruling out sabotage, things got even worse. A *Los Angeles Herald Examiner* rock journalist James had frequently insulted for his poseur taste in music and clothes heard a rumor about the boardroom outburst and saw his chance for revenge. He dropped a blind item in his column wondering whether the limey punk at Real could have caused the crash, which brought the LAPD knocking. Hard to believe now but back then, LA's finest had a serious hard-on for and were strangely threatened by the few punks who roamed LA, so they were all over him. Drawing on his noir heroes, James wisecracked his way through the interrogation. The law made it scarily clear they'd like to nail him, whether he'd done it or not, but with no supporting evidence coming to light, he eventually walked. God knows what would have happened if they'd have gotten their hands on the tape of his boardroom rant.

In the meantime, his prophecy about the Confederacy's posthumous record sales came eerily true and Denny's shaky career turned around. Far from grateful, though, and determined to punish James for questioning his leadership in the first place, Golden kept him to his contract but never signed any of the young exciting bands James brought in. This also ensured, of course, that there'd be no risk of James taking any of those acts to another label and showing Denny up.

He ended up at the Whisky A Go Go most nights, wired on amphetamines, downing Scotch, letting his punk energy dissipate into anger and bitterness. Terry had been supportive but once he married Jacquie, the Englishman's friendship was reduced to seeing the occasional band or sporting event together. To her, James would forever be a symbol of death, destruction, and loss.

When James's contract expired, he'd gradually pulled his life together. He was more or less unemployable, but started a small club in the then low-rent, somewhat dangerous, and definitely unfashionable Silver Lake end of Sunset Boulevard. Enough of the young bands he discovered and booked went on to successful careers to help ease his passage back into the record game. He'd managed artists with moderate success, balancing his affinity for their passion with a growing business sense that gradually evolved from his street-punk smarts.

In the early 90s, he was asked to help a young independent filmmaker choose some cool new songs that fit the emotional needs of the situations and characters of his film. He instantly fell in love with the role of music supervisor. Getting paid to lose yourself in fiction and music suited him like no job ever had before. It also involved huge chunks of time to get the legal permission to use those songs from record companies and publishers but to him it was worth it. Making better deals than anyone else became a source of pride to him. By 1996, he'd completely immersed himself in this world and had stopped managing altogether. He hadn't yet missed the three a.m. calls from the road.

Highsmith wandered past on his way to take a leak and raised an eyebrow in his direction. James, duly prompted, put some bread on to toast for both of them while he tried to figure out what to do next. The girl was obviously the key right now, but he had no way of getting right to her. What the hell was her deal? Where had she gotten the tape from? Did she know who he was when they met, or had someone at Denny's table told her? He hoped the latter, as she'd been the first woman he'd sparked to in a long time.

That would be about my level of smart, he chided himself. *Get a thing for someone who's got something to hang right over your head*. If the law ever heard that, it could still bring a lot of grief. Who had had the tape all these years? Had to be someone in the room that day. He hadn't realized it was being made at the time, not that that would have made much difference to him then. The question was obviously Jacqueline and Denny did, but what about the rest of them? With Jacquie missing and Denny clearly not an option, Terry was the most obvious one to start with while he waited for what he figured would be the inevitable call from the girl.

The ping of the toaster oven brought Highsmith bounding back upstairs from the beach. James buttered and jammed some for himself and distractedly slid Highsmith his lumps dry.

"How much would it suck if she's a blackmailer, Highsmith?" The dog gave him a knowing look. "I know, I know, I just met her, but we really seemed to have a lot in common." Highsmith listened until his slice of toast was all gone and then disgustedly headed to his bowl of water.

James had a nagging hesitation about revealing the existence of the tape to Terry. It would probably make him even more scared for Jacquie. He grabbed a cordless phone from the kitchen wall and went out through the blue slatted wooden French doors onto the small deck he had built out over the cliff. There was just enough room for a small table. It was flanked by two bench seats at either side of the balcony. In order to give himself some shade, he had stolen an idea from his favorite hideout, a series of shacks on the south coast of Jamaica known as Jake's. He'd laid down roughhewn branches on top of the roof and nailed them across the beams of the balcony.

He called Lainey first, wondering how much he should tell her. She'd never asked about his past and considering she naturally spent most of her free time with people her own age, she may well have no idea.

"What's up?" she asked.

"Let's go over what paperwork came in first. I may not be in until much later."

"Well, you'll be happy to know we got the approval on your offers for the last songs for *Lavish*."

"That's genius. All done a week before the mix." He was

genuinely pleased as the nature of getting music legally licensed for under-budgeted independent films normally meant last-minute drama. "All right then, I need you to do a bit of detective work for me."

She was used to tracking down songs and artists for him.

"Okay, cool. What do you need?"

"This is a bit different. I need to find some old-school label execs. Odds are they're here or in New York, of course. There's Jeff Stanley; he's in retail. Fawn Hill, publicity. Ann Landry, artist development. Charlie Major. I'm pretty certain he's still in LA. He may even have a place in Malibu, but either way, he's in radio promotion. Last, I may get a call from a Canadian girl. If I do, make sure you get a number and let me know immediately."

"Gotcha, boss," she said, rather mockingly, he thought.

He went back inside and retreated to the comfort of a long shower. As much as he'd inwardly railed against what he thought was an overabundance of clichés in his life, this was all coming too thick and fast. Maybe he should leave Terry to it. Jacquie hated him, after all. Deal with the Canadian girl and get life back to normal as soon as possible. Maybe it would go that way, but deep down he didn't think so. He liked to think he often had his best ideas in the shower, but not today. He got out to find a message on his voicemail from Lainey.

"This was easy. Ann Landry's got her own marketing company, Ann Landry Marketing, 8600 Beverly Boulevard, 323-555-6324."

Apart from how easy she'd made it to find her, James was impressed she'd managed to resist most of her competition's habit of having cutesy company names to impress you with their cleverness. He called and managed to get her office to set up a 4:00 pm meeting under the pretext he wanted to discuss a film soundtrack release. He left his office number and hoped the meeting wouldn't get canceled once Ann saw his name on her schedule. He'd head out at two, to beat traffic into Hollywood. He invited Highsmith to come along, who happily jumped into the front passenger seat.

They made the twenty-four miles down PCH into Santa Monica in thirty minutes and drove through the McClure Tunnel and onto the 10 Freeway. They had almost passed the interchange with the 405 Freeway before traffic slowed to a crawl. The weather had still felt hot, sunny, and the Santa Ana winds exhilarating while they were on the Coast Highway, but now as the city heat became dirty and oppressive, James reluctantly put the air conditioning on and the windows up. Highsmith sighed as he lost the abundance of smells but appreciated the cool air on his long hair.

They finally got to the Fairfax off-ramp and headed north on the old surface street. They passed through the residential blocks until they slowed to a crawl as they hit rundown laundries, appliance stores, Middle Eastern restaurants, and carpet shops. As they passed Third Street, the legendary deli Canter's loomed on the left. Its famously obnoxious waitresses were beloved of many, but it had long ceased to appeal to James, who had had plenty of that kind of service when he lived in England. He turned right onto Beverly past the CBS TV complex and found a one-hour meter. He pulled in gratefully and slipped a harness and leash on Highsmith, who wasn't yet familiar with city streets. They got out and walked past several newish boutiques and restaurants.

Ann's company was upstairs in a two-story Spanish building whose ground floor housed a retro clothes store. There was no formal lobby, but one of the six black workstations faced the door that he and Highsmith entered through. It was occupied by a twentyish spikey-redhaired girl. The walls were adorned with a modest array of platinum and gold sales plaques strategically placed among a wide variety of CD and tour posters. It was noisy, as several probable interns stuffed envelopes wherever they could find floor space. The occupants of the workstations were four youngish women and two men who worked the phones. The redhead got off the phone and asked if she could help.

"Yeah, please. James Dual. I have a four o'clock with Ann. I'm a bit early."

"She's on a conference call, but I'll take you through, as there's not really any room here."

She led the way to one of two doors that James hadn't noticed initially, as they were obscured by several boxes of CDs. He kept a tight rein on Highsmith, who was eager to get involved with the packing operations all around them. The girl opened the door partially and stuck her head in. She made sign language gestures to presumably not interrupt the call. They were ushered to two comfortable seats that faced Ann, who sat behind a black Ikea desk. The afternoon light poured in through the window that covered the upper half of the wall and illuminated her long sandy hair and weathered, lined face. She wore a vintage, multicolored Forbidden Fruit dress that belied somehow the authoritative strategic marketing plan she was describing.

She hung up after five minutes or so, stood, offered her hand briefly, and appraised him coldly.

"Thanks for seeing me, Ann. I had a feeling you might not."

"It crossed my mind, but I'm an independent, so as long as the bills get paid, I'm not too choosy about who my clients are."

He winced. "Truth is, I do do soundtracks, but that's not the reason I'm here. Please hear me out. I know this is a horribly sensitive subject, but I promise you my intentions are good. Jacquie has disappeared and Terry asked me to help find her. She'd been threatened, probably blackmailed and blamed me. She's had nothing to do with me since the Confederacy plane crash, so we believe this must be related. Have you heard from her or anyone connected?"

Her eyes blazed in anger.

"Atonement twenty years too late? I've always believed you caused that crash, either by direct involvement or at the very least invoking the wrath of the gods."

Highsmith had stiffened as her voice rose and leant supportively against James, which helped him resist saying, "Still the fucking hippy, eh?"

"I didn't do it, Ann, but if there's blackmail involved, it's likely someone's surfaced who knows what really happened that night. Help us find the truth."

She sighed. "The only people I've talked to recently are the group of family members that the Confederacy left behind. Our personal losses bonded us and I've tried to help them—Real never paid them any record royalties."

"What do you mean? The live record from the Roxy Real put out after the crash was multi-platinum," said James.

"Jesus Christ, James, didn't you ever grow up? You know how record companies work. They recoup all the marketing, radio promotion, advertising costs, etc., before they start paying a dime and their position is the band is still unrecouped."

In truth, he'd been shocked for years by stories he'd heard from huge acts, especially from the 50s and 60s, who had similar tales.

"What about the publishing money that goes to the songwriters? That's a statutory amount that is paid on every record."

"Real produced a film of that Roxy concert. The band had to sign waivers that night to allow the filming and buried deep in the contract was language that assigned publishing rights for all songs performed to the production company, which Denny happens to own."

"Fuck me! That's outrageous, even for him. Do you think any of the family members are angry enough to try to get to Denny through Jacquie? She would have been the one having them sign everything that night," said James.

"Hopefully they would have come after you first, James, if that were the case," she said malevolently.

He flashed on the tape.

"I don't think so, though," Ann continued. "Meantime, maybe you've changed but have you ever thought about this from anyone's point of view but your own? Who the hell were you to roll into town and tell us our time and their lives were over? Jacquie and I thought you were wild enough to do anything, including murder. If you really want to find out the truth, you'd better give some serious reflection on what you conjured up back then."

CHAPTER 7
1978

Terry had insisted James attend the Confederacy's Roxy show, which he sulkily did. He liked going to The Roxy usually, and looked at Mario, the manager, as a patient and protective uncle. Mario had always comped him, for some reason, even before he had a record company job and didn't have the money to pay. Whether the club boss had initially mistaken him for someone in a band he'd never know, but he'd always appreciated it and treated both Mario and Luigi, who ran the notorious rock 'n roll watering hole next door, the Rainbow, with the utmost respect and affection.

He'd started the night by sticking a tablespoon into a bag of amphetamine sulphate and swallowing it. He'd brought a bottle of Bell's whiskey into the limo that Terry had pick him up. By now he felt great, and although he still hated guitar solos, he'd not let the frequency of them ruin his night so far, but by the time the set ended and the requests for encores started, he knew he was only a song away from lobbing a beer bottle at the stage.

He leaned across the table, which was on a slightly raised, reserved section at the left hand side of the four hundred person-capacity club. "Look, Terry, I've been a good boy but enough's enough. If I have to listen to any more of this Southern fried shit, I'm gonna have to side with Neil Young."

"You just haven't been in America long enough to appreciate this music, James."

"It's not a matter of time—it's taste, innit? Just because you went from being a junior hippie straight to the Eagles and missed glam and now punk, don't expect me to."

Terry chuckled. "James, I hired you because you bring something I don't, but dial it down a bit, all right? I mean, you have to admit the Eagles write great songs."

"Those fucking cocaine cowboys? Look, I stopped pretending I was a cowboy at ten. 'Desperado.' The only thing they're desperate about is if their tour manager packed the blow. After reading that *Rolling Stone* article where they were talking about abusing their groupies, just fucking disgusting. Arrogant pricks."

The audience's clapping grew more intense as a couple of roadies wandered across the stage to check guitar connections, suggesting the inevitable encore was imminent. James rose. "Look, I know these cunts are reaching for their cigarette lighters. I've got to get out of here. I'll meet you at the Rainbow. I'll grab a booth before they're all gone. All right?"

James knew as well as Terry did that Fawn would have arranged tables for them. He moved easily through the crowd of fired-up but Quaalude-and-Jack-wobbly fans, nodding a knowing amphetamine grin to a couple of the ex-biker security guys as he passed into the foyer. He didn't see Mario, who was already likely at the small upstairs private club known as On the Rox. He pushed open one of the double glass doors and instantly felt the Friday night street life outside on the Strip. His buzz was perfect.

The Rainbow Bar and Grill was, and is, next door to The Roxy, separated only by a crowded driveway that led to a small parking lot where cars would be triple-parked by the red-jacketed valets. A steeply sloped dirt hill at the back led up into the side roads above Sunset. The parking lot was packed with way cooler kids than were in The Roxy, who clamored to get into the Rainbow. A hybrid of hard- and soft-edged glam rock girls mixed with the beginning of Valley girls, along with more than a few daughters of fading film royalty.

Luigi stood mock-delightedly and heralded the surging crowd. "Everybody's a star at the world-famous Rainbow Bar and Grill," he announced to nobody in particular. "Ah, Mr. James, come right in." He looked like a classic Italian from a 60s film. He wore a slightly ruffled white shirt on top of black pants, his tight curled hair shiny in the illuminated lights.

"Oy, Luigi, any chance of a booth, mate?"

"Mr. James. There's a table reserved for the band. You don't want to sit with them? Fawn also reserved a table for the label. It's very crowded right now, so everyone is eating the wonderful Rainbow Bar and Grill food—pizza's a specialty."

Wired as James was, he still found a smile. "Have you put the band in the corner?" he asked as Luigi led him in past the ticket desk cum maître d's stand. The corner booth at the back left side of the room was the prestige one, usually held for the likes of Led Zepplin or Fleetwood Mac level bands whenever they were in town.

"That is for Thin Lizzie tonight. They play the Forum."

"Yeah, right. Fair enough, Luigi. Drop me at Real's table and we'll see how it goes, eh?"

If the genial host took that as a sign of trouble to come, he didn't show it. "Please take this fine young man to table eleven, Wanda." Wanda was a stunning California blonde, slightly dialed down from the Playboy vibe and with a rock girl edge. She'd always been here, handled the frequently surreal behavior of the Rainbow's denizens with ease and charm. A lot of the waitresses came and went, usually because they became (somewhat understandably) too bitchy with customers or too friendly with visiting bands.

"What's new, James?"

"Nothing much. Been stuck at The Roxy all night. Now I gotta sit with a bunch of wankers and pretend I liked the show."

She tilted her head slightly. "You know, it wasn't so long ago that you were relying on Luigi to comp you in, and for whichever Rainbow girl you found that night to pick up your tab and take you home. Poor James," she mocked. "I guess you still have your English accent if you want to go back to that."

"Oh piss off, Wanda." He shook his head mock disgustedly as he slid into the red leatherette booth. He was halfway through a tall Scotch and water before the Real staff wandered in, led by Fawn, Jeff, Ann, Terry, and two statuesque women. Wanda artfully ushered people into the booth in a manner that left James flanked by the two women, who he realized were the backup singers. They smelled musky from having just come off stage, maybe some patchouli mixed in there.

Sue Ann swayed into the booth on some really tasty black-and-red cowgirl boots, with an ace of hearts on her matching skirt riding high as she slid across the leatherette, upper body and blonde hair getting entangled with the instantly-in-lust James. Her partner, Holly, came in the other way and hip-bumped him in. Fawn, unsurprisingly, had left the various assistants to fend for themselves, presumably Jacqueline among them.

"Denny came backstage to congratulate the band already," she gushed to no one in particular.

Such was his concentration on Sue Ann that it was only after everyone had ordered drinks that he noticed the band had been situated in the far right corner at prestige-wise the two booth, slightly smaller than the other corner where Thin Lizzy now held court. Phil Lynott, heavy-lidded, happily nodding, instantly hypnotic as his bandmates soaked up the attention. The Southerners seemed oblivious of their slightly secondary status, but maybe in among the jacks and rebel yells, they wondered just where and if they counted.

Sue Ann said, "So what's your story? How come you're so skinny? Don't you get fed out there in England?"

"What you talking about? I eat all the time."

"You look like you like to eat chemicals more than anything else."

"Oooh, maybe we should be talking about how you're wasting a soulful voice on these guitar-soloing shitkickers. I mean, come on, you've got a voice like Judy Clay, but I bet you don't even know who that is, do you, country girl?"

She feinted mad, as if she was going to swing on him, but grabbed his shirt front at the last minute, pulled him with a snap and started singing a note-perfect "Private Number" in his ear. His memory filled in the William Bell lines silently to the Stax classic duet. If Alex's *Clockwork Orange* ecstasy was with Ludwig von Beethoven, this was James's.

He sunk into her shoulder and was increasingly aware of the breast he was pressed against; he wondered how she would react if he kissed her. He eased himself up slightly, his hand using her hip to do so, stayed close but now looked straight into her green eyes. "I'm impressed."

She grinned happily. "I was born just outside of Memphis. Typical story, you know: singing in church, then a nice little fake ID got me into Beale Street clubs. My dad had all those Stax records."

"So what happened?'

"We moved to Alabama when I was seventeen. All the kids in school were into Southern rock or Clapton, so you know, I wanted to sing—that's what the bands were singing."

James shuddered at the mention of Clapton. The first time he'd seen "Clapton Is God" scrawled on a bathroom wall, he'd known for sure that while they spoke the same language here, the religion was very, very foreign. "Do you write anything yourself?" James wondered out loud.

"Sure I do."

He took a long swallow of Scotch and water while he tried to ascertain how fucked up he was by now. "Look, why don't we look at some of your songs together? I could book us some time, do some demos, maybe a couple of killer soul covers?"

"Baby, no one's listening to that anymore. Haven't you noticed disco?"

"Fuck that shit. I want to make records with emotion. There has to be a place for that. Like Joe Strummer's a soul singer. He means every word—you understand what I mean?"

She looked at him, still wondering whether he meant every word he said. "I think so."

"Look, I'm thinking we could draw on classic soul and maybe even a little country, but make it tough and modern the way The Clash drew on reggae, see?" At her vaguely uncomprehending look, he continued, "Look, why don't we meet up tomorrow and you can play me some of your stuff and we'll see how it goes, eh?"

Almost surprised he hadn't wanted to go back to his place right now, she said, "You know, James, that sounds nice. I mean, I don't have things recorded, but I could sing a few on acoustic..." She trailed off. "What am I saying? I have to be at Burbank Airport at three thirty a.m. for the flight to Phoenix."

"What the fuck are you flying then for? I thought you lot have your own plane?"

"Well, the boys like to keep partying and then crash when we get to the next city. It's easier for everyone than trying to wake up early and get anywhere on time." She laughed.

He smiled. "You know, they aren't quite as dumb as they look."

Her hand rose as if to slap him, but it landed gently and stayed flattened against the side of his head. "I don't know quite what to make of you."

"Well, think about it for a minute, but I've gotta take a leak. Then maybe we should think about getting out of here. Whatever you do, just don't ask any of this lot what they make of me." He glanced around the table. Somewhat surprisingly, Ann and Fawn were immersed in conversation.

He eased through the throng of mostly women who congregated at the bar and up the black steps to the bathrooms and waited for a stall door to open. He pulled a plastic bag out of the zippered back pocket of his black drainpipe Fiorucci jeans, and poured a moderate mound onto the crook of his hand between thumb and forefinger and snorted up a good amount of amphetamine sulphate. He typically swallowed the drug at the start of the night and then topped up along the way with the occasional snort to keep the buzz going.

Duly refreshed, he bounced down the stairs and wondered whether he should have offered some to Sue Ann. He offered a respectful smile as he passed Phil Lynott and got a friendly grin in return. As he eased into the booth, Terry and Holly made a move to join the band and Sue Ann was obviously discussing her immediate future.

"Think I can leave safely with this one?" she asked Terry mockingly.

"Only because he's not driving."

"Fuck off, Terry, I'm a brilliant driver." He leaned in. "Be nice or I'll go look for Jacqueline."

Terry shot him a look. "Just make sure Sue Ann's at Burbank to get on that plane."

"Can't promise you that, mate. We have an album to do."

"Huh? James, don't fuck around. This band's just picking up steam and you're on thin ice already."

"Thin ice? No one's said that to me since school. Let's go find the car, baby. Oy oy, Fawn, Real's got the tab, right?"

Even in her presumably partly inebriated condition, her glacial look was all the response he got. On reflection, he was relieved that she or Ann hadn't intervened. Sue Ann linked her arm with him. He would usually have felt uncomfortable with that sort of thing, but it felt strangely natural.

A slight bottleneck was caused by actor George Peppard, who walked with the very delicate steps of a serious drunk into the Rainbow parking lot. "Goodnight, Mr. Banacek." Luigi, as usual, was right by the entrance. It was hard to tell whether he was taking the piss, which he probably was, but he had such a beatific smile, it conceivably could simply be his delight at an actor adding an incongruous touch to his circus. James, himself, was amused when he saw the 1941 Packard 180 that waited was the same as he drove in his show. Personally, when it came to guys solving crimes from the back of extravagant cars, he preferred *Burke's Law*, but even so...

The Dav El limo Terry had booked him waited on Sunset, just forward from The Roxy, but that did mean they had to move through what was probably a hundred and fifty or so rock kids who hadn't gotten into the Rainbow. He thought he might have seen

Jacqueline briefly and it crossed his mind he should give Terry a heads-up, but dismissed the thought. If he and Holly were at the band table, it wouldn't look too suspicious and besides, it really wasn't his problem what Terry might or might not be up to.

"Look, we've got a couple of hours for me to talk you into staying. Do you need to get anything or can I have us taken for a drive or something?"

"We had day rooms to keep costs down. Everything but what you see is loaded already. The crew leaves with our stuff as soon as they pack up."

"Great. Why don't we take Sunset to PCH and head up to Malibu? Then depending on who wins, we can come back or head over to the 101 and down to Burbank Airport." The portly driver nodded, opened the door for them and vanished into the front.

"There's only one winner here, limey."

"Ohhh, we'll see about that." James tried to play it cool. The only cassette he had brought that wasn't punk or dub was Robert Palmer's classic *Pressure Drop*, which he pushed into the overhead sound system. Cool never materialized. They tore into each other. Both his black T-shirt and her red pearl-buttoned cowgirl shirt were on the floor of the limo before they'd passed the Beverly Hills Hotel. Trying to keep well balanced as the driver flew along the curvy turns on Sunset, James knelt between her legs to better pull off those red and black boots.

"That's a good position for you." She laughed. "Stay here awhile and get used to it."

Sometime later, with their positions reversed, she had a lot more trouble getting his Fiorucci jeans off. "Do you have these printed on, boy?"

"Gotta work hard to get what you want, Sue Ann."

"Like you'd know." She finally pulled both legs at once, narrowly avoiding any rips.

Robert Palmer singing, "Give Me an Inch Girl," was the only voice heard for a while until she had James pinned against the back seat on the brink.

"Who's in control?" She stopped.

His eyes went wide, unbelieving, for a second. "You." But as soon as she started moving back and forth and relaxed a little, he flipped her off and so it continued.

They sat at opposite ends of the long back seat, knees together, sweaty, giddy and grinning when the partition partially slid down. "Decision time."

"All right, pull over for a minute. Stay."

"James, I can't let these guys down. If you really want to do this, you'll wait until the tour ends. It's only five weeks. We finish in Nashville, and if this was just a fast way to fuck a country girl, then it won't matter, will it?"

He looked at her, hurt, and for once knew there was nothing he could say to get his own way. He couldn't tell whether the wave of sadness that hit him was postcoital, the speed wearing off, or something else.

"All right. Burbank." He grabbed the bottle of Bell's Scotch and poured them both drinks. The speed wore off but somehow he didn't feel he should either offer Sue Ann any or do any in front of her.

The driver turned off Pacific Coast Highway and the fifteen-minute canyon ride to the 101 Freeway felt almost like a reprieve. They had the windows down and enjoyed the sharp gullies, the smell of sage, and the occasional coyote yip. But when they got on the 101, they raised the windows against the still heavy freeway traffic. It was three fifteen a.m. when the driver arrived at the small, beautiful airport which James imagined was unchanged since the 1940s.

They continued around the fenced perimeter of the airfields, now meeting no traffic on the quiet Valley streets. They arrived at the entry gate for private flights. The guard didn't ask for ID once the driver had given specific flight information. They dressed again, although both were seriously disheveled.

She took out an eyeliner pencil and wrote on the inside flap of the Rainbow matchbook. "I don't have a private number to give you. It was cheaper to give up my apartment while we're on the road. But this is my folks' phone in Alabama."

"I just thought—Muscle Shoals Studios, right? Maybe we can record there." He brightened momentarily but his words were thick and slurry now. The alcohol was taking over.

They got out onto the tarmac as Terry stepped down the short steps off the plane, which presumably meant Holly was on board. Charlie Major, still bullshitting animatedly, was on the runway with a couple of band members and indie promo man Ron Deutch, old school-looking in a suit. Everyone had individual bottles of Jim Beam in hand, although the tour manager was up and down with bags and seemingly not too much the worse for wear.

"I guess I oughta get on." They held each other. James realized abstractedly they were the same height as her body contours melded with his again.

She let go, turned quickly and strutted towards the plane, her body swaying but she had no trouble walking upright in those killer boots.

Terry came over. "Can I hitch a ride? I let my car go."

"Yeah, of course. Let's get out of here." James, faux tough.

A day later, the *Los Angeles Times* headline read:

SOUTHERN ROCK BAND THE CONFEDERACY
& 7 OTHERS DIE IN PLANE CRASH HORROR.
Investigation underway on tragic end to flight that left
from Burbank Airport.

The meter clicked to expired. He snapped out of his reverie before the hovering traffic cop could pounce. Highsmith, who had been asleep, stirred. He half wanted to go back up to Ann's office and tell her he'd lost someone he loved that night, too, but didn't.

CHAPTER 8
ELMORE LEONARD

The blonde receptionist at the silver paneled entry to Real Records put down her Anita Loos book when she spotted Elmore coming through the elevator doors and ushered him to Terry's office. Almost too quickly for the author, who barely had time to soak in the mix of hopeful artists and bored executives who waited on the circular purple couch. He did happen to catch the framed triple platinum record of the Confederacy's *Live Forever at The Roxy* posthumous hit alongside the platinum one for their last studio record *Railroaded*. Terry rose from behind his desk and led them to a black leather and chrome couch that looked out through floor-to-ceiling glass at the wildfire-burnt Burbank hillside.

"So, Terry, along with your industry insight, I'd like to know what the story is with you and James. I'm curious what your history is."

"Well, I promised James I'd help you although I doubt this is what he had in mind. I'd often bump into him running round the London clubs in the mid-70s when I was out looking at bands for Real before I transferred to LA. He always seemed to be at the 'next' band's gigs just before all us A&R guys. Dr. Feelgood, Eddie & the Hot Rods, Kilburn and the High Roads. Graham Parker and the Rumour. You get the idea. Not necessarily the big sellers but the authentic ones."

"Was he working for another record company?"

"No. He was too young, wild, and in a strange way, cared too much. Very unforgiving about anyone he deemed a poseur. I guess he was a punk before anyone used that expression. By the time they did, I'd moved here. I loved all that California stuff: Gram Parsons, the Eagles, Linda Ronstadt."

"So how did he end up here?"

"I ran into him at the Whisky A Go Go one night. I was shocked. Punk, and The Clash in particular, had obviously galvanized him but London was a brutally depressing place to live then. Conservative government, controlled power outages, strikebreaking riots, droughts, IRA letter bombs. A generation of kids getting sold down the river. When Freddie Laker started his discount airline from London to Los Angeles, kids like him could scrape together cash for a trip like this for the first time. He hated most of the big artists here but I found out his vision was filtered from childhood through noir books and film. He came looking for what might be left of that."

Elmore smiled. "So did I."

"Did you arrive in time?"

The author shrugged. "So what happened?"

"He'd hate this, but it was like the Eagles' 'New Kid in Town' song that was out then. Within days, he'd assimilated into the street scene here in a way I couldn't and wouldn't want to have. He wasn't impressed by anything or anyone, so was taken to everything. He found a few kindred spirits, mostly dark-natured girls who'd been into The Velvet Underground and then glam rock when they were twelve or thirteen and had grown into decadent ways. They all had a confrontational edge, some of it harmless—throwing bowls of Rainbow Bar sugar along with torrents of abuse at would-be Sunset Strip icons like Kim Fowley and Rodney Bingenheimer—but there was a dangerous fatalistic spirit that scared most they came into contact with. It did give him serious credibility in the burgeoning art punk band scene, though, something other label execs and I at the time frankly didn't have. James's bullshit detector was in permanent overdrive, so he was just as likely to question their authenticity as anyone else's.

"Despite our differences in taste, I genuinely liked him; he could be funny and engaging. When I realized punk was his call to arms, it made sense to offer him a job. It's my job to see where music might be going. No one knew if punk would be as big here as it was by then in England but I wanted to be prepared."

"How'd that work out?" asked Elmore.

"Something tells me you know how it worked out," said Terry.

Busted, the author conceded, "Obviously I knew about the Confederacy tragedy but it wasn't until after we'd met the other night that I realized you both worked here then. I knew you hadn't seen each other in a long time and I wondered why."

"After the crash, word got out that James had advocated killing the band. Whatever he may have really felt, on the outside he was completely unrepentant. He embraced the rumors as the ultimate punk credentials. My wife Jacquie, who was also at Real, had become terrified of him despite their initial friendship. She'd lost her best friend in the crash. I came to realize over the years that she wasn't ever going to fully get over it, despite our having two great kids. It just became impossible for me to stay close."

"And now?" asked Leonard.

"And now we are going to talk about the modern-day realities of signing artists, why they are signed and how long it's likely to last," said Terry.

CHAPTER 9

The office garden was lit by the late afternoon sun as James and Highsmith returned to work. My Bloody Valentine's "Glider" blasted through the office.

"Jesus, Lainey, can you hear the phones ringing?"

"Absolutely." She waved pages of messages at him.

He walked into the meeting room, where he dropped onto the couch, frustrated and depressed. He realized maybe for the first time in any honest way that he'd been so fucked-up on drugs and self-preservation that he'd never really mourned everything and everyone that had been lost that night. He just kept pushing forward like some wannabe shark, never felt more than he could handle. Highsmith found his rubber bone with miniature soccer balls at each end, put his front paws on the couch, pushed the bone towards James, and growled in a mock tough-dog tone. James smiled despite himself as he was forced into a tug-of-war tussle for the next ten minutes.

His mood lifted. Maybe he should forget all this dredging around. He couldn't afford not to work for long. It's not as if he were some private eye getting a fee from Terry, anyway. Maybe Terry should hire someone. He could find his next film to work on. Jacquie hated him, anyway. If she knew he was looking, she'd be even less likely to come back. Fuck her. Terry'd be better off without her anyway.

"Oy, Lainey, let's go over these messages."

She strolled in and looked at him with a slight concern, as he rarely acted irritably, although she was smart enough not to pander to it. She tilted her head just a bit and up to the left. "Okay, boss." Her tone was ironic as hell. "Pat Lucas called from EMI Publishing. David Bowie approved the song for the ridiculously low fee you begged for. You're lucky the film's good, and now go find something with a budget."

"That's the message?" James laughed for the first time in days. "All right, what else?"

She rambled through the day's minutiae, and then said, "Oh yeah, on the detective front, found Jeff Stanley for ya. He's still in retail but in Nashville. Head of sales for Rodeo Records. I got a number on Fawn in New York, and Charlie Major's in LA. His home number's unlisted but he does have an office at *Charts Magazine*."

James looked up, impressed with her. "Maybe we could expand into the private eye business."

"Maybe so, but meantime, there's stacks of music in your office that it would be great if you could actually start to listen to."

He called the 615 number and got lucky. It was almost seven pm in Nashville and Stanley picked up his own phone.

"Jeff, it's James Dual here. Sorry to call out of the blue after all this time, but I really need to talk to you."

"What about?"

"Well, it's kind of complicated, but Terry's wife Jacqueline's disappeared, and we think it's got something to do with the old days."

"Really? She was a good kid, but I don't know how I can help." He sounded old and not quite as slick, maybe genuinely concerned.

"Well, I know you and I aren't friends, Jeff, but could I talk to you about the time around the crash?"

"The crash…?"A little more wary now.

"Well, yeah, that time period anyway."

"Look, James, I've seen your name on a few film posters lately, so I'll take a chance on the fact you're older and smarter. I doubt there's anything I know that can possibly help you find her, but I'll talk to you."

"Great. I really appreciate that. Do you have time now?"

"I said I'll talk to you, but not on the phone. You can come down here and buy me dinner."

"Jeez, Jeff, things are kind of hectic here, I dunno…"

"Look, that's the deal. I'm on my way out the door. Call my office and book a time if you're serious. Otherwise, don't waste my time." *Click.*

James stared at the phone. Weird. He tried Fawn's New York number but it went straight to voicemail. Only she would have some British assistant with an aristocratic accent telling you to leave a message for Fawn Hill, Senior Vice President, Corporate Communications…blah, blah, blah. Clearly Fawn had continued to scratch her way up the ladder, and now held a role that wouldn't involve talking about music either. Perfect. He tried *Charts Magazine* and got through to Charlie's assistant.

"He's not in, but I can take a message."

"Yeah, thanks, tell him it's James Dual. My number is 310-555-5657. I haven't talked to him in a very long time, but please tell him it's important. When will he be back?"

"He's in Pebble Beach for the *R&R* magazine charity celebrity golf tournament, until Sunday. He's partnering with Gene Simmons—from KISS," she said proudly.

"Of course he is. Thanks for your help." He hung up. Interesting. He guessed Charlie must be doing indie promo for the notoriously corrupt and proud of it. *Charts Magazine*. So why be that visible at *R&R*, its main rival? That was quintessential Charlie, though. Fly as close to the fire as possible because there wasn't any situation he couldn't glibly bullshit his way through, whether it was business or women. James smiled, reassured of some continuity in the world.

He called Terry. "Let's have dinner and I'll bring you up to date. Nothing great, just more to sift through. Do you mind coming this way? I've got Highsmith with me. The guys at Chez Jay will let him eat with us in the back room and we'll have privacy too, okay?"

"Yeah, all right, I'm going to the Damaged rehearsal later downtown. How's seven thirty?"

"Done. See you there." He picked through the biggest pile of unopened CDs and called Jay Fiondella, flamboyant owner of Chez Jay's.

"Okay, James. Don't make a habit of it, though, okay? When you get here, let Mary see you at the bar and then head round to the back of the building. I can't have you walking the dog through."

"Thanks. See you at seven thirty." He flipped through CDs, although he still got a fair amount of demos on cassette. With limited time, he went to the ones that had a visual style that made him think the music would connect to him.

At seven ten, they went down the front stairwell. The lawyers on the ground floor were gone. He liked the dark 1930s wood paneling and wainscoting that covered all of the offices downstairs. Highsmith, who was persona non grata down here, nosed around the corners of the skirting boards as they walked through the foyer out into the front yard of the building. Ocean Avenue was quiet. The lingering Santa Anas blew up over the top of the white stone rail across the street. Highsmith pulled him across the street to the ocean side. It was dark and dusty as they picked their way along the path. The homeless started to bed down for the night.

As they walked past the pier a couple of blocks down the way, the lights of the Ferris wheel flipped on and illuminated the old wooden boards. The blocks before Chez Jay had a seedy, slightly dangerous feel that the Santa Monica gentrification hadn't yet completely erased.

The jukebox played Roxy Music's "Amazona" as he and Highsmith passed the open door entrance, narrowly avoiding a half-staggering male patron who was beseeching the forty-year-old blonde who sidestepped his embrace.

"Baby, I've loved you true for so long. Give me a try," the guy pleaded in his Southern, sad, almost sincere voice. The fact that you might hear Roxy Music just as likely as the Allman Brothers, or as likely as Jack Nicholson to be the guy having a slow time of getting up from the bar beseeching the girl, was part of what made this joint unique. The bar in question was three deep and the drinkers leaned all over the diners at a dozen tables with red-and-white checkered tablecloths, but longtime barmaid/trouble shooter Mary saw the man and his dog and nodded. They walked around to the alley and entered, thanks to the grace of Jay, who unlocked the back door with a grunt of greeting.

The stocky, leather-faced owner was equally capable of slinging out overly obnoxious drunks or making the right kind of celebrities feel as if they were being shepherded into the back room of an old mob joint, which for all James knew, they might well be. He'd been coming in for years without ever learning much about Jay's history. The menu was small, kind of overpriced, ranging from spaghetti to so-so fish dishes, to the incongruous roast leg of lamb dinner, a bone from which Highsmith was treated to while James looked at the wine list.

Terry showed up ten minutes later, by which time James had ordered a really expensive bottle of Barolo. He looked haggard as he entered via the narrow corridor that separated the rooms. The din from the bar dropped into the background as the door swung shut behind him. Over the course of linguini with mussels and clams and the first of two bottles, James told his old friend about the tape and that he'd contacted their ex-colleagues, but expressed his misgivings about his qualifications to get to the bottom of things. Whether fortified by the wine or just having some things to consider, Terry had become more focused and sounded decisive when he spoke.

"Okay, James, I see it like this. I'll pay any and all expenses related to this—Nashville trip, etc. If you'll take a fee, I'll pay whatever you're getting paid to do films these days. Fair enough? Before you say anything, you should consider this. Whatever the deal is with this girl you met, it has to tie into Denny somehow, right? I don't think you can just walk away from this, even if you want to. If we can get to the bottom of this together, great, but if things get too heavy, I'll get professional help, okay? Besides, you did help with that murder and missing persons case during your club days, right—or so I heard?"

"Terry, it's not like I have proper experience. Are you sure you don't want to go to the police?"

"Look, I could file a missing persons report but truly what the fuck are they going to do? Just so you know, Jacquie never mentioned the tapes to me, and I'll not say a word to anyone, no matter what."

James looked at him with a wry smile. "Think they might be

enough to send me over, huh?" James filled both their glasses during the silence that followed his question.

Terry took a long swallow. "You know what? I think you should become Damaged's manager, too."

James looked at him incredulously. "Yeah, that's just what I need to take my mind off things."

"Listen, think about it. Denny will have a fit, but he would be forced to deal with you or lose the band. You'd at least get a chance to dig a little, see how he reacts."

"Maybe, but even so, there's the band to consider."

"Look, James, you really liked them. You know how to do this in your sleep. Come to rehearsal and talk to them."

"Be careful, mate. You know if I were to do this, you wouldn't necessarily be the person we'd sign to."

Terry snorted. "Nice."

"Look, as far as I'm concerned, your company's just as likely to fuck up this band's career as Denny's. You've got a bunch of frat boys working there, most of whom are in the business for all the wrong reasons. All this fucking rap/rock hybrid shit you're putting over these days suits them perfectly. I'm not sure that they'll get Damaged."

Terry was clearly nonplussed at having to justify all this to his friend. "Look, I'm going to get them on the road and—"

James put his hand up. "Save it. I'll come down tonight and let's just see how it goes, all right?"

They got on the 10 freeway a few blocks up at Lincoln, and slid into the still moderately busy freeway, making downtown within twenty-five minutes. They passed the high-rise core of official buildings—immigration, courthouse, etc.—and drove a bit farther past the garment district. James didn't know the area well and had rarely been here after his immigration interviews during the green card process and hitting the long-gone punk rock clubs that were the Hong Kong Café and Madame Wong's. He smiled wistfully as he remembered various altercations with bands he'd deemed inauthentic, including a table through Madame Wong's front door, which ended his visits there. Quite a feat, considering the entrance was up a flight of stairs. He had a vague notion that the Atomic Café, with its genius jukebox, still existed, but he couldn't have found it to save his life.

These days, there was the beginning of a reviving art scene and some loft conversions but other than the incongruous sight of two smartly dressed couples, they didn't pass a living soul for several miles. They pulled up by a chainlink fence that surrounded a three-story warehouse. James hopped out and pushed open the double gates; they pulled up alongside a primered green vintage pickup truck and a beaten-up Toyota hatchback.

Terry led the way to a single side door and they headed towards the noise. They went through another door that led into what looked like a makeshift recording studio control room. There was even glass that looked through to a larger area, where the band played. Must have been some sort of dispatch office originally, that looked onto a work area. Two large Wolfhounds jumped off a battered couch and loped over to a wary Highsmith, but everyone's scent checked out and once mutual asses were sniffed, all was well.

Davey spotted them after a few minutes and exited the floor area to reappear by the same door they'd entered through. "Do you guys want to come out here? I'd leave the dog, though; it's kinda loud." He introduced the affable, stocky, crew-cut drummer, Steve, and rangy, somewhat older bass player, Bill. Kat, the singer, wore an "I've Got My Own Album To Do" T-shirt, which cracked James up and led into a discussion of Ron Wood's solo record and on to Mick Jagger, whose line had inspired the album title. It was easy fun and he found them infectious.

The band went back to work, and played three new songs Terry apparently hadn't heard, before they turned to an impromptu cover of the Stones' "Monkey Man." They retired for beers back with the dogs, although Davey declined, having apparently a voracious appetite for chemicals and alcohol that had demanded moderation if he wished to remain alive. He said he'd had his limit for the week at Denny's dinner.

Kat popped a can with a slightly guilty look at Davey. James wondered whether she had a similar history. Young as she obviously was, that haunted look in her eyes suggested the possibility. After half an hour of musical talk and banter with the band about whether Davey's music or Kat's seemingly effortless, anthemic lyrical skills drove the show, Terry said, "So, I wanted you to meet James properly, because no matter who you sign with, you'll need a good manager. I think he could really help you. We are old friends, but you'll find everyone knows everyone else in this business. Besides, he's already told me he's not sure you should sign with me anyway." This got a few laughs.

"Sorry to interrupt you, Terry. In case you haven't figured it out by now, everyone you're hearing from right now will tell you anything they think you want to hear. I like what you're up to a lot, but other than the fact I really like what I do these days, the main reason I haven't managed anyone for a while is that all of these companies are fully capable of losing your record and there's no manager who can guarantee it won't happen."

Davey and Kat conferred quietly. Kat ended up spokesperson. "Eric's been setting us up with a lot of manager meetings and we've had some pretty big people interested, but no one that really felt right. We take what we're doing really seriously and we know we're probably only going to get one shot at this. When we saw how Denny reacted to you, we got curious and asked around about you and him. Had to get to asking really old people before we found anyone who knew much." She laughed. "Seems like in amongst all the shit you stirred up, maybe you actually cared more about music than protecting your gig. Is that accurate?"

Terry rolled his eyes at James but knew saying nothing right now was smart. James, vaguely uncomfortable but mostly pleased with that assessment, bit his lip ruefully. "Yeah, maybe then. Now I'm all about the money."

Davey chimed in. "We'd like to get some money too, but on our terms. We're uncomfortable with the idea of everyone being in bed with everyone else, but we're really more worried about Eric, his manager friends, and Denny than you and Terry somehow."

"If you want me involved, I'll do it as a consultant for a couple of months and see how we all feel about it after that. I gotta go to Nashville, but when I get back, let's meet without Terry so we can really strategize."

CHAPTER 10

Thirty-six hours later, he was boarding American Airlines' only direct flight to Nashville. Lainey had booked him dinner with Jeff Stanley for that night. He squeezed into the tiny window seat, pulled out his Walkman and cranked Primal Scream's *Vanishing Point* so he could enjoy take-off. Once they'd been cruising for a while, he used the hefty phone in the seatback to call a pal, Shelton Hank Williams III, figuring he might get through in time to do some serious drinking and see a bit of the town. He got an answering machine with some surreal cinematic excerpt that suited Hank down to the ground. He left his number at the Union Station Hotel.

The short flight breezed by. He'd made a vintage country music tape for the flight and George Jones played as the plane smoothly descended into Nashville. A short cab ride later, he checked in and showered at the Union Station Hotel, which had been converted from the old station in the center of Nashville. He called Stanley's office and his assistant suggested he come by the Music Row Rodeo headquarters and they could head for dinner from there.

He exited the hotel at six to catch a cab for the meeting. Always hard to explain his feelings back and forth on country music, but as this was his first time in Nashville, he wanted to see as much as possible and didn't give a fuck if it was total tourist time. The dichotomy for him was that he didn't "get" country at all until he lived in America, because there was no context in

England and it had always seemed a bit cheesy. By the time he'd wised up and discovered the authentic soulfulness of everyone from Hank Williams to Bob Wills, Nashville had long since moved on to crossover shit that nauseated him all over again. Somehow, from his label days, though, he'd always liked the label guys who were slinging the shit.

Mildly disappointed to see a PF Chang's as he looked out of the window, soon James felt the mood pass at the edge of Music Row. Compared to LA, with its huge sprawl of scattered labels and publishers, it was amazing to realize that a huge percentage of companies here could be entered simply walking down one street. The cab deposited him outside a two-story converted house, which was typical of a lot of the buildings along the street.

Once inside, Stanley's assistant looked pretty much like he'd figured she would, right along with that lovely drawl. She walked him into an office big enough for him to size up Jeff's weight and look while he walked over to the guy's desk, which was partly bathed in the shadows of dusk. His handshake was a little less sweaty than he remembered. He'd aged, but maybe not in quite the coke-ravaged way James semi-expected. Not altogether gone country—no boots or necktie—but a long jacket acknowledged he ain't in LA.

James shook his head a little. "Somehow it's really good to see you, Jeff."

"Thanks for the halfhearted, you schmuck."

James grinned. "So how did you end up down here anyway?"

Stanley got up. "Let's talk on the way to dinner." He glanced at his assistant. "See you in the morning, Bethany. We have a reservation, right?"

"You sure do. A booth just like you told me."

They walked out into the chilly evening. James hadn't realized

Nashville got winters. In his ignorance, he assumed the South was warm all year. There was a thin layer of ice on the sidewalk, so they tread carefully as they exited the building into a small parking lot in back that housed Stanley's dark blue Cadillac Eldorado. As they made the five-minute drive, Stanley explained the history of the joint they were headed to.

"The legendary Ryman Auditorium, which was home to the Grand Ole Opry in its classic years, is a dry venue, having been converted from a church, so every night between performances, various artists from Patsy Cline to Waylon Jennings slipped through the alley to Tootsie's, where they could both have a drink and sleep it off through the night if that was the eventuality."

"That's really cool, Jeff, I appreciate the idea. Tell me, what about you moving here?"

"Well, Gabby and I moved here in '92. Ronny Marin at Sony was really trying to push his acts into crossover pop, but he couldn't get into the chains outside of the South. It was a bit of a lifeline for me. It was a good change for us, too, to leave the 70s and 80s LA thing behind and start a normal life."

They slowed down on a busy street and looked for a spot. James could see the legendary Tootsie's. Outside, a rockabilly trio with slicked-back, Gene Vincent-inspired looks played with a stand-up bass player. Stanley pointed to a brick wall with a door. "See, there's the side door to the Ryman. People swear Hank Williams haunts this spot."

Once they entered the glass-windowed Tootsie's, the hostess evidently knew Stanley and slipped them past a long line of people who waited for tables. Most were modern cowboys, who shuffled their feet to a shit country band that played at the back end of the room. She leaned into Stanley as she nudged them into a nice red booth along with a plastic menu that had so many things he wanted on it, James instantly wished he was here for a week. He was having catfish everywhere he went though.

Stanley ordered a steak and a Scotch. James, not giving a shit, ordered red wine to go with the large order of catfish, fries, and greens. He half-listened to Stanley's affable but slightly false anecdotes about a bunch of people neither of them had either talked to or thought about for years, until he got round to Terry.

"So how is he?"

"Well, like I said, Jacqueline's gone missing." The food arrived. Stanley was on another Scotch. James liked the good, if not mythic, cornmeal-covered catfish. "So Jeff, I need to help him out and I'm pretty sure it all dates back to '78 and I think you must, too—otherwise you'd have told me to fuck off or said what you had to say on the phone. Seems like you still have some fat, cushy job so you certainly didn't do it to get a free meal, right?"

Stanley wasn't drunk yet, or too obviously scared, but in a kind of world-weary tone that James thought might be honest said, "After the crash, Denny had me into his office and told me there was a large push to get the live album into the pipeline within days, and to accommodate that, we'd be receiving product from an outside manufacturer as well as the usual from our own plant. The band were outlaw heroes overnight. I'm getting a three-to-one count from this other plant. Denny doesn't say shit for weeks, but it's obvious when it continues that they're manufacturing cleans. Basically bootlegs, counterfeits—call it what you will. Bottom line is all the money was going to Denny, not Real, or of course the estate of the band. It's pure profit for him. Nothing's going on the company's books. Nothing against the band's advance. No royalty, nothing. Anyway, what am I going to say, right? End of that year comes and I get a nice bonus. What the fuck?"

"Why are you telling me now?"

"Well, when you talked about Jacquie, I knew you might know something else. See, I got a phone call out of the blue, asking me if I ever felt guilty about the 70s. First of all, I'm laughing 'cause who doesn't, ya know? But then last week, I could have sworn I'm being followed places. I wasn't saying this on the phone, but I'm convinced that either someone from the family found out they'd been royally fucked, or else Denny's worried and he's getting ready to clean up loose ends. Either way, it's no good for me. I've been trying to live a simple family life here."

"I'm sure, Jeff. Tell me you haven't fucked your assistant. Maybe even on the job interview. Look, anyway, I ain't here to judge you. I don't care that you cashed in. Personally, I could see the family coming after Denny, but why Jacqueline? Doesn't make sense. Did you have any sense who the voice was? Could it have been Deutch?"

"It was a woman."

James's heart sank. "Oh no. Did she sound Canadian?" The catfish was now cold. Didn't taste good at all anymore.

"Didn't notice. She was kind of neutral, you know, more mocking than accusing. But she was obviously about money. Told me to dwell on my sins and she'd be in touch to discuss my salvation."

James ordered a beer. "I would have figured Deutch telling you to make sure you kept your mouth shut, or maybe just pushing you in front of a car one day." He laughed to keep it light but felt pretty sure it was the same girl he'd met at Granita. Fuck. Just a blackmailer. He shifted mode. "So back then, did you ever hear from the relatives' lawyers, anything?"

"Nothing at all until the late 80s and then only little odds and ends in *Billboard* that lawsuits had been filed. It was a joke, really—I mean, no computer records back then, and there are so many ways to hide every cent of record sales against marketing, promotion, that most artists never see a dime, never mind when there was seventy percent of sales not going on the books at all."

James sat, quietly digesting. A couple of drinks and the nouveau country folk bugged him less. The room got louder, which helped him think. He watched Stanley devour the rest of his steak between mouthfuls of Scotch. The ice had melted so it didn't rattle on his teeth now.

"How long would it take Denny to set up an alternative manufacturing plant?"

"Why?"

"Well, let me ask you something else first. Was this the first time, or had he been moving cleans on other records?"

"Not as far as I know."

"Could he have done it without you knowing?"

"Probably at first, but unless it was spread nationally on a fairly small scale, I'd have noticed sales patterns shifting, I think."

"So let's say he'd set it up this way. The live record was the first time. He'd made a killing." Stanley winced at James's choice of words. "No one else inside the company would likely be suspicious because the band hadn't sold much in the past, right? Some sales spike on a posthumous release. An unknown factor. Impossible to predict."

Their waitress came by. Stanley stared at her chest while she leaned across him to remove their plates. They ordered new drinks. The band had finished. "Mercy, Mr. Percy" by Varetta Dillard played over the sound system, which sounded way better than the homogenized shit that had preceded it, that was for sure.

"So how long, Jeff, and what happened next?"

"A couple of months, maybe, I dunno. What does it matter?"

"Because Denny's a planner and a schemer. He's had his whole fucking system set up and when that plane went down in flames, he was ready to roll. It's too much of a coincidence. Don't tell me this never crossed your mind."

Stanley looked gray-faced. "I tried to convince myself he'd been getting set up and that this was a good chance to get started, but…" His voice trailed off into the past.

James finished the sentence for him. "But you knew in your gut that he knew the plane was going down. That's why you're fucking scared now. Which is why you'd talk to me, but not on the phone. You're hoping I'm still the same loudmouth so you'll be safer with someone else knowing Denny's a murderer."

Somehow saying it out loud had shocked them both into a stunned silence that lasted through several songs. It must have been Oldies Night because one after another came classics: "I Fall To Pieces," from Patsy Cline and then Connie Francis's version of "Just A Dream." His eyes burned with sadness and behind it a still-unacknowledged rage.

Finally Stanley spoke. "So what now?"

"Was Jacquie ever around when you and Denny discussed the cleans?"

Jim Reeves sang, "I'm Beginning to Forget You."

"Denny never really discussed it with me. He told me what to do. I got bonuses. Obviously he knew I knew but we never directly discussed it."

"Do you think he recorded you?"

"What? I don't know. Why?"

"It might explain the girl's phone call, if you'd implicated yourself somehow."

"I don't think we ever talked about it, but I was doing a lot of liquor and blow then. I'm not certain." Stanley groaned.

James shook his head. "I've gotta take a leak." He walked through the throngs of dancers to the restroom, and asked the waitress for the check as he passed her. He called the hotel from the payphone and retrieved two messages. First Lainey, "Charlie Major's office called and we arranged dinner for you two at the Sandcastle, and Kat left word saying that Eric got an offer from Denny but it's only good for two days so please call her ASAP." Then Hank, "Hey, man, don't know how long you're in town, but if you wanna meet tonight, I'll be at 3rd & Lindsley after about ten. It'd be good to see you."

Back at the table, he paid the check. Stanley said, "Why don't we have one for the road at the bar?"

"Thanks, Jeff, but I'm gonna go to 3rd & Lindsley to see a friend. I'd appreciate a lift if it's not out of your way. Come with us if you want," he offered halfheartedly, having become vaguely depressed at the prospect of more alcohol with his dinner companion.

"No, James, perhaps it's better if no one much sees us together. I'd had Bethany get us tickets for the George Strait show at the Stadium, but the more I think about it, the more I'm hoping you'll keep my name out of all this."

They braced against the cold night air. The rockabilly band was still blazing, seemingly impervious to the chill.

"If it was George Jones, you'd have me there. I'm heading home tomorrow. If you think of any slight thing that might help find Jacqueline, call me."

Five minutes later, the Cadillac pulled up outside of a smallish-looking bar with storefront windows and blue wood paneling. James could see the gaunt, angular grandson of Hank Williams at the bar.

With his long hair not visible from this angle, he looked hauntingly like his forebear, the man at once out of his own time. James got out of the car without shaking hands. He braced his hands against the top of the passenger door to avoid slipping on the icy sidewalk. He almost said, "Watch your back," but stopped himself. "I'll let you know anything you should hear, Jeff. I appreciate your talking to me, even if I know you did it for yourself."

"So long, Slick," said Stanley.

Inside the bar, a five-piece band was playing. The singer, a fair-haired, blue-eyed woman with the sweetest country soul voice James had heard since the likes of Maggie Bell of Stone the Crows fame back in his early teens prowled the stage. The guitar player rolled beautiful slide guitar lines that washed across her vocals like a dusky dream. James ordered a beer but he and Hank saved the conversation until half an hour later when the band, who went by the name of Blue Mother Tupelo, took a break.

"That was fucking great, Hank, thanks."

"All right, James. I thought it was worth getting myself out the door on the early side to see them too. Glad you liked it. What finally got you to Trashville?"

"Jeez, Hank, it's a long, dark tale." James grinned.

"Those are my specialty."

"I'll fill you in, but let's hear from you first."

"Well, I'm making another record, hopefully this time it'll be more of me than what these motherfuckers at Curb forced me into last time."

His father, Hank Williams Jr. of *Monday Night Football* infamy, in a rare moment of paternal attention, had introduced his son to Mike Curb, ex-lieutenant governor of California and owner of Curb Records. The record man had signed Hank to an onerous label and publishing deal, proving some shit just never seems to get any better. He'd promptly forced him to co-write with a bunch of Nashville cheeseballs despite the artist having a fat notebook full of haunting tales of darkness and despair that would have made his granddaddy proud. With both the talent and balls that had clearly skipped a generation, he denounced his own record to the press in a brave but unsuccessful attempt to get kicked off the label.

"Yeah, no co-writes, right?"

"No fucking way."

"What I don't get," said James, "is the country market isn't doing so great right now. It's been shrinking. Why won't they embrace you?"

"Think they wanna keep the last piece of their pie the bland flavor it is, you know. Circle the wagons. Anyhow, why don't you and I step outside and smoke a nice fat joint? I'm gonna play a few new ones acoustic and see how they feel, all right?"

A few minutes later, as the first chords of "Alone and Dying" drifted across 3rd & Lindsley, a beautiful cherry red pickup truck with a cow catcher grille on the front slipped up the roadside embankment that speed-trap-loving Tennessee cops employed. It quickly sped up to move alongside Stanley's slightly weaving Cadillac Eldorado. It cut in front of him once, just to spook him a little, and then allowed the Eldorado ahead again. Then it jammed up an inch from the rear fender and put the full beams on, which half-blinded the disoriented New Jersey man. As Stanley sped the car up to around eighty-five, the truck cut across to the far side of the road. Now catching up, the driver angled the cow catcher towards Stanley's passenger door. Happily for the pickup driver, who really hated to have to deal with his slow working car body shop, Stanley tried to accelerate into the impending curve but instead launched the Cadillac far into the night air off the road and crashed down across the embankment and straight into one of the venerable oak trees that lined a five-acre homesite.

The pickup truck driver pulled up and carefully reversed his truck to the edge of the road, where he awaited the hoped-for explosion. When this was not forthcoming, he shrugged, his rising anger kept in check by considering how his beautiful paint job was still intact. He turned the truck lights off and with a small flash light, picked his way carefully down the embankment and across to where the wrecked Cadillac lay. The debris of leaves and bracken made avoiding telltale footprints a relatively easy task. He opened the driver's door carefully with gloved hands and saw the bloody form. He removed one glove briefly and could feel a very slight pulse in the stricken man.

With his still-gloved right hand, he leaned across and released Stanley's seat belt. He carefully pulled Stanley's head off the steering wheel by the remaining hair at the back of his head. He thoughtfully peered into Stanley's unconscious eyes and thought there might be a slight flicker. His right hand then slammed Stanley's head back into the steering wheel with a shattering crunch. He paused, looked to see whether any lights had come on at the somewhat distant mansion. He needn't have worried. As it happened, the owner of the land, one George Strait, was onstage at the Nashville Municipal Auditorium that moment with all of his household in attendance.

A minute or two went by, and he found that Jeff Stanley's pulse, along with any chance of uttering inconvenient words at some point, was completely gone...

After a now only half-remembered night of debauchery with Hank,

James had swung by his hotel, packed, caught the one direct American flight back to California, collected Highsmith from the beloved ex-Bank of America manager turned dog minder, Bette Fechtman up on Busch Drive, bought some cooked trout from Malibu Seafood, and enjoyed it with half a bottle of Bordeaux. He asked Lainey to call Damaged, and assure them he'd be in touch with everyone about their deal in the morning. For once he listened to his body and went for a mercifully nightmare-free night's sleep.

CHAPTER 11

It was about 12:30 pm when the phone rang in the lousily constructed wooden attic above Damaged's rehearsal space. Davey was completely dead to the world, but Katrina half awoke, rolled over in the old iron bed and grabbed the phone from the bare floor on the fourth ring.

"Hey, James. Are you back?"

"Yeah, I got your message. Did you tell Eric we are going to work together?"

"Yeah." She half-yawned, half-chuckled throatily. "He did suggest we continue our managerial search, but we told him it's a done deal."

"Your message said Denny's made an offer?"

"He's offering to pay for demos if we do his fucking afternoon showcase and will give us an option for a record."

"How sweet of him. What do you guys think?"

"Well, we wanna do everything on our own terms but despite all the labels talking, it's the only offer we've had to record so we didn't tell Eric no."

"Right. Obviously there's no love lost between Denny and me, but ultimately I want you lot to have the best chance you can get. I hate all the bidding war crap because sometimes the expectations get so high that it becomes a weight around an artist's neck before you ever have a record. On the other hand, if a label has put up a good-sized advance, it does set a certain tone inside the label to take you seriously. Let's agree to play somewhere with a good sound system but I'd round up all the label suspects and see who'll actually make offers. And to make it fun, we'll let Denny book and pay for the venue."

"James, we trust you, but are you sure we shouldn't just say fuck you all and come to the Dragonfly? Wouldn't you have done that in your heyday?"

He sat on the branch-shaded deck with a relaxed Highsmith asleep across his feet. Maybe she was right. Maybe he was too fucking comfortable.

CHAPTER 12

James took the elevator up to the seventeenth floor of the Century Park East high-rise that housed the legal partners Levine, Brody, and Hauser. This building was where he had experienced his first earthquake, the sensation of which had been enhanced by the rollers the building had been built upon in order to allow it some movement during the big temblors. At the time, he'd thought the whole building was about to topple.

He'd left Highsmith at home, as he'd not wanted to impose the antiseptic aesthetic on the impressionable young dog. Where would he pee, to start with? It would be impossible for any latter-day archeologist to detect a semblance of the old MGM lot that had once stood here. He announced himself to the middle-aged receptionist, who gave him a vaguely disapproving look and buzzed Brody's office. James flipped through a copy of *Charts Magazine* while he waited. Irreverent rival to *Billboard*, it was the only music trade he bothered to look at. Their gossip columns predicting hires, fires, and band signings always amused James, knowing, of course, there were multi-layered editorial agendas and a refreshingly reckless attitude. He saw that Damaged was listed along with a few others in the Buzzing section.

Brody's paralegal, Jim Davis, came and walked James through the elegantly appointed offices back to one of the corner offices that housed the partners. Two of the four walls were glass from floor to ceiling. The walls were ringed by a series of photographs: Brody with a mixture of label heads—Irving Azoff, Walter Yetnikoff, Clive Davis—along with artists like Michael Jackson, a young Bruce Springsteen. He didn't rise to greet James, who dropped into one of the two cushy black leather chairs that faced the lawyer's old-school wooden desk.

"Is this to be the beginning of a very uncomfortable working relationship, Dual?"

"Not if everything you say is as straightforward as that, Eric."

"Hmmm." He pursed his lips and touched his hair line which, James noted idly, seemed to be a little nearer the pudgy man's eyebrows than he remembered. Probably using one of those new hair restoration products.

"Why are you advising Damaged to take Denny's insulting offer? Like I don't already know the answer to that," said James.

"It's more than your friend Harper has put on the table thus far," Brody noted acidly, and James realized, accurately.

"Have you let all the weasels who are sniffing around from the other companies know there's an offer in?"

The lawyer shifted in his seat. "I don't see the advantage, given it's really just a demo deal."

"Come on, Eric, like you need to give them details. Bluff a little. This just confirms what I thought about how cozy it would be for you and Denny to make this nice and easy on yourselves."

Brody bristled with indignation; whether faked or not, time would tell. "How dare you come in here and question my integrity? Denny and I may be friends, but that doesn't extend to selling him artists on the cheap."

"Okay, Eric, here's the deal. Call the other labels, including

Real—tell them there's an offer. The band will do one show that they can bring their senior execs to. Tell Denny no SIR showcase. He can pay for the Viper Room and they'll play a mid-evening show as long as I can invite who I want."

Brody pursed his lips once more. "Surprisingly reasonable by your standards. Let me talk to Denny."

James hit the elevator button as he realized he'd let his instincts for the band take precedence. If he'd really wanted to wind Golden up, he would have done what Kat suggested and told him Dragonfly or nothing.

By the time he'd driven to his office, there was a message from Eric's office to confirm the showcase. He called the band and got Davey, whom Kat had obviously filled in.

"So, Thursday night, Viper Room. You can go in at three pm and sound check. There's normally a DJ Thursdays, and no band, so the club will take any walkups. You can have as big a list as you want, which should help this feel a little more natural."

"Yeah, but not as natural as Dragonfly."

"But the Viper Room has great monitors and Katrina should really be able to hear herself for once. You said her voice has blown out screaming sometimes."

"Yeah, I guess."

"Davey, if you're not ready for this, say so."

"Fuck it, James, I'm ready. It's just I've been waiting all my life for this."

James smiled. "I'll see you at sound check."

CHAPTER 13

James decided to head over to the Viper Room for the late afternoon sound check, ready to help steady any nerves, if needed. Eric's office had faxed over an impressive guest list of A&R weasels from all the majors, significantly including a couple of label presidents: Interscope's Tom Whalley and Giant's Irving Azoff. The legendary manager and ex-MCA head was an interesting addition that would definitely elevate Denny's blood pressure.

As he turned right onto Sunset off Doheny, he got caught in the slow crawl of traffic, but got lucky and found a parking spot right by the Viper entrance which was on Larrabee, the sloping side street. He remembered to cramp his front right tire into the curb, as they ticketed if you didn't. Ridiculous scam, considering no one drove stick shifts in LA, so the likelihood of your car rolling down the hill was pretty much zero. The club had been called Filthy McNasty's when he'd first arrived from England and then the Central until Johnny Depp had taken it over, doing a nice job of fixing it up. Less than half the size of The Roxy across the street and the Whisky, it had never been able to compete with them for the English touring bands. River Phoenix's drug OD demise on the street outside was sadly how the club was remembered the most.

Currently, a bunch of amps were being loaded out of the band's van onto that spot of Sunset. For some reason, the Viper only used the Sunset double door as an entry for load in and load out.

Punters were all entranced via the side which typically, by night, would have (in James's opinion at least) an obnoxious red velvet-roped way of admitting. Damaged was still at the roadie-less stage so all but Katrina were doing the humping. Davey grinned happily as he put his amp onto the high stage.

"All right, then?" James asked.

"Yeah. Can't wait. I came down last night to check the sound out. You're right—we'll tear it up here."

Steve had erected his kit and began a few little flourishes to inadvertently punctuate the conversation.

"So how about your vampiric crowd? Think they'll come here this early?"

"I think so, enough at least to fill this room up a bit. How about the business end?"

"Have to say, quite impressive. Want details?"

"Nah. Tell me after."

James was more than a little relieved. He'd feared Davey, needing all this a bit too much, might tense up, but so far, so good. He wandered over to the bar where Katrina was astride a stool and stared into the middle distance. He slipped onto the one next to her.

"'K?"

"Yeah—bit reflective."

He looked into those black eyes but didn't speak.

"No matter what happens tonight, everything's going to change, right? I mean even if we don't get signed. 'Cause this will have been the moment."

"In a way, yes. Can you live with that?" he asked.

"Look, I started this for fun. I'd never sung before—no lessons, nothing at school. This voice just came out of nowhere. Davey…it's been his life. He's been in bands since he was fourteen.

It's what drives him on. We were both pretty fucked up when we met. There was dark shit all around us, and writing and playing together gave us something to focus on while we tried to get cleaned up a bit. If it ended here for me, so be it. I'm just not sure if Davey…" She trailed off.

"Yeah, I've been wondering a bit too. Look, he seems all right. If you lot just deliver like normal, it'll be fine. Try to keep it light with the band and then go kill."

She smiled.

"Look, I'll be here for sound check, but you need to make sure the monitor mix suits you. It should really help hearing yourself, but I'd suggest you don't have it so loud you get distracted, all right?"

"Yeah, thanks. There have been nights my voice just tears up by the time I get to 'Cool as Fuck.'"

He smiled. "Once we get this out of the way, I'll sort you out with a good vocal coach. You're gonna need to sing five or six nights a week once you hit the road. Listen, who has your list? I'm gonna get this stuff out of the way now."

"I got it." She pulled a couple of handwritten sheets of paper out of the back pocket of her black Levi's.

He wandered back across the floor to a black (like the rest of the club) door that led to Johnny Depp's partner's office, Bobby Aren. The short, curly-haired, affable New Yorker was seated behind a desk in a tiny office halfway down a narrow corridor that continued on to a dressing room. He stuck his head in.

"James? What the—" he exclaimed in his nasal but pleasant tone. The office looked much the same as when James had last entered, except for the absence of a mirror with a large pile of coke and two musicians from a somewhat notorious rock band from Manchester.

"It has been awhile, Bobby. You good?"

"Yeah, not bad. Spending more time than I really want in here these days, though. Gotta book more bands, 'specially to keep the weeknights in the black."

James knew it was tough to keep any LA club flying for the long haul, especially one that had been celebrity-driven from the get-go.

"The weekends have kinda gone from young Hollywood actors to Valley and Orange County weekenders. The LA version of New York's bridge and tunnel crowd, ya know?"

"Oh, fuck," said James with a pained grin.

Bobby shrugged. "What ya gonna do, right? Jeez, it's been too long, James. When were you last here?"

"Me and Michael Hutchence from INXS came down," he remembered suddenly.

"Oh God, right. So sad that he went, especially like that. You guys were close. Sorry."

"Yeah, I miss him. No one lit a room up like Michael. In a way, it seems like he was the last of the true rock stars."

"Yes…"

In the silence, he again thought about the tragic and inexplicable end of the charismatic singer hung on the bathroom door of his Sydney hotel room—supposed accident of autoasphyxiation. Hounded out of the country by the scumbag English tabloids for his doomed romancing of "Saint" Bob Geldof's wife Paula Yates, she now lost to an OD, her baby orphaned—a sad, sad waste.

"Yeah, Johnny was pretty broken up about it too. It makes no sense." A thunderous guitar riff crashed through the wall. "Jesus Christ!" exclaimed Bobby. "That's loud!"

"That's actually why I'm here."

"To complain about the noise?" Bobby tried to lighten the mood.

"I'm managing them," said James.

"Really? Thought you'd given that up."

"Yeah, I had. Long story that I won't bore you with."

"You thinking about signing with Denny Golden? I know he's springing for this."

"We'll see." James gave a rueful grin. "Couple of things you could help with, Bobby. First, can you get your sound man to give them as long a check as they want? If it costs you overtime, I'll be happy to pick up the tab."

"Don't worry about it."

"Thanks. Second, I know the label publicists will call to get booths reserved." The Viper had a handful of VIP tables and the rest of the upstairs part of the club was standing only. "I'd love it if there could be a mix-up so Denny doesn't have a table. Give them to Azoff—and Terry Harper."

Bobby laughed. "Glad I had Olympian send a check in advance. What are you up to?"

"Would you believe me if I said this isn't a band you see sitting down?"

"If you say so, James. Denny's a prick and I can deal if he never comes back."

Katrina's voice was now in full cry.

"Thanks, mate, I really appreciate it. If things happen the way they should for this band, I'll make sure they come play here when it will mean something. I better go see how they're doing. Oh, yeah, here's their list. Did you get the A&R one from Eric's?"

"Yeah, all good."

They hugged quickly. He walked out and remembered to

slide his form-fit earplugs in as he opened the door back into the main room. The empty room intensified the sound that rumbled through his body, but it felt good. The stage, which was very high for a room this size, would help Kat, and its being small would obscure the fact that she didn't move much, which would likely bother the senior American A&R people.

The sound man, who had a strong Scottish accent, was getting good levels quickly and, unlike a lot of the bitter, nasty club soundmen in LA, seemed to be enjoying himself. Davey had set up stage right, opposite to normal, but would directly face the tables where the guys who could actually write checks would be seated. Smart.

Kat was on her haunches now and helped the Scot get monitor levels. "Fuck one, two, fuck three, four." She laughed and started growling and yipping; she threw in lines from the Stones' "Monkey Man" here and there, but sounded like Iggy Pop in her dangerous abandon. James shivered in anticipation.

CHAPTER 14

At six, he headed across Sunset to the Rainbow Bar & Grill. To his immense pleasure, Luigi stood in his familiar spot by the entrance, although it was way too early for any Roxy concert-going crowd to be about. His old friend was slightly heavier-set and showed a little gray in his thick black hair, but looked amazingly well, especially considering the business he was in.

"Mr. James—what a surprise. How are you?"

"Better for seeing you, Luigi."

"What brings you to the world-famous Rainbow Bar and Grill?"

"I was at the Viper Room sound-checking a band I'm managing and realized I was just up the block from you. Came on the off chance you might be here."

"I'm always here," Luigi said, perfectly seriously, his Italian accent undiminished by time.

James shook his head, empathizing. "I had a club for a while. It's hardcore being around high people all night, every night, but you look great. How do you do it?"

"Clean living."

James wasn't quite sure if he was kidding. "Is your kitchen open yet?"

"Yes, chef's ready. Would you like the Rainbow Bar and Grill world-famous pizza for old times' sake?"

Despite never eating pizza, James nodded. "Sure. That sounds great. Got time to join me?"

Luigi looked inside, where the unchanged red booths and checkered tablecloths were wholly unoccupied. "Oh, for a minute."

They walked over to one of the smaller booths on the entrance side of the horseshoe configuration. A pretty, but not stunning, black-haired waitress came out of the shadows; she looked surprised to see her boss seated, for much like Rick in *Casablanca*, Luigi did not join the punters.

"A pizza on the house for Mr. James, and what about a very tall Scotch with a drop of water?"

James smiled. "A glass of whatever Italian red you have would be great, thanks." She slid away. "I don't suppose Wanda's still here?" he asked, naturally remembering the iconic waitress.

"She is. We created a job for her to be in charge of the waitresses. Hiring and firing."

"That was very cool of you, mate."

"Funny. It seemed like a kindness, as she was like family by then, you know, but it turned out to be a big plus. She can tell the ones who will fit in here, so things go much smoother than they used to."

"Yeah, you want good bad girls, right?" laughed James.

"Exactly. So where have you been all these years that you don't come visit us?"

"Sitting here, I got to admit I feel sad about that, Luigi. You and Mario really looked out for me, and I should have stopped by. Some things have happened lately that brought up those times. I don't expect you remember, but I met a girl here the night of the Confederacy plane crash—she went down on that flight. After that, as you probably do remember, I was hitting everything pretty hard.

Once I got straightened up, I think I didn't want to be reminded of her."

The red wine and thick-crusted pizza arrived, adorned with a nice mix of green peppers and some really good-looking anchovy filets. He cut a piece of crust and slid an anchovy on it, chewing appreciatively. "I've always tried to keep moving forward, no reflection, no looking back. But bottom line is I'm sorry, because in doing that I didn't honor our friendship."

"That's nice, you say, James. Don't worry too much. We are still here now, right? Can I ask why you are thinking about that time again?"

James didn't hesitate. "Terry Harper's wife Jacqueline has disappeared. Maybe you remember her? She used to be Denny Golden's assistant back then."

He nodded. "Pretty girl. Seemed a bit innocent to be among all the Rainbow children, though." He waved his arm expansively around the still-empty room. As the arc of his arm pointed towards the entrance, Wanda strolled in. In the dim light, she looked unchanged. It was only when she headed towards them that the age lines were apparent and, like Luigi, she had filled out a little. Her hand went to her mouth.

"Oh my God, James! Well, you are a sight for sore eyes," she exclaimed. She bent down to hug him as he half stood.

"You too, girl." He felt a rush of happiness.

"Mr. James is telling me that Denny Golden's old assistant, Jacqueline, is missing."

Wanda paused, obviously trying to place who they were talking about. "Oh yeah, Jacqueline Dean. Man, she was a green one."

"Actually, Jacqueline Harper these days. She's married to

Terry Harper," James interjected.

"Wow, you're kidding me. Last I remember, she was in a fit over him going off with that poor girl from the Confederacy."

James stiffened. "Are you sure? How the hell can you remember all that way back?"

Wanda had one hand on her hip and adopted a pose he was all too familiar with. "Maybe because I wasn't shit-faced every day of my lazy ass life the way some people were." She glared at him, he hoped only partly serious. "She knew you were trouble for Terry and a threat to them as a couple. He'd see you leave here with a different girl every other night. She was convinced he'd feel like he was missing out, and that night when he left with Holly from the Confederacy confirmed she was right. I told her she should pretend she never saw a thing, but the way she went crying out of here, I figured they were done."

James got up and hugged her. "I love you, Wanda. Thanks."

"Sure you do. I've got to get ready for my shift. Really nice to see you alive, though. I wouldn't have figured you'd make it."

"Wanda, could I call you? Maybe take you for lunch when I get this situation sorted?"

"Lunch? You get up in the morning and everything now, huh? Who'd have thought? I'm here five nights a week. You know the number." She sauntered off and James thought maybe she was just slightly exaggerating the swing of her still very beautiful ass.

As James went back to demolishing the pizza, Luigi quizzed him a little. "Please tell me you don't think this situation is connected to Denny Golden."

"Can't do that, mate. I think all roads lead to him right now."

"This is none of my business and I don't want it to be, but be careful. You seem to have got your life back and you look really well. Why go there?"

"Thanks. I appreciate your concern, but I promised Terry I'd try. It's too late to turn back now. If you know something I should know, please spill."

"Nothing specific, my friend, but I hear whispers, as they used to say. Trust me, you don't want to get too close to his business."

Luigi walked him back to the parking lot, which was partly filled with early arrivals for the show at The Roxy.

"Look at all the boys and girls of the Rainbow parking lot. They still come."

"Funny, but the way fashion goes, this could be 1978."

"True. Look at that girl." Luigi pointed at one who could have been an eighteen-year-old Stevie Nicks if she'd been raised by the Manson family. "She looks just like that friend of yours, Drea, daughter of those actors."

"The more things change, eh, Luigi?" James left the old adage unfinished and walked back up towards the Viper Room.

CHAPTER 15

As he turned onto Larrabee, he saw a three-hundred-pound, shaved-headed black man in a gray Armani suit bluntly dealing with the line of people, a mix of music business insiders and Damaged fans who moved slowly and impatiently. James walked down past the rope to where he could see Asa, the excitable but friendly Persian cashier (like many exiles, he preferred Persian to Iranian) who crossed off names in a slow, deliberate manner.

Asa called out, "James, come on in. Bobby told me you are manager." The security guard wordlessly unhooked the rope.

"Thanks, Asa. This lot driving you crazy yet?"

"Same as usual, James. They all think they are a VIP."

He walked past the booth down the short corridor, at the end of which was a dark lounge area that typically played low-key chill-out music. Due to the slope of the street, you had to go up a flight of stairs to access the main room of the club, which he now did.

He could see a petite waitress with cropped hair over by the booths on the far side of the room in heated conversation with a woman who looked suspiciously like the female Olympian exec at Granita. He smiled contentedly and slipped through the door, deciding to stay out of the way until showtime.

The band sat quietly, maybe pensively, in the sparse dressing room and sipped from bottles of water.

"All right, you lot?" he asked. Everyone grunted in the

affirmative. "Mind if I have a look at the set list?"

Davey handed it over. James nodded appreciatively. Light—shouldn't run more than thirty minutes, only slightly more than half their usual gig. He frowned though, as just before the closer "Cool as Fuck" there was a slot that just said "Cover."

"What's the cover? Dunno if I'd be doing a cover, ya know?"

"It's a surprise. We think you'll approve," laughed Katrina.

He shook his head. "It's your funeral. Seriously, I want you to just go and have fun. I'd suggest that you don't acknowledge that this is a showcase on stage. Just be how you'd act at Dragonfly or anywhere, ya know?"

A few minutes before they were due onstage, the door burst open and a seriously flustered Lainey entered. "James, I've been trying to find you for hours."

"Girl, the band's about to go on. Can't it wait?" he said.

"No."

"All right. Let's go out here." He ushered her into the corridor, wanting to minimize any distraction to the band. "What the fuck's so important?"

"The Nashville Police Department called, looking for you this afternoon. Jeff Stanley's dead. They said you were the last person to see him alive."

"Oh God, what happened?"

"Car wreck. He hit a tree and was dead when they found him."

James's mind reeled. He shook and his gut was in a knot. "What do they want me to do?"

"Call them as soon as you can. I have the officer's name for you."

Bobby came up. "Ready to get this going, James? Place is

packed and I don't want to turn my regulars away later if I can help it."

"Yeah, all right. Lainey, can you run out and make sure Irving Azoff from Giant and Tom Whalley from Interscope are in their booths? Also, try to spot Denny Golden."

"I'm not sure what these people look like."

"Then ask Terry. Be quick, okay?" His jangled nerves betrayed him now. He leaned against the wall and tried to compose himself. Was Stanley's demise an accident? He'd been probably driving drunk for thirty years or more—why now? He'd have to think very carefully what he would say to the cop. Last thing he needed was another Nashville trip right now. If they were convinced it was an accident, they might settle for a phone statement. The still-flustered Lainey returned.

"All the ones you want are here."

"Okay, thanks." He stuck his head into the dressing room. "All right, you lot, let's go."

After an initial blast of lead guitar feedback that had many covering their ears, Damaged settled into a rock solid performance. By three songs in, Kat was clearly loving the feeling of power the high stage gave her, as she glared down and howled at the dense throng of bodies. He spotted the huge frame of Deutch standing in the middle of the room, directly behind Golden, ensuring no one came within a foot of the label head's space. Pete flanked him, head bobbing. Davey was glorying in the moment, without overdoing the guitar heroics. Rhythm section note perfect.

They finished "Surviving You" and Davey briefly stepped next to Katrina, singing "Oooooh, Oooooh" like a backup singer, and as he said, "Got a light, James?" the Englishman realized they were about to launch into one of his all-time favorite rock anthems,

"30 Days in the Hole," by Humble Pie. As the girl roared the drugs and booze drenched lyrics, odds were few would even know it was a cover, but it didn't matter because despite the original iconic Stevie Marriott vocal, she owned it right now.

As the song ended, he heard a particularly loud yell and spotted John Van Put, an old-school English manager: a short, rotund, perpetually sweaty man who was rarely far from his next drink. James wondered whether Eric had invited him in hopes that the band would have a change of heart.

"Cool as Fuck" left James elated, forgetting all else for the moment. The band wisely resisted their fans' calls for more tonight, saying simply, "Thanks, we're Damaged," and ducked off stage. He left them to enjoy making their way through the crowd. Whatever anyone said to them tonight would mean nothing until the cold light of day when the phone calls and faxed offers would either come or they wouldn't.

He looked for Terry when Van Put rolled up along with Barry Gordon, the slick, soulless head of A&R at Pacific Records. "Brilliant, James. What a show! Would you take us over to meet the band?"

"Us?" He raised an eyebrow quizzically.

"Ha, ha. Yes, us. We are giving John here a label deal and Damaged could be the perfect first signing."

Despite his revulsion for Gordon in particular, it was an interesting thought, and he knew for the band's sake he shouldn't blow anyone off out of hand. "Sure. Let's go."

They pushed their way against the small tide who gradually headed towards either the bar or exit, and found the band about halfway towards the door to their dressing room. Katrina hugged James, and spoke into his ear. "Irving *fucking* Azoff told me I'm a rock star."

"He should know, right? Seriously, good show, girl."

They separated; James gave Davey and the guys a quick thumbs-up. "So, guys, this is Barry Gordon from Pacific Records, and John Van Put here who, along with managing a number of bands you loved at one time or another, now has a label deal there."

John was all over them but it seemed as genuine as the bourbon that he reeked of. "Fucking brilliant—the Humble Pie cover is a great idea. We could be all over rock radio with that. You remind me of when I first met AC/DC."

Barry half turned so he was talking only to James while the band soaked up the praise from Van Put. "John wants the band. We are ready to make a preemptive offer if that's something you'd be interested in. I'll say this now, though, before we involve Eric and our business affairs people. We are about to announce John's label deal and need the momentum, so it will be a good offer, but I don't have time for a protracted bidding war. I need them in the studio soon, so at the latest we have a record to set up this fall for a first quarter release."

"All right, Barry, you understand I'll really need to discuss this properly with the band, but it's an interesting notion and I do take it seriously."

"Fair enough. We'll be in touch."

He wanted to find Terry but realized he should get the guest list so they could tell exactly who'd been there. Lainey was over at the bar with a couple of girlfriends, so he decided to do it himself. The place had emptied considerably as this joint wasn't where Damaged's fans would hang out typically—the drinks were too expensive, for one thing—and the majority of the A&R weasels were probably moving on to the next gig, so he had no trouble as he made his way back down the stairs, at least until he got to the bottom where the massive Deutch stood in the shadows. He didn't speak, but grabbed James by the front of his T-shirt, lifted him off the ground and threw him effortlessly through the beaded curtain, where he landed in a sprawl on the floor of the chill-out room. From James's perspective, he could only see Golden's gut looming over him.

"Last time you fucked with me, Dual, I decided to let you continue to exist. Barely, of course, but it amused me as you count for less than nothing in the world. Your pathetic attempts to annoy and humiliate me of late, though, have brought my gaze upon you again, something you should fervently wish to avoid."

Out of the corner of his eye, James could see Deutch filled the entrance ensuring the privacy of the moment. The next thing he noticed was that Denny wore the same carefully scuffed shoes as at Granita, as the right one came crashing with full force into his stomach. As he choked for air, Golden advised him, "Don't make me look at you again." Three swift brutal kicks to the ribs followed in quick succession.

Unable to catch his breath and barely hanging onto the Rainbow pizza in his gut, the next thing he realized as the foot swung back, this time slamming into the back of his head, was that apparently Savile Row shoemakers were using steel toe caps this year.

Deutch looked down at the unconscious body as Goldfrapp's neo-noir "Lovely Head" played. "Denny, why not let me take care of this kind of thing like usual?"

Golden smiled contentedly. "I needed to deliver this particular message personally. What's he going to do about it? We have insurance if he were ever stupid enough to try to press charges.

Besides, I rather enjoyed it—like pulling wings off a butterfly. Can't let you have all the fun now, can we, Ron?"

On that note, the happy couple made their way out to the waiting Music Express Town Car, which whisked them the few blocks to Denny's West Hollywood penthouse, which he hadn't had the opportunity to enjoy for several weeks.

CHAPTER 16

He came to in an unfamiliar double bed, the size and color of which he figured meant he wasn't in hospital. He had a not-at-all-noir, neo or otherwise, nauseating, aching, spinning sensation that was completely new to him. He did, however, try to recall every self-pitying tough guy inner monologue he'd ever seen or read, milking the moment, while he tried to prop himself on one elbow to get a better look at his surroundings.

A white framed window, about an inch and a half open, let in some serious dirty heat. On the other side was a wooden table with a plastic bottle of water, a few silver rings, and an ankle bracelet. The walls were Caribbean red, which he very much appreciated right now. He grabbed the water, which was warm, but finished it, coughing in a way that caused the bedroom door to open. Lainey's lanky, quizzical frame entered.

James smiled, guessing and appreciating a lot, but said, "I wouldn't have figured you'd go for these nice warm walls, given your rainy-day, dream-away disposition."

"Glad you still have some wits left. We kinda wondered there for a minute. Actually, you're in my absent vacationing roommate's room. I didn't want the mental image of you in my bed, boss man."

"Yeah, well, given I'm acknowledging most of my wits have gone, how'd I get here?"

"The cashier, Asa, found you. Terry and I took you to

Emergency at Cedars, which was nearest."

"You took me to Cedars? You know I hate that place."

"Well, they didn't like the look of you either. Diagnosed you with three cracked ribs and a concussion, but wouldn't admit you when the insurance card that was in your wallet wasn't paid up. My place was nearer than Terry's, so here you are."

"Okay, thanks, girl. I appreciate it."

"James, I'm thinking you were too far from the bottom of the stairs to have fallen, and last night you didn't want to talk about Jeff Stanley's death. You've got me helping you find all these people from your past, so I think I've got the right to ask you what this all means."

He tried to sit up, felt a wave of nausea as he did so and noticed he was mostly undressed. "Yeah, you do, but who undressed me?" Fifty/fifty horrified either way.

"Well, actually, I did. Terry got embarrassed and impatient when we were trying to pull those drainpipe Levi's over your ankles. Jesus, how do you deal with that when you're on your own?"

"I manage. Anyway, where did you get the 'drainpipe' expression from? You're way too young."

She rolled her eyes. He noticed and tried to act like he was in control. "Tell you what. Throw me a towel, point me to your shower, and I'll take you to whatever breakfast joint you use to nurse your worst hangover."

She demurred to this and returned with a pink towel. "Bathroom's one door down."

He thought he was doing okay. No serious dizziness after she left him to pull it together and made it into the small bathroom. The opaque glass shower door and turquoise tile felt familiar, the slightly lowered interior welcoming. He tested the two water control handles whose markings were too faded to tell which was hot or cold. Eventually the balance was right, so he was about to step into the welcoming heat when he felt a wave of nausea. He just managed to spin, grab the toilet seat up and finally give back the Rainbow pizza, along with everything else in his gut. After he flushed the toilet until his puke was gone, he spent ten minutes getting blasted by the hot water; his aching ribs strangely gave him an angry strength, but his usual clarity of thought from a shower was entirely absent.

Back in the roommate's bedroom, he pulled on yesterday's clothes and made his way through the similarly turquoise tiled kitchen into the living area, where Lainey lounged absently reading the *NME* on a somewhat tatty beige couch.

"All right, you, let's go eat and talk."

"Mmmm," she said. "I think Duke's. I can drop you at your car easily after if you're up for the drive home?"

"Yeah, I'll be fine. Oh, wait—Highsmith."

"Don't worry, I called Bette. She grabbed your key and picked him up."

They walked out of the 40s Spanish duplex's front door into the hot late morning sun. The Santa Ana winds were not so noticeable here in Hollywood, although the eighty degrees was still high for this time of year. They got in her white Volkswagen Jetta and went north from Willoughby up Poinsettia. She turned left on Santa Monica Boulevard. It was only when she hit a right on Crescent Heights and then a quick left onto Sunset a minute later that he remembered Duke's had moved from where it had lived within the legendary Tropicana Motel until that mythic low-rent joint was torn down. Put it this way: if you were Led Zeppelin, you stayed at the Hyatt on Sunset but the Ramones would be at the Tropicana. And if you were Tom Waits, you lived there.

As they walked in the new black-walled narrow joint, he realized whoever was in charge of design had completely embraced the spirit of the old place's habitués more than its actual décor—which made sense to him. They flopped into a booth and a Guns 'N Roses-era waitress wordlessly dropped menus. Lainey ordered huevos rancheros and he French toast with bananas, both with black coffee. She wondered, not for the first time, if she'd made a giant miscalculation when she chose to work for/with this guy. He looked straight at her as they took their first tastes of coffee.

"Girl, I don't think there's anything I can tell you for sure. Jeff had been drinking with me at dinner. I'd be guessing about anything else. It's better for now if we pretend I did fall down the stairs last night. That way you'll have nothing to worry about. I trust you, but I like having you around and don't want you to know anything that could put you in harm's way, okay?"

"All well-meaning, I'm sure, but I need a bit more than that. Jesus, I'm fucking curious as well as scared. Spill."

"Everything started with Terry's wife leaving. He asked me to help find her. The rest is a lot of pointless guessing right now."

"You don't seem to be exactly in mourning for that poor man."

"Jeff and I were never friends. I didn't like or respect him, so to fake emotion over his death would feel like the worst kind of sentimentality."

"Wow, a little ruthless but I guess I understand," she conceded.

The silent waitress slid their meals across the black vinyl booth top. The French toast sugar rush jacked his system up and he had what in his dazed state felt like a brain wave.

"If you want to help, we need to find the actor girl who was at the Granita dinner. I'm pretty sure she called Stanley and threatened him. Did you see that Olympian exec at the Viper Room last night? She was the same girl who was with our actor at Granita."

"Jenny Jones? She's their director of media and artist relations. I see her out and about. She's okay." For Lainey, *She's okay* verged on a compliment. She forked her huevos in neatly chopped bites.

"Think you could get me a number?"

"I could maybe do that. I think you're talking about a woman called Aurial something but why? What could she have to do with Stanley or you, for that matter?"

"Look, if I tell you, you're into this all the way. Why would you want that?"

"Dunno. Bored, I guess."

"She has some tapes from twenty years ago, one of which includes me suggesting how to send the Confederacy to a mythologizing, fiery death."

Her mouth formed an *O*. "Well, they did have some way too long guitar solos."

"I knew there was a reason I hired you. You realize we're both crossing a line, though."

She nodded sagely.

"I think Denny's in this up to his neck, and when he kicked the shit out of me last night, I got a bit surer."

They got the check. "You all right to drive home?"

"Yeah. Give me that number. I gotta call the cops in Nashville."

She drove him the few blocks to where his car sat in the late morning light. Not feeling like taking the freeway, he U-turned and made a left on Sunset and took his time back to PCH. The Pacific Ocean was a sharp blue and the Santa Ana winds blew whitecaps so vivid he understood why so many unsuspecting tourists became transfixed by the view and drove right off the highway into the ocean.

He couldn't quite make the yellow at Porto Marino and stopped right in front of the heavily weathered but stunning Deco building where in 1935 actress and club owner Thelma Todd was found dead in her chocolate-colored Lincoln Phaeton, outside her own joint and home.

Sometimes no matter how famous those involved were, murders don't get solved—not publicly, at least. Ask Biggie Smalls, right? Or better yet the LAPD.

CHAPTER 17

He made it to Bette's in thirty minutes, and could hear her dog boarders barking from the top of Busch Drive long before he made the turn in to her ranch, which was spread over an acre or two. The dogs all had runs built out of her friendly-looking kitchen. A cacophony of barks rang out as he crunched over her gravel driveway up to the ranch split-door entrance. Highsmith's paws were over the lower level by the time he got there.

"Hey there, Bette. Sorry for any inconvenience."

"You okay, James? Your assistant seemed worried."

"Yeah, I'm all right. Highsmith been good? Glad you had room for him."

"Well, honey, I was actually fully booked, but he slept with me. He is a charmer, ain't he?"

Faking that he was not on his last legs, James hugged her and left extra money. He and Highsmith headed back down the hill onto PCH and home. Aching like fuck, he ran the first bath he'd had in years, hoping it would help the ribs, at least. He put Keith Richards' *Main Offender* solo record on the living room stereo loud enough so "Wicked As It Seems" would drift into the bathroom, stripped off and eased himself gingerly into the tub, where he began to sift through everything.

First off, Denny's attack seemed out of character, which presumably meant he'd gotten under his skin finally. Surely he wouldn't have done this just over the wind-ups dished out during their Damaged dealings? Did he know about Stanley yet? James shivered for a second despite the intense heat of the water. Fuck, what if he had Stanley killed—tidying loose ends? No, surely not. Unprovoked after all this time. Not unless Stanley had threatened him. By the time "Demon" played, he was thoroughly bored with the bath, although as he stepped out he felt a bit better and decided to call Nashville PD.

Detective Perkins—Dwayne to his friends—took the call at his gunmetal desk and fingered through the almost two-foot-high pile of case folders. A sliver of late afternoon Nashville sun came through the half-closed blinds of his pint-sized office, which cheered him slightly, as he was thoroughly sick of winter. He was about thirty-five, slender, in good shape and had all his brown hair, slightly long for a cop—not at all the pudgy cliché James imagined on the other end of the line.

"So, ah, Mr. Dual—I understand you had dinner together at Tootsie's Restaurant on the night of Jeff Stanley's death."

"Yeah, that's correct."

"Had you been drinking together, too?"

"Uh, yeah, a couple."

"Mmmm, more than a couple, based on the restaurant's copy of the check. You the wine drinker or the Scotch, or you boys mixing it up?"

"Wine was me."

"Yeah, figured as much, you being from California and all. Bit irresponsible letting your friend drive after, wasn't it? Supposing he was your friend, of course."

James was irritated now, but stayed cool and didn't respond.

"I'm curious, Mr. Dual, what was his demeanor like? Was he troubled or was there something about your meeting that upset him?"

James, not liking this at all, realized he should have thought through his story. "No, I hadn't seen him for a long time and we just swapped tales from when we worked together years ago. Is there some point to these questions? My assistant told me he was in an accident."

"I'm trying to see the picture of his last hours on earth. That a problem for you, Mr. Dual?"

"No, sorry."

"So did you leave the restaurant together?"

"Yeah, he gave me a lift."

"Really. So were you in the car when it crashed?"

"Of course I wasn't. What kind of a fucking question is that?"

"Maybe we'd understand each other better if we were in the same room, sir."

James got up from the couch and walked onto the wooden balcony. He hoped the white-capped waves would help him focus on getting off the phone with a minimum of damage. "All right, to be clear, Jeff dropped me off and seemed fine to me. He wasn't driving erratically."

Dwayne tilted his chair onto its back two legs to get a little more sun and smiled, enjoying fucking with this music business asshole. "Dropped you off where? At your hotel?"

"Um, no, he dropped me at a bar called 3rd & Lindsley."

"Okay, you see anyone there who could corroborate that?"

James stifled the words "Shelton Hank Williams III." He figured the arrival of police at his door might not go well with the mix of liquor, drugs, dangerous Nashville girls, and loaded shotguns that in all likelihood would greet them. "I'm not sure, but probably the bartender." Not a lie, as he'd bought many drinks, he figured.

"Okay, so just to finish up for now—what brought you to Nashville? Was Mr. Stanley the purpose of your visit?"

James leaned on the wooden rail. Highsmith had glanced at him with a quizzical eye before he walked down the steps to the beach. A moment of slight inspiration. "No, I came to see a band, Blue Mother Tupelo, and just checked in with Stanley for old times' sake."

"Okay. Guess that about wraps it up. Oh. Do you remember if he was wearing his seat belt?"

"Uh, not certain, but I think so."

"Well, he wasn't when we found him."

"Is that significant?"

"We will be in touch if anything significant happens when we get the autopsy." Perkins did his sarcastic English imitation best on "significant" and hung up.

Truth was, Detective Dwayne Perkins was looking for anything that would explain how Jeff Stanley's head was all caved in from impact but his ribs were in better shape than most people's— among them James Dual's, who gingerly followed his dog down those worn wooden steps, and tried not to wince as he did so. The briny air smelled great, but a fog bank rolled in and by the time he gingerly took the step off the last plank onto the sand, the temperature had dropped ten degrees.

The ocean was flat, no surfers—not even any other dog people, who were usually the only beachgoers during what passed for winter at the Point. Four homes, much larger than James', hugged their own section on the lip of the cliff above, their respectively red, pale blue, yellow, and green exterior walls the only colors against the now-gray sky. He gazed along the curves of the coastline to the pier that extended out from the Sandcastle and remembered suddenly that he was having dinner with Charlie Major there tonight. Highsmith had found an ocean-worn tennis ball, but James, who threw it from habit, was in instant agony and had to stop. He cursed the pain, cursed his stupid overreaction to the detective's needling questions, and lastly, (and out loud, he realized) that motherfucker Denny Golden.

He took some 800 mg ibuprofen left over from a root canal, fed Highsmith, and left a message for Eric to find out what action had occurred on the label front. The showcase felt like a week ago.

CHAPTER 18

As he was about to head down to the beach for the walk to the Sandcastle, the phone rang.

"'ello?"

"Boy, I can't take my eye off you for five minutes, can I?"

It was her. Granita girl. And if Lainey was right, Aurial.

"Your name Aurial?"

She didn't miss a beat. "Well, you got that part of your homework correct, but I hear you are getting into all kinds of trouble without me."

"Yeah, could be, although I'm not sure you're not the source of all that trouble."

"Double negative there, kiddo. Thought you English had the grammar down pat."

"Maybe I need a lesson or two. I already did my history revision with the cassette you gave me last time."

"Good. I like pupils who don't have to be ridden too hard to stay on top of their homework."

He enjoyed the sexual tone, but pressed on. "What kind of a student was Jeff Stanley?"

"Not the teacher's pet, which you might be in the running for if you keep up the good work, but he seems a bit slow on the uptake so far," she said.

"What? About the school fees?"

She stifled a chuckle at this. "You might say that."

"You have harsh late fees, huh?"

"How's that?"

"Stanley's dead."

There was a sharp intake of breath on the other end.

"How about we have a private session here?"

"School rules preclude unaccompanied teachers visiting students at their homes."

"Look, if you are operating on your own and got those tapes from who I think you did, it would be better for us not to be seen together."

She paused. "Okay. When?"

"I'm tied up tonight. Why don't you come tomorrow at seven?" He gave her directions and hung up before she changed her mind.

He carefully pulled a black hooded sweatshirt on and locked the front and back doors, something he rarely bothered to do, given the crime-free neighborhood.

The old gray wooden boathouse to the left of the steps loomed in the dusk. He was slightly startled to see a strange aquatic contraption in the sand behind it. It was a jury-rigged catamaran with two ten-foot-long foils painted in three stripes of red, yellow, and turquoise, joined by a wooden driver's platform in the middle. Two plastic chairs whose legs had been cut off faced forward, and a bigger red swivel seat faced backwards towards a large outboard motor. It made him think of Jamaica and he was half tempted to borrow it for the ride around the half-mile of coastline to the Sandcastle, but realized he didn't have the strength to drag it the dozen or so feet into the ocean. He shook his head and headed off, as Highsmith's sad bark at being left behind rung in his ears.

It was almost dark by the time he trudged up the steep bank of sand to the concrete parking lot at Paradise Cove. The lights from the trailer homes on the other side of the parking lot illuminated the whole area. There were a few tables occupied, but he had no trouble acquiring one of the dozen booths that ran along the ocean-facing side of the old joint. He skimmed the surf and turf menu while he waited for Charlie. Fish was sadly the last thing you'd want to order here, unless you were fond of overcooked slabs, well-buttered. Cheeseburger and fries would be far safer. On the plus side, they'd always carried a bottle of inexpensive but decent Bordeaux in among the list of overly fruity Californians. It arrived as he heard "Buddy," and saw Charlie swagger across the dimly lit room. They hugged, perhaps both feeling more pleasure than they would have expected at seeing each other after so long.

"You look good, Jimmy." Charlie poured them glasses before he'd even sat down.

"You, too." James meant it. Major was a little more florid of face, but had all of his hair, albeit largely silver-gray by now, and was still physically his imposing larger-than-life self.

"Thanks for coming out so early, Jimmy. I did not want to cancel out on the young lady I'm seeing tonight."

"Glad to see there are some constants, Charlie. So you never married?"

"Hell, no. I have no sense that that would be good for anyone. The fact that I am lucky enough to not age at all makes frequently meeting new young girlfriends the best solution." He grinned. "And this one in particular is a true firecracker."

It was funny, but somehow Charlie's whole persona had aged well for James, the way a lot of the cheesy 70s songs he used to hate so much had, and he found himself smiling, happier than he had felt for some time.

They took a minute to look over the black vinyl-covered worn menus, pointless, considering they'd been the same for twenty-odd years. A middle-aged waitress, black hair in a bun, whom James didn't recognize, took their T-bone and baked potato and cheeseburger and fries order, and somehow seemed disappointed she couldn't talk them into overpriced shrimp cocktails to start.

James sat back and took a long sip of the wine. "So how's the wonderful world of radio promotion?"

"Funny you should ask that. I still get paid handsomely, but it's just not as much fun as it used to be. The golden age has passed. The PDs at the stations are so corporate now. The playlists so tight, all you can give these guys are competitions—bands to play at their fucking dumb acoustic Christmas or summer BBQs. There is a distinct lack of proper inducements like drugs, women, cash...I used to feel like a freebooter, a pirate. Alas, it's more like being a goddamned travel agent, sending contest winners to Hawaii and such shit."

"What are you gonna do, right?" James asked rhetorically.

Their food arrived, looking uniformly dried out. Charlie, undeterred, cut a chunk of steak, chewed meditatively for a minute, and then pointed out towards the cove. "You know the history of this spot, Jimmy?"

"Well, I know *The Rockford Files* was filmed here. James Garner's trailer's in the lot outside and they shot in the restaurant a fair bit."

The promo domo shook his head. "No, the real history. Back in Prohibition days, the rumrunners and bootleggers used to bring the booze in at Paradise Cove."

"Really? That's genius," enthused James.

"Yeah, and then later in '38, Tony Cornero had a gambling ship just outside the three-mile limit."

"How fucking cool."

Charlie, warming to the subject, smiled. "I had a feeling you might think so. Can you see that row of lights in the distance?"

James peered out into the darkness, needing a minute before he dimly made out what Charlie referred to. "Yeah, just about."

"That, Jimmy, is the past hoving into the immediate future."

"How do you mean?"

"That is my ship. It's going to be the best fun anyone's had in years and make a lot of money in the bargain. Completely private club, invitation only—I'm gonna have a little gambling. A little something for everyone—you know what I mean?"

James smiled. Charlie's voracious appetites would indeed think of everything.

"See, Jimmy, apart from being a great time, it will give all the music business a place to get crazy without anyone interfering. The way the world's going now, too many fucking morals mixed with the fucking paparazzi—everyone's getting too uptight. I'll shuttle everyone in and out on cruisers. We'll drift on outside the three-mile limit."

"I love it, mate. If anyone could pull it off, you might."

"No might about it. I've already got all the dollars I need. Now you may be wondering why ol' Charlie thought to tell you all this?" Not pausing to wait for James's response, he continued. "When you called, it started me thinking. See, I know everyone I could possibly need to know in music to get this thing rolling, but you have one foot firmly in the film business. I'm thinking you can quietly invite just the right film A-listers and actors to make the whole thing even larger than life, right?"

"I tell you what, Charlie, I think all great clubs come from people starting joints they create because there ain't a place like that to go to."

"So you're in?"

"Look, mate, honestly I have no interest in going back into the club business, but I'll tell you what. I need to pick your brain a bit and if you're up for that—I'll try to help."

"Okay, son. I had wondered why you wanted to talk. You definitely didn't have any interest in my world when we both worked at the same place. Subtle as you were then, I got the distinct impression you didn't care for me or the wonderful world of promotion."

James grinned ruefully. "Yeah, I thought you were a bunch of cunts."

The Georgia man raised a bushy gray eyebrow. "And now?"

James paused and reflected for a minute as Charlie flagged down the waitress, and whispered his order in her ear.

"I can't quite explain it, but put it this way. I'm thinking you are like a lot of artists whose songs I hated in the 70s—Journey, REO Speedwagon, etc. You all have started to grow on me. I fucking hope it's not nostalgia creeping up on me."

"Perish the thought."

It was only when the table was cleared and the two men leaned back on opposite sides of the burnt wooden booth, James realized Charlie had conjured up a bottle of Château La Mission Haut-Brion '78. How he'd managed that in the Sandcastle of all places threw him completely but duly inspired, he started in. "So here's the story. I started out trying to help Terry Harper find his wife Jacqueline, but soon all the roads led to Denny Golden and the Confederacy plane crash. Jeff Stanley died in a car wreck just after I talked to him about recordings Denny may have made back then—ring any bells?"

Master poker player Charlie gazed out of the window, apparently imagining he was already on his floating palace, but no doubt the tumblers of what and what not to reveal were precisely clicking into place. "That's sad about old Jeff," he said finally. "Back then, me and Denny were thick as thieves. He'd hustled his way to president as a lawyer, business affairs guy, but he didn't have any relationships at radio, which was where the real power was and is, when it comes right down to it. He wanted more than just running Real—the boy wanted his own label. He sounded me out. Timing was good. He knew my deal was up at Real in a year. Offered me a chance to buy in for ten percent of his new label if I'd jump ship and work for a nominal salary for the first three years while he got things off the ground."

"Really? But you said no?"

"We negotiated back and forth, but I eventually said yes."

"Really? So what happened?"

"He fucked me."

"How and why?"

"Well, things had got started around the time you're talking about. I didn't connect the crash to ol' Denny's slow goodbye to our deal at the time—even I'm not that smart."

James, slightly drunk, took his turn at raising an eyebrow. "And now?"

Charlie shrugged. "You tell me exactly what you want out of this and I'll maybe fill in your blanks."

"I already did. Finding Jacqueline."

"So, no old scores to settle with Denny?"

"Purely fucking incidental."

"Even after last night?"

James laughed. "You do keep your ear, or is it nose, to the ground, huh?"

Charlie continued. "Denny played me pretty good. I even started putting regional promo guys in place for his company. Nothing was public, of course. Easier to keep things quiet in those days. He wasn't pushing me to deposit my investment and I'm figuring I'd rather keep my money making money for me until the last minute, so I hadn't troubled to get our agreement signed since I wouldn't be getting paid until we were out of Real. Then, out of the blue, he told me his plans had changed and he didn't feel comfortable raiding Real's key people to start his company, and he'd have to withdraw the offer. Well, I knew that second that he'd obviously gotten the rest of his investment from somewhere else. I started sniffing around and was pretty much convinced he was running cleans. You wanna make the leap that the safest way to do that was with an unknown sales quantity like the Confederacy, be my guest."

"So why would he do that to you, given you would have run his promo, too? Did he bankroll all the rest of the start-up costs himself?"

Charlie gave a lopsided grin at this. "Who you bringing to my boat? Listen, the little lady who is keeping my mojo working awaits. How is me telling you more going to help either of us?"

"Fuck, Charlie, I'll seriously get people out to your boat—it will be a pleasure—but I need to get the whole picture."

"All right. When he made his move and brought Gary Kalusian and Ron Deutch in, it wasn't hard, given their 'family background,' to figure where he got the rest of his financing."

"Okay. But if he was siphoning off all kinds of money, why would he want to be stuck in that sort of dangerous relationship?"

"Good question. That's why I didn't see it coming. It doesn't make obvious sense."

"Not obvious, but you eventually figured it out?" asked James.

Charlie leaned in. "Only one way. If he hired them to down the plane and they decided that for their investment in Denny's future, they should have long-term profit participation."

"Fuck me. That actually makes sense. But if you've known this for however long, why haven't you done something about it?"

"Never seen how it would benefit my bank account or life expectancy."

James sat back and took stock through the Bordeaux filter. Right this minute, it all felt right. It figured that Jacquie must have known all or most of this and likely come to the same conclusions. Difference being, Charlie was a shrewd sociopath who, other than the denied opportunities, wouldn't have lost a minute's sleep over any of it, whereas it would have eaten her alive. Reality was, though, they'd all buried it for twenty years, so there must be a catalyst to crash it all into the present, and of course he could see her face.

"Charlie, any chance you got a call from a woman bringing up any of this stuff?"

"Can't say I did," he demurred.

James, drunk now, almost but not quite resisted, and said, "Can't say you didn't either, right?"

"Listen, I'm moving my business outside of the three-mile limit, where everything's legal. I really don't intend to get too distracted by anything or anyone else—and if you're smart, you won't either. From what I know, Harper didn't help you when you needed it, and his missing wife fucked you over, right? What's in it for you?"

"Good point," James slurred.

Charlie grabbed the check out of the waitress's left hand and put it back in her right along with some crisp bills. James grinned as he realized he hadn't seen any record man use cash as opposed to the AmEx corporate card in a very long time. They rose, the older promo man noticeably more steadily than the weary Englishman.

"Thanks for the great wine, insight, and advice. I'm gonna walk home, see my dog, and digest it, all right?"

"Jimmy, despite the urgency of my next rendezvous, I'll drive you. No arguments."

They walked through the dark bar area past the retro jukebox and out the heavy wooden door into the parking lot. The lights at the trailer homes a couple of hundred yards out showed the way to the country star gifted Bentley that Major clearly still drove. James went to the wrong door, the venerable vehicle having obviously been imported from England originally. He leaned back into the sturdy leather seat abstractedly, and remembered some crazy teen night in a motor just like this. They eased out of the lot past the guard gate into the narrow, dark side road that led from Paradise Cove up to Pacific Coast Highway. Charlie pushed a 7" vinyl into the in-dash record player, which definitely impressed James. "White Room" by Cream was the choice.

Charlie had reached into the half-open ashtray and pulled out a joint so nicely rolled it looked like a commercial-sized cigarette. He took a reflective hit as they waited for the light to change at the dead end of Paradise Cove and Pacific Coast Highway. Charlie noticed James's expression. "Fuck me. We actually like one of the same songs? It's tilted me like a pinball machine. Y'all need to jump on my bandwagon—I could make you some nice cash. You've had that experience of starting a club and know the pitfalls, and you don't—or at least didn't—take shit from anyone. Look, I'm a great customer and I know how to be the center of attention at a great party, but the rest of it…" He spread his arms expressively, joint in mouth, the Bentley not wavering despite the lack of hands on the wheel.

His right hand ejected the Cream single and replaced it from a nicely built-in rack with Little Eva's "The Locomotion," as his left eased the car into the left turn lane for Heathercliff. "I had Carole King somewhere around here," he said, referring to the song's writer.

"Yeah, I see her at Granita the uvva week."

"No, this was back when I was working 'Tapestry'." The Bentley made the left turn off Dume, down the steep slope of Grayfox. James started out of the door and winced slightly. Charlie handed him the joint. "You finish this up and sleep on what I said. You'll feel a whole lot better in the a.m."

James added a beer swigged on his deck as Highsmith snuffled around, and forty-five minutes later with the dog lying diagonally across the floor near the open window, the warming weather encouraged them both to a deep sleep.

CHAPTER 19
DENNY GOLDEN

As the temperature shot up, the smog crept back into West Hollywood, ensuring that Denny Golden woke up Saturday in an even worse mood than when he went to bed as the wicked cake mixture of toxicants he'd ingested now had its icing on top. The mood worsened when he realized it was Saturday and there would be no one at the office to vent at. Not that that would help, he quickly realized. Truth was he still didn't know who had taken the tapes out of his safe. They'd given him what he thought of as an untouchable insurance policy and their absence hung like a fucking sword of Damocles over him.

He'd opened his safe thirty-six hours ago and, while he grabbed his pharmaceutical-laden briefcase, it had occurred to him to reach a little farther and pull out his cassette box, but he didn't feel its reassuring touch. This wasn't something he removed or mostly thought of, so he initially thought it had merely been nudged to the back of his expansive safe as various confidential items had gone in and out. It wasn't until he'd yelled at Ron Deutch to put on all the lights and had poured a gin and tonic to go with the long line of coke he'd chopped for himself that he went in for a second look and gradually got seriously crazy. His calculating mind raged between thinking specifically who had access to the safe and what the tapes' absence could mean. Deutch had been conciliatory but less proactive than usual and had left around two a.m. Thursday night.

He'd spent Friday at the office, ostensibly conducting business absolutely as usual—seething—but considering he was a condescending and dismissive asshole to most of the employees he dealt with on a daily basis, no one really noticed any change in his demeanor. He had told Eric directly that his demo offer to Damaged stood, but that he wasn't so blown away by the show that he would up the bid much. Meantime, most other business slipped to the back of his mind as he wracked his brain to figure who the fuck could have gotten into his safe, how, and most importantly, why. He decided to head out to his Malibu estate in hopes the change of scenery would help shake the feeling of dread that enveloped him.

CHAPTER 20

James had woken shockingly refreshed. The dope and alcohol worked wonders for his aching ribs and by late afternoon, he was ready for Aurial.

Highsmith lay by the front door. His knowing Springer eyes looked back at James as he changed into a slightly newer pair of 501s he'd had the talented dry cleaner down at Dume Plaza seriously drainpipe for him. He looked at a couple of barely worn shirts, but defaulted to a black T-shirt. He passed by the various Converse and pulled out a pair of squared-off, if not quite pointed, narrow shoes. He remembered worrying about the cliché of buying Prada shoes, but it seemed like all the other men's shoes were bulky with huge surrounds that made him feel as if he had clown feet. The fun, early 80s days of Melrose Avenue's original boutiques were long gone. He allowed himself a moment's reminiscence of Cowboys & Poodles and Let It Rock. Now, if you didn't want high-street crap, you had to look to the Italian designers for shoes. And if you had serious money, you could get your jackets made at Richard Tyler's place on Beverly and Poinsettia.

He wondered how he could focus on stuff like this when there should be so much to worry about. Being English when all was said and done, it didn't occur to him that he might be more than a little repressed about dealing with emotion. The closest he got today was listening to O.V. Wright's "Drowning on Dry Land." Given all the shit that had and was likely to happen, maybe it was just as well.

He had the shoes on—resisted the jacket, though—when he heard a screeching crunch of tires and gravel as if a Formula One race car had just navigated the dead end outside. Highsmith pawed at the old wooden door and barked up an excited storm as James pulled it open. She strode up to him from a beaten-up '76 white Dodge Dart, instantly in his physical space, radiant in her neo-noir glory: black sheath thigh-length dress highlighted her blonde hair and perfectly oversized mouth bathed in retro red lipstick. They both resisted any attempts at opening lines. He led the way to the kitchen and offered her a drink.

"Scotch, if you have it."

He did have a bottle of Bell's even though he rarely, if ever, drank it himself these days. He made the drink as he would have for himself. A tall tumbler, a little ice, a lot of Bell's topped with just enough cold water to belie the inherent lethal nature. He leaned across the turquoise tile kitchen counter, and pulled the cork out of a half-empty bottle of Cote du Rhone to pour himself a glass. She raised a disapproving eyebrow. He tilted his head slightly sideways, more or less like Highsmith did. She slowly shook her head. Reluctantly, he poured the glass of red down the sink, created a mirror of her drink and walked them through to the living room, where he put on the second side of the Stones' *Sticky Fingers*.

Highsmith jumped territorially between them as they seated themselves on the blue Deco-style couch that faced the darkening ocean view. James took a sip of the Scotch, liking the adrenaline rush of "Bitch." He wondered which clichéd line to open with, for he was sure the situation demanded one. He finally settled on, "So is this where we put all our cards on the table?"

She smiled. "Well, putting all of them out would be rather boring, don't you think? But a few? Yes. I think I could show a few."

"I thought hearing Stanley was dead, likely murdered, might encourage you to realize you're in way over your head."

Her green eyes looked straight into his: insolent, unwavering, tough. "Look, kiddo, don't make the mistake of thinking I need rescuing. If anyone does, it's you. I came here to maybe give you a break."

"Oh yeah? How's that?"

"I could bleed you for the long haul with these tapes. Once I realized the Confederacy crash was a murder inspired, if not executed, by you, I knew I was in like Flynn. Set. You'd at the very least go down for conspiracy."

He took a long swallow of Bell's and instantly wondered why he'd more or less given it up. "Look, girl, all that's a long fucking time ago. I'm not gonna pretend hearing that tape didn't shake me, but I know I didn't actually do it, so you won't be getting any cash out of me. I'll start with the card dealing and see how it goes. I didn't know about the tapes, but I'm betting they were made by Denny Golden and that you somehow acquired them from him. If he's aware of that, you may need more help than you think."

She put her hand idly on the black-and-white nape of Highsmith's neck. The dog sat upright, still sizing her up. "You're warm. Go on."

"I think you made the leap that Stanley and I might have something to hide and decided to try to weasel in. Did you try the same stunt with Jacqueline Harper?"

Aurial smiled. "On the tapes, she sounded like an irritating goody-two-shoes, which considering the nefarious stuff all around her, made her hypocritical to boot. So yeah, she was first port of call. I really put the frighteners on her."

James stifled a smile at the retro London gangster expression.

"Where'd you get frighteners from?"

"Well, I could have got it from my British gangster film class if I'd finished it, but it actually came from the advanced Stones course, which led to *Performance* and an A grade."

"I'd have been a little bit more intrigued if you'd actually had a protection racket rather than turning out to be a cheap blackmailer, never mind an on-the-make actor."

"Disappointed in me?" she asked evenly.

As he finished the tall glass, he vaguely wondered whether there were classes like that, but remembered that they'd both bailed on formal education before college, so it was somewhat of a moot point. "Girl, I've got an open mind that is definitely predisposed in your favor, but I need a convincing origin story from you."

"Go fix us another drink and then I'll begin," she said. He wasn't sure whether that was ironic or patronizing, but he did as he was told.

Highsmith relaxed slightly, lying between them as James returned, drinks in hand. It was dark outside, but the rising, almost full moon bathed the room. She took hers but started in without drinking.

"Okay, how about you shift your wanna-be-noir perception and see me as a budding cat burglar. I'd done the usual round of ingénue auditions and the only offers that resulted were thinly veiled seduction attempts and party invites. I accepted some of the latter. I started having this fantasy cum notion that I could case some of these joints—you know, come back a little later and clean up. I needed money and was having fun. I was determined to climb up the outside of the homes. First place, I just pushed open a second-story bedroom window and went back the following day when I knew the guy was out. He'd been trying to score while his wife was out of town, so I grabbed all the jewelry and cash I could find. There'd been fifty people in the place the night before, and he wouldn't ever want the details out."

"And so you end up at Denny's?"

"Yeah. Jenny Jones invited me. We'd hit it off one night, plus she told me Denny lived in the penthouse of Sunset Tower. Imagine climbing that!"

James sipped and grinned.

"Okay, so there's a small crowd. Denny takes selected people to his bedroom to snort long lines of exquisite coke. I've been listening appreciatively while he tells me self-aggrandizing stories about keeping various rock stars happy, so I'm first of the night. This means I am in this vast curved room with a 180-degree view south down Doheny and west towards the beach, which is stunning, but not stunning enough to distract me from keeping a keen eye on Denny while he heads to his wall safe to bring out the night's supply. 07 left, 3 right, 9 left, 2 right, click. He brought out a gold box and pours out a good pile from a chalky-looking plastic bag onto the mirrored table in front of his overstuffed, gold frou-frou bed. While he starts chopping very long, careful lines, I pull out my lipstick and make a nice careful note of the combination on my yellow American Spirit cigarette box."

James nodded appreciatively. "Uh huh."

"Well, everyone's happily and maniacally wired for a while. I'm figuring out my way back in but realize, of course, that these places don't have windows that open far enough for climbing through, so unless I'm ready to take out whole panes of glass, my fantasy is going to stay just that. Fortunately for me, Denny's late-night decision to drop downers to take the edge off gives me another option. I've been drinking hard, so all I'm really thinking about is doing a line or two to pull me together enough to drive home, but that controlling fuck is clearly not offering any more. He's pretty much on the nod, but there's still enough activity that I can slip back into his bedroom unnoticed, pop the safe, pull the box out, tip a bunch into my compact for later and a palm full I snort quickly. As I put the box back in, I feel it bump against a steel box. I grab that on impulse, figuring it might be cash. The fact that it's locked only confirms the fact to my drunken brain.

"I leave it on the table for a minute. I go back out and hear that Jenny's bailed with the manager of a band whose name I forget. No one's paying any attention to me, so I duck into the bedroom one more time, grab the box, make a beeline for the door, hit the elevator, and as they say, head for the hills. The coke's straightened me out enough to drive home, albeit faster than I should. Fortunately, no meetings with the sheriffs along the way. I came to in the morning and find this box beside my bed and hazily remember acquiring it. I spent half the day unsuccessfully trying to hack it open. Couldn't take it to a locksmith, not knowing what might be found inside. Eventually I thought to get over to the espionage store on Beverly and Western."

As much as James wanted her to get to the point, he couldn't resist interjecting, "You're kidding, right?"

"You don't know about it? Invaluable. They have everything. Bugging devices, you name it. I got my wall climbing suction pads from there. They sold me an old-school oxy-acetylene torch. Had to spend more than I wanted from my last job, but I figured there had to be something valuable. So after all this, I finally burn through the lock and am not amused to find a bunch of fucking cassettes. I'm thinking unless they're lost Beatles demos or something, this has been a total waste."

"I don't think they had cassettes back then," James felt compelled to mention.

"Whatever. I'm pissed because I only have a CD player at my place at the time, so I end up driving around in my car listening. An hour or two later, it all starts to make sense and I realize I'm sitting on a gold mine."

"Okay, obviously I heard a copy of one with my performance. What else did you get?"

Now she drank, grinning broadly. "That would be all the cards, boy."

"Wild Horses" segued into "Dead Flowers." Fighting nostalgia, he couldn't stop the certitude he'd felt when he first heard those songs that he and those close to him weren't likely to live very long, having given their lives over to the lyrics. Punk had sprung partly out of the disappointment of being let down and geographically deserted by the likes of the Stones, but with a lot of water under the bridge, he was feeling the dark cool of *Sticky Fingers* vividly right now. He took a drink and looked straight into her eyes. "So all business and fortunes aside, when we met at the Granita bar, did you know who I was?"

Being a smart, albeit possibly a bit damaged girl, she realized the implications of what he asked, but kept a poker face while "Moonlight Mile" played. She held his gaze and eventually replied, "No, actually I did not."

Elated and happily surprised, he did his best not to react.

"Why, were you thinking all this was a setup?" she asked.

"Fuck you." His right hand reached out and laid along the side of her forehead and high cheekbone. She leaned in and kissed him. He wanted to let go and get lost, but just couldn't risk that. "So how come I find that tape in my pocket?"

"Just my good luck, boy. I'd decided to keep close to Denny to avoid any suspicion if he realized what had happened. So when Jenny asked me to join the wine-and-dine-the-band dinner, I tagged along. It was only when Denny started making disparaging cracks about you and Terry that I realized I'd hit a bit of dumb luck. The tapes were still in my car, so I decided you deserved a little surprise."

"You mean I have the original?" James asked incredulously.

She grinned a little drunkenly. "I didn't actually say that."

"So what's the story? What exactly do you want out of this? Are we teaming up in some way?" His would-be tough guy pose was all over the map.

"I could ask you the same thing."

"First and foremost, I've got to find Jacquie and her kids. Did you hear from her after you put the 'frighteners' on her? She pay you anything before she split?"

"She agreed to get $10K to the spot I told her to, but when I showed up at the Greyhound station on Vine, there was nothing. I kept calling, but she never answered."

"Kind of a clichéd spot to have her leave the cash, huh?" he posed.

"Hey, that place has a lot of advantages, easy not to be spotted. There's a reason it's a cliché. Anyway, I didn't think a married woman, secure with a family, would risk fucking it all up for $10K."

"Yeah, but she is, or at least was, a girl who saw everything in plain Midwestern black-and-white. If she knew Denny's secrets, she probably felt the guilt of never saying a word in an almost unbearable way. Maybe you're the trigger that brought it all back…"

"With you as the bullet, huh, boy?"

He looked straight into the riveting green eyes and tried to

143

match her gaze. "Yeah, I'm a bullet." He realized they were back to *Performance* dialogue. "So you've had no contact with her since?"

"No. When I couldn't get hold of her, I decided to move on to Jeff Stanley. I was having some fun with him while I figured out just how to get him to deliver me money in a safe way."

"Did you go to Nashville?"

She paused just long enough for him to wonder if she was considering the ramifications of her answer and whether to tell the truth. "No, I thought about it, but apparently you or the Grim Reaper beat me to it."

"The Grim Reaper—nice turn of phrase. Well, if you think I might have done it, you are either crazy or brave coming here tonight, huh?"

"Oh, I'm both of those, kiddo, but on reflection, I decided it unlikely. Besides…"

"Besides what?"

She shrugged. "A few other things tipped in your favor."

"Like?"

"Let's say those tapes gave me a broader perspective."

"How so?"

"That truly would be showing far more of that mythical hand of cards we were talking about than I have any intention of doing. So let's talk about how we find this annoying Midwestern neurotic broad, and preferably getting well paid in the bargain."

He shook his head, half smiling. He figured he'd have to draw any more tape details out of her gradually, hopefully as the liquor took hold. She'd just downed the second Scotch, though, without any noticeable effect, while he started to feel his.

The phone rang. Terry was on the other end and sounded energized.

"Jacquie's mother called and has the kids."

"Since when?"

"They've been there the whole time." His old friend sounded mightily relieved. "So much for Mexico."

"Surely you'd called her before."

"Of course I did, but apparently Jacquie had insisted she tell me nothing."

"Why?"

"Jacquie told her things were really bad between us and she needed some time away. Told her mother I wouldn't be able to handle the kids on my own. She got worried, though, as Jacquie hasn't checked in with her, to talk to the kids, in days. I mean, you know this all came to a head when she said it was your fault but she obviously didn't tell her mother that."

James didn't answer. Terry continued, "You know, there's always stuff. I had to travel and obviously when I'm here, I'm out a lot seeing bands at night. I dunno…"

James tried to decide how much to tell Terry about the girl when a thought occurred. "This should make it easier to track Jacquie down. Let's get the date she flew in to Illinois. We can check flights out to Mexico from what—Chicago O'Hare? "

Terry cut in. "Her mother's in Palm Springs. She moved west when Jacquie's father died five years ago. Property was cheaper than LA, of course. Her and another Midwest widow bought a place."

"Ohh, so maybe she still did head to Mexico. Easy enough to drive down to Tijuana from Palm Springs, right?"

"Yeah, could be. At any rate, I'm going down to get the kids in the morning."

"Look, Terry, do you think that's wise? Maybe it will be safer for them to stay out of the way until we get things sorted."

"Safer?"

"Didn't Lainey tell you about Jeff Stanley?"

"Tell me what? We had our hands full getting you out of the Viper Room. How the hell did you fall like that, anyway? Drink too much? Calming your nerves before the showcase?"

"Stanley died in a car wreck the night I saw him, and the Nashville detective obviously doesn't think it was an accident. Meantime, Deutch tossed me up in the air before Denny shined his shoes on my head, so yeah, I think your kids might be better out of the way. By the way, I'm sitting with the girl who tried to blackmail Jacqueline. She's all right, though. I think I like her."

CHAPTER 21
RON DEUTCH

Ron Deutch was a troubled man, and at times like this, he found that driving the immaculate 1973 white Lincoln Continental he looked after like a child helped him think. He thought even more clearly when he listened to the songs of his hometown Philly icons Leon Gamble and Kenneth Huff. Indeed, 1974's "For The Love of Money" pulsed through the gliding auto's speakers at this very minute.

He was heading north on La Cienega after he dropped author Elmore Leonard at LAX for his Saturday night Detroit flight. He wished he could have had the freedom to talk all this through with the author, as no doubt he would have made sense of the pieces of the puzzle, but didn't dwell on that fantasy. More problematic was worrying about discussing things with the increasingly erratic and volatile Denny Golden. He'd always unquestioningly done Golden's bidding and would never betray him, but for the first time he worried about exactly what information he could safely share. Golden's sudden impulse to kick the shit out of an insignificant punk like James Dual in public, no matter what their history, was really out of character.

Now that the tapes Denny had believed gave him absolute power were missing, who knew what was next?

He'd spent whatever free time he had from the day-to-day promotion biz to explore what the renewed connection between Dual and Harper might mean, as he'd been instructed. Ironically, he'd been helped by an offhand comment from Leonard, who told him that when they were at Dominick's, it appeared that the pair hadn't seen each other in a long time, and for sure that the show that night had been the first time Dual had seen Damaged. He had wondered at length about why Harper had told Denny to stay away from his family. He couldn't imagine that Denny would have anything to do with an ex-assistant, and why would Harper think otherwise?

He'd got part of the answer when he asked Jenny Jones to see what she could find out about Harper's seriousness in signing Damaged. Jenny had had her assistant get on the case. In both the music and film worlds, assistants knew everything and shared most of it with one another. So it didn't take long for the news to come back along the rumor mill that Terry's wife had left him. Rumors being what they are, the details varied from Terry had been fucking or trying to fuck Katrina, to Jacquie running off with the guitar player in the newly reformed Foreigner.

His reverie was interrupted after he braked sharply to avoid running a red light at La Cienega and Washington. The occupants of a gold Lexus behind him, which had almost plowed into the rear end of his pride and joy, evidently were of the opinion he should not have braked so sharply and had swerved alongside him at the light to voice that opinion in a manner that, had Ron been able to hear them above "If You Don't Know Me By Now" he would undoubtedly not have approved of. The four red-bandanna'd junior gangster occupants gave it all they had, and the one riding shotgun tapped his breast, suggesting weaponry was just a grab away.

On another night this might have gotten ugly, but keenly aware of his musings on Denny's recent volatility, he powered his driver's window down, turned his steely visage upon the group and in his somberest tone said, "So sorry to have inconvenienced you fine young gentlemen on your journey. Good day to youse. But since we are talking, can you tell me are the Crips red and the Bloods blue, or is it the other way around? I can never fucking get it straight." The light changed and he moved into traffic without getting a clear answer.

He turned the volume back up, pleased with his restraint, idly hoping the Lexus occupants were really gangsters and not rappers masquerading in case he'd unwittingly given up another song for sampling in a manner he would not approve of.

He saw the 10 freeway west onramp entrance and impulsively took it. By the time the old Route 66 turned into Pacific Coast Highway Route 1, he realized that he was going to drop in on Denny to straighten things out. His fast cruise through Malibu was briefly stopped at the light to Cross Creek Road, as was an old Dodge Dart headed in the opposite direction. He wouldn't have registered the blonde driver except the crazy broad looked across at him, mimed pulling her first and second fingers out of a holster, and aimed them straight between his eyes. As the light changed, she pointed the fingers up, blew the smoke away, and accelerated into the waiting pack. He sighed. Five minutes later, he made an illegal left across the PCH divider and pulled up close enough to press the entry buzzer in front of the imported English gates and ornate fence that surrounded Golden's estate.

CHAPTER 22

Terry reluctantly agreed to make the considerable detour on the way to Palm Springs to save James and his ribs a drive and came to Malibu to pick them up. Highsmith chose the floor of the passenger seat rather than a seat in the back while they zipped down PCH and onto the 10 Freeway, making it through downtown Los Angeles as the morning rush-hour traffic dissipated.

James filled Terry in as best he could on Nashville and the aftermath. They passed the windmill-like energy devices that signaled Palm Springs was close before conversation turned to the band.

"Look, meantime, what about Damaged? Did your dipshit business affairs person actually get an offer in?" said James.

"Yes, of course we did. I don't understand why you are being so aggressive with me about them. I introduced you to them."

"That's the fucking point, Terry. Like we are all living in your world—you took it for granted that I'd go look for Jacquie, manage your band, and put them in your lap. Now I'm going with you to your mother-in-law?" Incredulous, he put his head in his hands. They slid off into the two-lane blacktop that took you onto Palm Canyon Drive, the main drag into Palm Springs. James quickly relaxed as he drifted into the easy Sinatra/Bob Hope aura. The unusually wet winter in the desert had produced surreally colorful flowers that bloomed everywhere, giving a 50s sci-fi Martian red tone to the surroundings.

"Do you miss Jacqueline or are you just looking for her because it's the right sort of thing to do?"

Terry's eyes left the road ahead and looked at James reflectively. "Hmmm, I don't miss most of what our life had become. You know, just the grind of day-to-day interactions and petty resentments."

"You fuck around on her much?" asked James.

"Not since we were married. But I'm still slaving five nights a week in clubs on average. Crawling into bed long after she and the kids are asleep."

James, wondering about the life he hadn't led, pressed, "Glad you had the kids?"

"Glad, but somewhat guilty. I feel a bit like the worst kind of detached English father from stiff-upper-lip films."

James grinned. "They even gonna be happy to see you?"

"Well, I hope so. It's not like I beat them."

They cruised past the hodgepodge of pastel boutiques—swimwear a pervasive specialty—restaurants with unused misting sprinklers, a See's Candy store. They took a right on South Palm Canyon Drive, off onto Arenas, a side street that sloped up towards the brown grass-flecked mountain whose base was only a few hundred yards away. A hodgepodge of homes and 50s neon-signed bed and breakfasts ran along both sides of the road.

"Bang on some Sinatra, Terry. Let's get the mood right, eh?"

"We're almost here," said Terry, as a huge-stomached, 50s bleached-blonde woman stepped in front of the car, she and her blue and yellow bikini so oblivious that for a moment James wondered whether she was a California-filtered Fellini vision, or maybe he was.

They turned left onto Palencio and pulled up at a white stone adobe single-story home next door to the Cactus Inn. The short path was flanked by moderately sized cactus that Highsmith pulled back and forth towards but intuitively only sniffed gingerly, pausing to cock his leg perilously close to the last one on the right. The arched wooden doorway, which had pink bougainvillea flowing around it, opened to reveal a five-footish white-haired lady who smiled in greeting, at least visibly undisturbed by the events that flowed around her.

"Hello, dear," she said to Terry. "And you must be James, I imagine."

Terry bent down and gave her a brief hug.

"Hello, Martha. How are you and the kids holding up?"

"Oh, they are fine. Honestly, it's just a change for them and they seem to be enjoying the thrill of skipping school." She noticed Highsmith strained at his leash. "Do come in," she said, "and he's fine if you want to let him roam."

The door opened straight into the living room, walls adorned with a gallery of family pictures, including a variety of childhood ones of Jacqueline from proper little 60s girl to fresh-faced sixteen-year-old budding rocker ready to head west.

"The children are in the yard out back. Would you like to go see them or talk first?" she asked.

"Best talk, I think," Terry said. "I don't want them to start worrying if they haven't up to now. What can you tell us, Martha?"

She ushered them to a well-stuffed brown couch and she sat across in a matching chair. She was surprisingly succinct, James thought, as she ran through what she knew. Jacqueline had called, sounding very upset, and said she'd like to bring the children to stay while she worked things out.

"She arrived a few hours later in a terrible state. She wouldn't go into detail and, as I hope you would agree, I've always tried not to be a typical prying, judgmental mother-in-law, so I was as supportive as I could be without pressing her. All marriages have their troubles." Terry nodded, seemingly genuinely touched. "She said she needed time to think things through—at least a few days. I said she was welcome to stay here. My housemate Sheryl is back visiting her grandkids, so there's plenty of room, but she said she had to be on her own for now. I'm sorry, dear, I hated to lie when you called, but she made me promise not to tell anyone that I'd heard from her. But she should have called me by now, so I felt I had to talk to you."

"She said 'anyone'?" asked Terry.

"Why yes, she did, but I took that to mean you. Why would anyone else be looking for her?"

Terry and James glanced at each other. Both realized that Martha thought this was all a marital spat and that Jacquie had decided not to tell her mother otherwise. The old lady, clearly no dope, had her radar on, though.

Terry broke the brief silence. "Do you know where she is?"

"Not exactly, but I believe she went to Mexico. I saw her passport next to her wallet in her purse. She said she'd call me in a few days but that calling might be difficult, which made me think she was south of the border. It would make sense since she loved the semester at college she'd spent there."

"Oh, I'd forgotten that," said Terry.

"Yes, she'd been at Monterrey's Architectural College and studied language too."

"Is there anyone there she might still be in touch with?" asked James. Highsmith still pulled at the leash.

"Why don't you let him off? Everything's enclosed here, so he won't go far," suggested Martha.

The Springer Spaniel, true to his name, sprang and made deep snuffling noises as he covered every square inch of the low-ceilinged room and disappeared down the single corridor that led to the rest of the house.

"C'mon, you two," prompted James. Blank looks from husband and mother. "Terry, I know you didn't remember her college time there but were there ever any calls on your phone bill or letters from Mexico to her? Anything?"

Terry shook his head. "Nothing I can think of."

"Martha?"

"Goodness, dear, it was so long ago and she left home to live in Los Angeles right after, so it's not like I would have been around her to know. I do remember she loved her time there and the people she was at school with, but I can't think of her mentioning anyone specific in recent years."

"Terry, did you and Jacquie ever go together?"

"Well, just to Cabo, but not to Monterrey. You know what, though, she had said she'd wanted to visit Real de Catorce."

James looked at him questioningly. "I've heard of that place. Wasn't it a bandit stronghold in revolutionary times? I thought it had become a ghost town and got adopted by kids who did peyote, that kind of thing. Doesn't sound like Jacquie."

Terry interjected, "I don't know about that. I think she had said it was a holy spot for Catholics and she wanted to go for more like a pilgrimage, if that's the right word."

Martha smiled, despite the situation. "How nice she's still so religious. I didn't know if it meant much to her as an adult."

A door banged and a fair-haired, spindly, ten-year-old boy

narrowly led an eight-year-old, somewhat darker complexioned girl down the corridor, both hotly pursued by a bounding Highsmith.

"Hi, Daddy. Did you bring us this dog?" asked George.

"Yes, can we keep him?" asked Amy.

"Well, hi, children. This dog is Highsmith and he belongs to my old friend, James. Do you remember him?"

"No," they cried in unison. "We want a dog. We want a dog."

Terry shook his head, visibly relieved that dogs were their biggest apparent concern.

"Well, it has been a long time."

"Where's Mummy?" asked the girl.

"She's still on her trip, darling."

"I'm hungry. What's for lunch?" asked the boy, and that was it. No tears, nothing even awkward, really.

Despite Martha's offer to make lunch, it was decided they would all walk the few blocks back down to South Palm Canyon Drive where they sat at a dog-friendly outdoor patio of an old Mexican joint. The mix of tacos and burritos was decent, although a typically inauthentic Californian version of real regional Mexican food. With all the revelations James had imparted on the way down duly digested, Terry wisely asked Martha to keep the kids until they found her daughter. The old lady probably had plenty of questions but the presence of the kids kept things light and superficial until the two men and dog were back on the road.

It was only 4:00 pm but the light was fading fast, and the Sinatra Terry had put on now seemed pointless to James as they quickly hit the 10 Freeway. The towns like Fontana and Riverside that popped up on the exit signs made James think of meth labs strewn on wastelands. To shake the descending depressing mood, he asked whether he could use the bulky car phone that was nestled in the central console of the wagon. When Lainey didn't answer the office line, he was about to curse her until he realized it was the weekend. Terry turned his eyes from the road questioningly.

James shrugged. "I dunno what to tell you. I just thought of an artist manager I'd done some business with in Monterrey last year. Maybe he might have an idea. Perhaps you're going to have to hire a local private detective. I'm lost here, Terry. I've never seen it but I do know it's a pretty big city. Where would I start? I know there's some really cool bands coming out of there these days, but it's not like Jacquie would be out at clubs, etc."

"I know, I know," said Terry. "But the more I think about it, the more Real de Catorce seems possible. To be honest, she was pretty insistent about us going, but I just never took enough time off for holidays, on top of which until recently, flying with the kids was a pain in the ass."

"You sure there's no friend in Mexico?"

"I don't think so. You know what, though, maybe there's someone in our address book at home. I'll go through it."

"Yeah, maybe something will turn up. I'll call this guy Repo in the morning and see if he can fill me in on how big Real de Catorce is, and how we might find her if she's in Monterrey."

Terry dropped them back at Point Dume without coming in, to James's relief. His ribs ached like fuck and he didn't feel like the company of anyone but Highsmith. He chopped up some previously cooked chicken and dry food for the dog. Not for the first time lately, he thought how he'd like to know how to cook food he liked. Given he'd done nothing to that end, he called Malibu Seafood and ordered a tuna burger and fries to go.

Man and dog drove the six minutes up and down the coastal road hills, going far past their destination before a break in the PCH central divider allowed them to make a left and double back to Malibu Seafood, which was situated on the far side of the road from the ocean, but allowed its customers pure ocean views. The tiny 60s and 70s vibe blue and red wood shack was pretty quiet compared to its line-out-the-door summer norm. James entered and eyed the fresh fish and shellfish in the glass counter to his right before he crossed the three feet to the take-out side. He looked up at the whiteboard with handwritten logs of grilled fish choices. The only customers ahead of him were a rotund family of German tourists, likely making the most of the off-season prices at the trailer park that nestled in the hillside above the restaurant.

Bonnie, always cheerful, had his order ready. James eyed the small rack of fish cooking books, intrigued, but as usual, intimidated, left without purchasing one.

By Monday morning, he felt way better. He rang off a string of calls, Eric still happily surprising him with some serious bids on Damaged—including one from Terry's Real lawyer that actually was more than competitive, to his relief.

He called Damaged's joint and talked to Davey and Katrina. "Looks like you'll have serious choices to make. Let's go eat some food together and plot."

The pair was buoyant and agreed to meet at the Formosa Café for lunch, along with the rest of the band.

"Hola, Repo," he greeted the soulful Uruguayan Mauricio Oropesa with his next call to Monterrey, where the rising manager called home. James explained the gist of the situation.

"Well, James, my business partner, Javier, was at that school, maybe a bit younger, but he might be able to help. As for Real de Catorce, I know a young singer, Belu Suarez, a cool but maybe a little dangerous girl who takes peyote journeys there frequently. She would perhaps know if an American woman was new there."

"Brilliant, Repo. You gonna be around? I'm thinking I need to finally make it down there and meet you."

"Of course, James. Let me know, I'll have you picked up from the airport. Fly Air Mexicana—it's direct, and customs and immigration is easier."

He put the receiver down, revved up, but his hand didn't lift it up for the inevitable next call right away. When he did, she answered, "Yes," on the third ring.

"Hello, Trouble. Wondering if they taught you any Spanish back there in teacher training school?"

"I get by."

"Good. How about I buy the tickets on Terry's dime and we go look for his wife?"

"As long as I can collect my $10K from her if she's there."

"Fair enough." He grinned and figured he'd deal with that problem when the time came. "We'll be going to Real de Catorce by way of Monterrey."

Lainey pointed out to him after a bit of research that it was easier to get there from Mexico City, but his gut was that Jacqueline would have taken this route if indeed she was there at all. Either way, he wanted to meet Repo and get a sense of the city's burgeoning music scene. She got coach flights direct for Thursday afternoon for about three hundred bucks a ticket.

Highsmith sprung around the living room, chasing and mostly catching the sand flies that buzzed about the kitchen. He remembered Monday evening was the beginning of the puppy training classes he had promised himself they'd take. As the black-and-white critter flew through the air, mouth agape and beautiful ears flying back, he remembered the rescue job from Glendora police station. The woman from the English Springer Spaniel Rescue Association had said there was a pair of three-time loser Spaniel puppies at the 50s Happy Days-like town lockup.

James had pulled up after having followed the directions of the animal control officer, who had strongly recommended, "Take the boy. He's a serious character and you can't tell now, but he's going to have amazing markings," a prediction that was coming very ying-yang, black-and-white true. Apparently he'd led his sister on three escape missions from their home with a white-trash family, including two kids and dogs who predated the Springers.

As he entered the lobby, a heavy thirty-ish shirtless Mexican guy was being bailed out in a sweet manner that could never happen in the still post-Parker/Darryl Gates, fascist inner city climate of Los Angeles.

He was led past the human cells to a dog version. Glendora, evidently too small for a pound, had maybe a dozen cages set up. An aged German shepherd looking sad and forlorn stood out to James, looking like an institutionalized career criminal. He'd wondered on the way out what to do if he didn't connect to the dog when he got here. He saw the black-and-white critter sitting upright, looking completely unconcerned despite the fleas that crawled over him. The officer opened the meshed cage door. Man and dog looked each other square in the eye. Dog slightly lifted his chin upwards.

A cop loaned James a thin leash he'd put on the three-month-old miscreant. "Yeah, this one took his sister on the lam three times from their home. An old broad took the bitch for her grandson earlier." They walked around to the now empty lobby check-in desk, where James scrawled his name at the bottom of a few forms. As they prepared to leave, the dog tugged backwards on his leash to pause them for a moment. He proceeded to shit all over the lobby. This time, the head shake was more than clear: "Let's get the fuck out of here." If James had ever been sure of something in his life, it was that this was a kindred punk-spirited partner.

CHAPTER 23

Damaged dressed as if they were going to a gig—which only differed from everything they usually wore insofar as they discussed it to make sure there was no clashing. They pulled their old green Dodge pickup on the right side of Formosa Avenue into the one available spot on the street slightly north of Willoughby and walked the long block and a half. The Warner Brothers lot across the street had started out in 1919 as the Pickford-Fairbanks studios, but it was stills from the many Elvis films that were displayed inside the Formosa Café, along with pictures of the Memphis Mafia and their King in the red booths that most remembered it for these days.

They strutted across the baking asphalt of the old parking lot and ducked into the welcoming gloom. The long, somewhat narrow room was still relatively quiet and it was easy enough for the band to grab a window booth, where they continued their ongoing debate about what to do next. Steve, the drummer, whose girlfriend was more than a little pushing for marriage along with at least a Valley condo, voted for the highest advance. Stoic bass player Bill, who'd been close too many times to count, tried to disguise his melancholy sense of déjà vu with creative ideas for the best producer.

James bounced in, childishly happy at having found a spot in the lot to park. He figured that unlikely event was a good omen, not to mention he held a fistful of newly faxed offers. The short walk also avoided additional wear and tear on his ribs, but in truth they were feeling way better. He spotted the band and slid onto the end of the booth next to Davey and across from Katrina. It was clear, as the elderly Chinese waiter dropped off the sizable menus, that the band knew nothing of the Viper Room aftermath that had left him in that condition and he chose to leave things that way.

They ordered, and a variety of glowing nuclear 50s red food duly arrived while James broke down the situation.

"So there's five offers, all in the same range of advances, but of course those numbers can change as they potentially bid against each other. I'd advise that you don't get caught up in that part. Anyway, they'll all expect to take you to expensive dinners at what they perceive to be a cool restaurant that will reflect on them well." James poked unenthusiastically at the shrimp-fried rice that beamed back at him. "So trust me, this is the shittiest food you'll eat in a while."

"So we eat good, and then what?" asked Katrina.

"It's all like an elaborate courtship dance where everyone tries to convince you that they love, understand, and care about you the most and will work unceasingly hard in the quest to make you the biggest band on the planet."

The band gave variations on the same rueful grin.

"I'm just trying to give you a realistic perspective. We all know you're leaning towards Terry, and he's introduced me to you. Mercifully, his business affairs guy put in a competitive offer."

"Azoff in?" asked Katrina, deadpan.

James grinned broadly. "Oh, ready to sell your soul to the devil, eh? Listen, if he was still in management, you'd be set, but keep in mind he's going to be most concerned about the label he's running, which might not run parallel to your interests. They did check in with Eric, but haven't made a written offer. The best offer is from Pacific Records for John Van Put. They want you in the studio quick and release in September to launch his label. I can't see anyone putting you out in the fourth quarter, though, when the majors are releasing superstar acts for the holiday season."

"What about them? John's been aboard for some fucking great guitar records?" asked Davey.

"Yeah, maybe. You're in a somewhat magic moment. As ridiculous as it is, go to all the lunches and dinners that these people want to do. Ask questions but remember to shut up and listen to what they say because that's when you have to trust your gut a bit and hope your bullshit detector is working. It's hard because they will all tell you what they think you want to hear."

Katrina asked, "You'll be here, right?"

"Here's the thing," James said thoughtfully. "I'm going to be away for a few days, but truth is I know all these people and if I'm not there, they might reveal a bit more to you lot as their guard will be slightly down."

They all looked at him a bit skeptically.

"Look, try and enjoy it. Have a laugh—don't get so out of hand you scare them off. You've come this far. If we don't fuck it up between us, you'll go make a killer record, right?"

The hard sun angled in through the window and reflected off the black-and-white 60s photos right onto the Formica table, leaving them all in a perfect frozen moment.

CHAPTER 24

He went home and fed Highsmith before they set out for their first training class. It was dusk when they took the quick left onto Malibu Canyon past the manicured green, rolling lawns of ultra-rich Pepperdine University and the immediate right onto Winter Canyon, which sloped down parallel to Pacific Coast Highway. The classes were to be held at a fenced-in area of a junior high school yard. They were greeted by Tawn the trainer, a pleasant, forthright sturdy woman, who would have been described as "tweedy" were it the English countryside. Highsmith jumped up at her and she put her knee up, knocking the surprised Springer back to all fours. She took James's check, attached it to her clipboard, and handed him a stapled class guide.

After an hour of hilarious mayhem filled with the twelve dogs' attempts at sits, heels, and stays, it was clear Highsmith was a very quick study, but easily bored. He was clearly enamored of Molly, a black standard poodle, and pulled them alongside her as they walked in the darkness. James chatted briefly with the rotund, bubble-haired lady, wondering whether it was true that dogs and their owners grew to look alike, thinking this pair had a head start. Certainly the elderly, aristocratic gentleman who proudly walked Archie the Airedale out didn't have far to go either.

By Wednesday, he'd taken care of a few loose ends. Lainey coordinated meal meetings for Damaged. He surprisingly hadn't

164

met much resistance from Eric when he suggested there was no real need to meet with Denny's people at this stage, given the recent dinner. It had probably helped that he'd also said he felt the same about Terry. Truth was, of course, that Terry was perfectly capable of arranging anything he wanted in the way of access to the band. He called Davey and Katrina, reassured them that by the time they got to the next round, which would likely include a bigger group of employees at the various label offices, that he'd be back in town. He and Aurial had agreed it was smarter to meet at the Air Mexicana gate, which they did, almost colliding as they both arrived late, clutching carryon luggage only.

She decided against telling him he was tardy, feeling that their scholastic sparring was close to running its course. "Thanks for arranging the transport, kiddo," she said, acknowledging the Town Car that had whisked her here.

They had a window (which James had edged her for) and a center seat. They had five minutes of hope that the aisle seat would be empty until a verging-on-obese woman and her similarly sized friend flopped down in seats 11C and D, causing their gingham print dresses to crunch. The one whose name was Edie expressed and acted upon a desire to remove her shoes immediately.

James was relieved he had the window, as he would have dealt with the situation with far more anxiety than the girl, who somehow seemd to exert her physical boundary effortlessly. He grabbed his CD player and flipped on his favorite take-off record: The Heart Throbs' *Cleopatra Grip*. He loved the adrenaline buzz of hell-for-leather speed buffered and amplified by the sensual soundtrack to one more safe escape or the perfect exit music. The plane took its sharp ascent and was instantly over water and curved south. He saw Point Dume and felt a twinge of homesickness—something he never felt for London. He didn't look across at Aurial until he changed CDs, by which time they crossed the border over Texas air space, a few miles from Austin, and he'd put on Los Alegres de Terán, a Norteño record that helped him get lost in the idea of searching for a missing wife in Mexico without unduly worrying about it.

She was rail straight and held a trade paperback Black Lizard novel at the height a finishing school would insist upon. Her long fingers just obscured the author and title; she put it in her Italian leather-looking black shoulder bag as the plane taxied to a stop in the shimmering heat of Monterrey. James was thrilled with the contrast from the institutionalized prison-like feel of LAX to this. The customs and immigration guys were pretty much what you might expect if you watched your vintage noir films, but no corruption on display, and as you exited into customs, you walked into a beautifully stylized area of sleek 60s Italian-like modular furniture: brown wood counters surrounded by immaculate stainless steel. They were spotted by the stocky, ponytailed manager, who swept them up in a happy embrace. Aurial, slightly looser than James might have expected, hugged Repo back and the Englishman followed suit. He led them through the big clean-lined glass doors to the turquoise 60s VW Bug he'd left illegally parked outside.

The first true sign that they were entering somewhere unique was the steel factory that had retained its structure while being turned into a rollercoaster ride for kids. They passed the Bohemia, Indio, and Carta Blanca beer factories that were now the blue-collar city's biggest industries.

"So what's with the rollercoaster?"

"Oh, man, it's actually a beautiful expression of a proud city acknowledging its industrial past while turning to the future with a sense of purpose and fun."

James grinned. "Yeah? I think I'm going to like it here. Anyway, it's brilliant to meet you finally. Thanks for coming out to get us."

"Of course. There's a bunch of people who want to meet you, whose songs you used, but first let's get you checked in to the Crowne Plaza."

Although James had always avoided chain hotels like the plague, he'd been promised that the original 1920 wooden lobby and bar area had been retained. There was no parking on the busy street so they jumped out at the curb, agreeing that Repo would come and pick them up at 7:30 pm.

The glare of the outdoors dimmed as they entered the high-ceilinged lobby, which exceeded James's expectations. The serious but pleasant forty-ish man behind the check-in desk adjusted his crisp black suit jacket slightly and decided English was the best bet for these two. Accordingly, they were assigned adjoining rooms and within five minutes, tossed their respective luggage onto generic double beds on the twelfth floor. Somewhat disappointingly for James, his room could have been any Hyatt anywhere, anytime, but he figured it would encourage him to spend more time in the classic bar.

He left Aurial to her own devices while he went back downstairs. He saw an open area he thought was a bar, but realized its red, green, and yellow surrounded area was actually an open kitchen. The hanging salamis and glass jars of thin breadsticks and olive oils suggested Italian. The impassive girl behind the highly polished tile counter wore a tall white chef's hat and overalls. She silently slid a menu, which confirmed the Italian-influenced antipasto on offer this afternoon. He sat on a bar stool and ordered *verdure en scapeche*, delicious grilled vinegary peppers and eggplant. There was a kick to the peppers that he guessed meant there'd been a Serrano chili added. He appreciated the local touch, and wondered where Repo intended to take them tonight. He sipped on a glass of red and tried to focus on his agenda. He'd asked Aurial on instinct, but realized she was a volatile wildcard who might end up being a huge plus or a huge minus. He needed to keep her close and get as much information about the tapes as he could. He, of course, wasn't going to let her blackmail Jacquie but figured Terry would happily reward her with $10K if all went well.

A lot was going to depend on whether Repo's partner, Javier Rios, had any leads on Jacqueline—a long shot at best. Ultimately, all he could plan was to ask for as much help as possible and make the most of getting to a place he wanted to visit. He put the meal on his room, went back up, showered, and dressed.

CHAPTER 25

They were called to the lobby. A giant bear of a man greeted them. He was clearly trying to grow an Afro, although not entirely successfully.

"Hola. Repo and Rios asked me to swing by. They are just finishing up at the studio with the Zitas and since I was rigging outboard gear, it seemed best I pick you up."

"All right, thanks," said James.

They followed him out to the curb, where a white paneled van was parked. The guy behind the wheel wore a vintage Run DMC-era gold chain around his neck and a *Straight Outta Compton* T-shirt. He was Guillermo and the Afro belonged to Sebastian. They were roadying and teching but had their own DJ and MC duo going, including a late-night slot tonight if Aurial and James stayed up late? It was perhaps both an invite and a challenge. She was wedged tight into the second row of bench seats between James and an old Marshall amp. She turned so their noses were an inch apart, raised her left eyebrow, and left him with the decision.

"Yeah. Can we come by after our dinner?"

Guillermo turned around, disconcertingly giving them his full attention, since he was the driver, supposedly guiding them through the hectic traffic that flowed out of the downtown area. "Yes, of course."

James tried to focus on the striking mountain range that,

bathed in sunset, surrounded the industrial city.

They pulled up on a desolate street that looked more like a business district than residential. Guillermo hopped out; he and Sebastian freed up back seat space by humping the amp through a set of double glass doors. They opened the back doors and removed the mixture of gear, its only common denominator being that it all looked twenty years old. Five minutes later, Repo bustled out through the same doors, followed by a shortish, somewhat preppy, earnest-looking fellow who had to be (and was) Javier Rios.

As they rode and got to know each other firsthand, James became aware that while they soaked into the unique strong, cool culture of a modern Mexican city, the proximity to the Texas border had rubbed off a bit on guys like these. Sebastian pulled up outside the vividly yellow painted restaurant and the four of them piled out. James stepped shoulder to shoulder with Repo. "So listen, aside from all the missing person talk, I wanna hear about what you've got going on."

They were quietly ushered in to a corner table at the bustling restaurant. Repo and Javier were clearly valued customers. They sat in the bright shiny yellow chairs.

"Well, James, things are good. The Zitas are making a great new record. We are busy with several really promising new artists like Chloë. The business is, of course, complicated here."

"How do you mean? Business is complicated everywhere, right?"

"Yes, but here," the Uruguayan's voice lowered slightly, "piracy is so prevalent it's like a shadow business." He noticeably eyeballed the room to see who might be in earshot.

"Really? I didn't realize," said James thoughtfully. "Nothing you can do about it, I suppose?"

The conversation paused as an orange T-shirt and jeaned waiter brought menus and took drink orders. James looked at the Oaxacan menu but couldn't comprehend the descriptions beyond a few key meat and shrimp dishes that his horribly limited Spanish allowed.

"Well, James, to answer your question, we are wrestling with some difficult decisions, but naturally anything I tell you needs to be treated in the strictest confidence."

"Of course, mate."

"Well, we estimate that when we do deals with majors like EMI, something like fifty percent of sales go to bootlegged copies."

"La Pretenciosa" by Las Hermanas Segovia set the easy tone. The drinks came, and James realized that Javier and Aurial were chatting away in Spanish, the girl seemingly fluent. He sipped on a pretty good glass of Rioja, and Repo returned to the subject at hand.

"So we've been approached by the, er, pirates to start doing deals directly with them and sharing the proceeds."

James couldn't stifle the astonished laugh. "You're fucking kidding me?" But he knew the answer.

"Classic if-you-can't-beat-them-join-them, right?"

James mused. "So what are you thinking?"

"Well, we are, of course, conflicted and a little nervous, but right now our artists are having a hard time surviving."

James shook his head. "I get it. I don't know what I'd do if I was in your shoes."

"Part of the reason I'm asking is when we sign to the major labels, we get the potential for releases in other countries if those territories choose to put them out, but this, er, situation would seemingly be domestic only." He smiled wryly.

"Right, of course," James mused.

"So, James, I know you've been supportive of the type of artists we sign, so perhaps you might be interested in helping us with foreign licensing deals if we decide to go this route?"

James nodded.

"Thank you. I'm sorry to bring this up when I know you are here for very different reasons, but it's clearly a conversation better had in person."

"No problem."

The waiter returned. James, lost, asked Aurial to order for them both. She grinned, enjoying his helplessness.

"By the way, while you two played the record game, Javier here told me he's pretty sure Jacqueline's been here." She leaned across him to dialogue with Repo and the waiter while he turned to Javier.

"Is she serious? You've seen Jacqueline?"

"Well, not firsthand," Rios smiled. "In actual fact, I wouldn't know her since she was graduating from school when I enrolled, but after I made some calls, it turned out we had some mutual student friends…"

"And…?"asked James, impatient for the point of all this.

"Well, she has indeed been here in the last week."

James froze, enjoying the moment beyond belief as mythic singer Lydia Mendoza's 1930's hit "Mal Hombre" started its haunting echo around the room. "You're fucking kidding me? After all we've been through—you found her?"

"Well, it just so happens I know Diego Kandracke, who owns the Havana Club here, and I thought he would be about the right age and he was at the same college. He saw her and is willing to talk to you later. We will go after dinner, but meantime, have a drink and anticipate the food."

The waiter brought a variety of *gorditas*, thick corn bread pockets stuffed with meat and cheese stews. He and Aurial looked at each other and grinned as they chowed down on the delicious layers of taste and texture, which sped up their mutual red wine consumption. Next came sea bass in *huitlacoche* sauce, a perfect, smoky, earthy taste like nothing James had ever tasted, but loved.

"What is that?" he asked Repo.

"Oh, man, you probably don't want to know. Think of it like a truffle or a mushroom, maybe." He chuckled to himself.

They were all close to drunk by the time they rolled out onto the street. James had barely won the grab for the check a minute or two before. They hailed a cab, a 60s VW bug missing the front passenger seat, and convinced the reluctant driver that all four of them could fit. As he sat on the floor next to the driver, James got a sense of déjà vu: he'd ridden home this way with his old Belfast-born mate Norman's similarly seat-deprived VW back in the nascent days of his club. Aurial was seated between the two managers, effortlessly swapping banter in Spanish.

Fifteen breakneck minutes later, they were deposited at the crowded driveway of the Havana Club. James's heart sank as they worked their way through the clubby throng to the crowded entrance, replete with velvet rope. Repo and Rios were immediately recognized and quietly ushered in to the pulsing club. The money was stiflingly apparent.

James put his hand on Aurial's shoulder as they walked into the crowd. "Fuck me, you ever walk down Rodeo Drive in Beverly Hills and wonder who buys that incredibly expensive, perfectly made, but horrible stuff?"

"It's all here, huh?" she replied.

The techno house soundtrack was good but incongruous, given this was a large bar with no dance floor. He would have bolted if there wasn't a compelling reason to be there. Mercifully, Repo sign-languaged them all through a small doorway into a much smaller lounge, where they took four of the six stools that surrounded a raised marble bar. A black turtleneck-clad bartender took their orders and exchanged a few words with Javier before he turned away to talk into the small headset that he wore. The manager, clearly enjoying all this, sipped on his Scotch and explained to James that Diego would join them shortly, which, ten minutes later, he did.

A tall, tanned, jet-black-haired guy, immaculate in what James guessed to be a Dolce & Gabbana suit, strode into the room and greeted them all cordially. The bartender placed a bottle and glass of mineral water in front of him without asking. James noted appreciatively that that was the only smart way to run a club. After a few pleasantries were exchanged, Diego continued in impeccable English. "So. I understand you are looking for my old college friend, Jacqueline?"

"Diego, you don't know the half of it, but yes, that's exactly it. Is she here? Have you really seen her?"

The club owner's coal black eyes looked hard at James. "I agreed to talk to you, as we clearly have a mutual acquaintance in Javier here, but might I ask the reason for you to come all the way here?"

James paused, it stupidly not having occurred to him that he might get quizzed this way. How much could he trust this guy? Instinct told him to tread carefully. "Yes, of course. Did Jacquie not explain the situation?"

"Well, certainly she was very specific about keeping our conversation private. The only reason we are meeting is because

Javier and Mauricio vouched for you."

James nodded. "Well, here's what I can tell you. Her husband, who is an old friend of mine, is very concerned and wants to make sure she's safe. I imagine you know she left her two children behind as well?" ventured James, curious to see whether he would react to that. Nope.

"Go on," suggested the club owner, impossible to read.

"I respect your loyalty and discretion. I promise you if you help me to see her, I will try to convince her to come back to LA but won't do more to force her return. I just need to make sure she's okay and put Terry's mind at rest."

Diego rubbed his thumb and forefinger against his chin thoughtfully. It crossed James's slightly drunk mind that he wished the generic techno that still pulsed could be one of dozens of songs that would fit the moment far better.

"We had occasionally corresponded since our college years, but I was surprised that she came after so many years. Our conversation will remain private, but suffice to say I had one of my security men drive her to Real de Catorce, a place she had long wished to go to."

Did this guy look a little wistful, James wondered. He decided not to press. "Thank you, Diego. Do you have an address?"

He got a smile in return. "You will hardly need one. Please honor your word and do not trouble her in any way."

Aurial grinned wolfishly and gestured to the bartender to give her another shot of mezcal. James nodded his acquiescence. As Diego strode out, having excused himself to attend to the variables of running a busy club, he was passed without apparent recognition by a striking woman who now walked towards them, her strong features framed by medium-length black hair. She wore what looked to be a vintage blue and yellow print dress that stood out simply among the sea of designer tat. There was a regal indolence about her face, somehow, as if cast from granite and reflected new and ancient Mexico. Repo rose and introduced them.

"James, this is Belu."

James shook her extended hand while Aurial nodded and half raised her shot glass in greeting. The Mexican took in the group appraisingly.

"What would you like to drink?" asked the bartender. She surveyed the small bar and chose a Carta Blanca from the limited choice of beers. James half turned so he could speak to her directly.

"You have immaculate timing. I just found out the woman we are looking for is in Real de Catorce."

"Oh, that's not what my band says," she said seriously. "They say I come in too soon and usually cause trouble."

He smiled, hearing absolutely no lack of laconic confidence in her self-deprecating words.

"But you can take us there?"

She grinned. "I was planning to go for a peyote journey, so you...and maybe her, too, are welcome to travel with me." She jerked her head towards the increasingly rowdy Aurial. "It's an arduous twelve-hour ride but it's possible my friend Abila will be able to provide a car."

"All right, I trust you. Listen, I have to ask. I've heard a lot about the music scene here in Monterrey, but this place is fucking horrible, right? No offense to anyone, but this reminds me of some cheesy suburban disco outside of London when I'm like seventeen."

"Well," she replied, "I can't speak for places or times that long ago."

"Please get me out of here," he pleaded.

"I can see that you are a punk of a certain time, so I might consider taking you to the Barrio Antiguo. There is a bar called Antropolis, I work at occasionally, but it is not a place for the faint of heart."

James was mesmerized by her, impossible to fully explain, but her eloquence and demeanor was a unique mixture of Shakespearean English blended seamlessly with the magical surrealist tones of her birthplace.

"I'm in."

Repo and Rios wanted to get over to their hip-hop gig and Aurial, upon hearing Antropolis was a beer joint, decided to join the managers, where she could continue her mezcal binge. James thanked them profusely for the huge step towards finding Jacqueline. They worked their way through the dense crowd and took separate cabs that were lined up outside.

The cab cruised through semi-lit, narrow streets until Belu directed the driver to pull over to the right on a dimly lit block that felt very old—medieval was the inappropriate word James thought of. The doorway felt like the entrance to a catacombs, dusty and ancient but heavily populated with cut-off-T-shirted kids either trying to squeeze their way in or sliding out for a little more air. Belu eased them in. A long wooden bar was to her left, three deep in beer-reeling patrons. It appeared that there was another area that people funneled out to once they'd grabbed their drinks. A bartender who brought cases of beer behind the bar as fast as he could still had time to spot the striking woman who entered purposefully and ask what she and the rubio wanted. She requested and got two Indio beers.

James took his gratefully, feeling the perfect ska-backed anthemic music that almost elevated the old foundations right through the floor. The second the beer hit the back of his throat, he was completely at home. His look told her everything, which was just as well, as all conversation was submerged when they stepped into the sweat-drenched interior. Dense groups of cool-as-hell kids were drinking hard and chanted along to the choruses of brilliant song after song by bands like Tijuana No!. It was the most joyous, honest atmosphere he'd been in for years. The spirit was definitely what he had gone for with his own long-gone club, the sweat dripping off the walls in a very similar manner.

She half tilted her head to an iron stairway that led upward. He followed her up, and took a long appraising look at her assured figure as it cut a swath through the mingled couples ahead of them. They arrived to cooler air on a rooftop that was covered by a green painted tin roof. There was an oblong bar in the center that was knee-deep in rotating punters. A dense mist of bud eased any tensions.

He got the next Indios that had gone right into his top five beers. "So tell me about Real de Catorce."

They raised and clicked bottles. While they drank, she told him stories of peyote adventures and dreams, as if recounted by William Shakespeare.

CHAPTER 26

As James woke, he had a distant sense of pissing many Indio beers back into a medieval latrine. His eyes opened on a blue, starlit sky that, he gradually realized, was a ceiling in a compact bedroom surrounded by candles that lay on a stone-tiled floor. Two yellow crates of vinyl records were against one wall. The Psychedelic Furs' first release was the one James's eyes focused on, and then Echo and the Bunnymen's *Crocodiles*. He raised his head slightly—it hurt. He closed his eyes and drifted. After a while, the door, also blue and covered with constellations, opened. Belu stood in the doorway with mugs of coffee.

"Hola. Here, drink this." She smiled warmly at his obvious confusion. "So we are at my mother's house, in case you don't perhaps remember. When we eventually left Antropolis, there were no cabs so we walked here. Perhaps the fresh air did not enhance your soberness. At any rate, we need to leave quickly. I just spoke to Abila and the car won't start, so we need to get to the bus station within the hour if we are to travel to Real de Catorce today."

"All right. Any chance of a shower first?"

"Two doors down. I'll call your friend and we can pick her up on the way to the bus station."

Dazed, and somewhat surprised by the girl's focus, he drank the mug of coffee gratefully and dragged himself down the narrow white corridor to the bathroom. It looked like it had been built in the

50s—pale green and white tile. He pulled back the red shower curtain and played with the painted hot and cold knobs. Five minutes later and wearing last night's clothes, he wandered down to the far end of the hall, which opened into a square, somewhat formal living room. Family photographs, mostly black-and-white, were neatly arranged around the walls. The handsome, heavily stuffed brown leather couch looked inviting, but somehow like it was rarely used. He went through into a more lived-in lounge, where a boxy TV dominated the room. To his right, with a very wide entrance, was a large kitchen presided over by a seventyish black-haired woman, clearly Belu's mother. She had several pans and pots on an impressive stove and the warmth of the room suggested that the oven had been in use for some time, too.

"I'm happy to meet you, James. You like my kitchen?" She was amused at his shambolic manner.

He felt possibly more at home than ever in his life, which made no sense, especially with the king-sized hangover he was nursing. He did know enough to roll the corn tortilla she flipped out of a cast-iron skillet up around the eggs, roasted tomatillo salsa, and other magical ingredients that brought life back into his veins.

Belu appeared, declining food while dismissing her mother, and ushered him back out towards the heavy wooden front door. She nudged him into the cab she'd conjured up, and twelve minutes later had a damaged-looking Aurial carrying both his and her bags into the cab, too. Bemused, he made no comment.

"You will need cash for the tickets," Belu informed him.

The two-lane highway that led to the open-air bus depot was flanked by a street market that mixed food produce of a dizzying variety with bootleg videos of films that were barely in theaters in the US. He poked through the assortment while Belu sorted the tickets with the pesos James gave her. Aurial looked surly, but determined as she inched through the food stands, helped by a chipper Belu who, tickets in hand, assured them gorditas were the only choice. She was more than right.

They hopped on the fairly modern white coach that was a third full as they pulled out of the urban center of Monterrey and quickly headed out past the high mountain areas onto a long open road that stretched to apparently nowhere. It sank in there was going to be twelve hours of this boredom. Small TV screens hung every ten seats or so, inexplicably showing a Sean Penn film with Spanish subtitles. James, curious about Belu's mother, pressed her for details.

"My father was in the OSS during World War II. They lived in Washington, DC, when they were first married. They moved back to Monterrey in the early fifties."

"Really, and that's been the family home ever since?" he asked.

"It's a really good home. My mother, who drives me crazy, worked with the architect who built it. She insisted on a really big open kitchen, being smart enough to know she would spend more than half her life in there and wanted all the family to enjoy that room together. The architect, of course, feeling a woman knew nothing of design, fought her, but as you saw, she is a quietly strong woman and she hands-down realized her vision."

He nodded, still analyzing his strong pull to this family history. "So what's your story? You look way too young to fit into that time line."

"My parents had four boys and then I came as an unexpected afterthought when they were on the verge of separating." She smiled. "We have been very trying of one another."

He smiled. "Yeah, I know how that can go."

181

"There was enough drama that I entered theatrical school and studied Shakespeare here, plus, of course, the band I sing for," she said.

"Yeah, Repo told me about that. I'm curious to hear."

"That's possible." She offered him a Walkman only slightly less battered than his from her shoulder bag. "There's six songs. If you like them, perhaps you can help me find ways to get them in a movie."

As he put them on, he glanced at Aurial, who lay against the window across from them in the two-by-two seat configuration. He resisted the urge to go across the aisle, not sure what he was feeling. The off-kilter keyboards of Belu's band kicked in and he looked past Aurial at the ever-browning expanse that lay on either side of the highway. With traces of the Psychedelic Furs filtered through a generation and a continent or two pulsing beautifully in his ears, his mind conjured up clichéd images of Robert Mitchum south of the border in noir films like *His Kind of Woman*.

Through the glaring light, he couldn't distinguish the details, but the bus driver clearly could and pulled over at the side of the road at the beckoning of a group of seriously armed *federales*. The driver popped the door across from him and two soldiers jumped up the steps and ordered him off. James looked out and down from his right side of the bus view and watched the driver open the luggage container that was directly below on the outside of the bus. His gaze locked onto a soldier, who pointed his automatic weapon towards the driver. The federale became aware and looked up, held James's gaze, and clearly sent a life-or-death warning to not look too closely. James got a sharp reminder that his living on the cusp of reality and fiction in Malibu was a whole lot different than doing it here. He looked away and the moment passed, but he wouldn't forget it.

The passengers' bags were hauled out, opened, and tossed thoroughly, like some extreme customs search. Belu looked at him, her head half tilted, seemingly accepting without particular rancor. Aurial hadn't reacted at all, but gazed out the other side of the bus. None of them had anything down below.

Twenty minutes later, they were waved on their way; the federales did not board the bus again. James put on a Miklós Rózsa mix of his best scores and wished for an Indio beer.

CHAPTER 27

Eight hours later, no one was in a good mood. There was now a 50s or early 60s Mexican lucha libre film on the TV screen. James was absorbed by it but frustrated by his lack of language. Belu had just awoken from a fitful nap and looked a little haunted. He stepped across the aisle and joined Aurial, who had barely spoken the whole trip.

"You all right, girl?"

They looked hard into each other's eyes yet again, both wondering whether they were projecting what they most wanted in some dumb fantasy or trying not to be scared of the best fun they might ever have. He tried to keep it practical. "If she's here, we have to figure the best plan to get her back to Terry, right?"

She bit her lip in a vaguely menacing way. He wasn't sure whether that was because she was pissed off that he'd peeled off with Belu last night or that she wanted to get maximum dollars from Jacqueline for skipping on her blackmail threats.

The moment was broken up as the bus slowed. Its brakes made hissing decompression sounds as the driver turned right off the highway into the dilapidated turnstile-cone, elongated beer and gas station that was Estacion 14. James wearily looked across at Belu.

She took the meaning. "This bus is too big to make the drive up the cliffs and through the very narrow tunnel to Real. We have to negotiate a ride or wait for the local bus."

There were a couple of gypsy cab drivers, but clearly not trustworthy to Belu's practiced eye. James and Aurial dragged their crispy, bedraggled selves and belongings off the bus and planted themselves on one of the stone benches that lay under the semi-covered parking area. The first thing James felt was the serious temperature drop. An hour and fifty-three minutes later, a classically worn and torn, faded gray and yellow bus pulled into the third of three slots. Clearly rural in nature, it off-loaded a mix of passengers. They clambered on; Belu grabbed a window and Aurial did the same five seats down while James scrunched in next to Belu. The rest of the passengers were mostly Huichol Indians on their annual pilgrimage.

The ponderous, worn-out-sounding bus pulled back onto the highway, but ten minutes later turned off onto a gradually rising curved road that took them onto a perilously narrow, steeply graded cliff road. It was essentially one lane, which even to someone who'd grown up with the English version, was unnerving. As half a wheel hung over a dizzying steep drop to hell and kicked small stones into the abyss, Belu asked him, "If this bus fell off the cliff, taking you on a horrifying plunge and your choice was to be permanently crippled or dead, what would you opt for?"

Her question remained unanswered when fifteen hair-raising minutes later, they rounded a high corner to face a high cliff with a small circular hole that the bus entered with an inch to spare. Their pace through the Ogarrio Tunnel was barely five miles an hour as a handful of pedestrians walked the mile and a half ahead of them in the pitch-black. James felt the history of the approaching place descend on him: post-Mexican revolutionary outlaw hideout that had become a true ghost town. The right wing mirror of the bus scraped along the wall and flew off into the darkness.

There was just enough room for the bus to turn left as it came out of the tunnel before it touched a double row of stalls that ran on either side of a further sharp hillside reddened with dry earth. A few people visible in the dusk bought Catholic icons as they climbed down the rusty steps.

"What's the story, Belu? Can we get something to eat and, more importantly, drink?"

"Maybe," she replied, "but we should establish somewhere to sleep. There are limited possibilities here and I fancy camping out would not be to your liking."

The three of them walked through the entrance to the whitewashed walled city and up the wide dirt street. The bone-chilling cold intensified as they got into the small town square. The only light came from candles and the occasional flicker of a gas lamp. Belu purposefully walked them past a small, inviting bar into an orange adobe building that turned out to have rented all five rooms it had. He sensed her worry, but she was clearly a dutiful host and encouraged them to another darker entrance three buildings down. The rotund woman who busied herself behind an old wooden countertop that passed for a lobby exchanged a few curt lines with Belu.

"Well, they have one room, which appears to be our only option for tonight." They trudged up the rounding stone staircase, its darkness only illuminated by a wall candle halfway up the flight that led to their room, which was entered by a heavy wooden arched door. The room itself was completely dark, with a large, low bed they discovered by grasping touch. It was freezing in the room, their breath causing clouds.

James felt a gloomy mood descend and immediately asked whether they could go to the bar. They left their bags in the room and wandered across the way. Their entrance was definitely taken note of by the seriously local bar habitués. Of the eight round stools along the bar, three of them were taken. Belu and Aurial grabbed two next to each other while James, who remained standing, leaned over the bar, pointed to a bottle of Indio while he glanced back to ascertain his compadres' order. Belu, sparing him, exchanged quick words with Aurial and a few with the disinterested old man behind the bar. He turned his back to them while he stirred a few white ingredients together.

James took his beer appreciatively and put some pesos on the counter. The candlelight flickered off the fading walls, red behind the bar and yellow on the surrounding ones. The brilliant Los Alegres de Terán recording of "Alma Enamorada" echoed across the room in its mono beauty from the old battery-powered boom box in the corner. One beer became two as the soulful Norteño vocal group sang from across the decades.

After three beers, Belu, who had left the bartender a good but not condescendingly large tip, asked him whether he'd seen a woman who fit Jacqueline's description. He said he'd last seen her two nights ago, that she'd been in on and off for a while, always on her own and mystifyingly to him, always ordered the awful white wine that he had to offer.

"I can't believe she was in here and we got that lucky," exclaimed James.

Belu shrugged. "I don't think with the descent of darkness that you can visualize how small a place you are in. If she likes to drink alcohol after about nine pm, this is the only choice, and earlier there are only two or three places to eat or drink. There are four or five places she'd be likely staying. I imagine you will find her tomorrow. Perhaps you should concentrate most on what you will say to her."

He raised his eyebrows and grinned as again she seemed to effortlessly get to the heart of the matter. What indeed, he wondered as he started the next Indio. Everything had been focused on finding her, but if he was really this close, did he even slightly think she'd be happy to see him or remotely decide he'd be the guy to solve her problems and bring her home? He clearly needed to have some very persuasive lines to convince her with. The more he somewhat drunkenly thought about it, the clearer everything hinged on her current feelings about Denny. She had to know on some level this was because of her time working for him, but would her almost pathological anger at James still foreshadow everything?

He turned to Aurial who, matching his beer with mezcal shots, looked at him with a knowing glance.

"Glad you came?" he asked.

"That remains to be seen," she said, deadpan. "It's been a joy so far. Just make sure you don't forget I'm here for my money. Tuition fees aren't what they once were, you know," she said, perhaps to make sure he knew she was still playing with him.

Playing or not, it lightened his mood and that, mixed with the beer, got him ready to confront Jacqueline in the morning. Meantime, they would drink. At about 3:00 a.m., Belu led them outside and there was an almost complete absence of artificial light. The vast constellations of stars were incredibly vivid against the still blue night sky. Belu pointed past the crumbling painted wall at the two or three small fires that burned in the distance; diffused music drifted towards them with the smoke.

"I will join them for some peyote later today. I think Aurial should come with me while you see this woman."

"Belu, you seem so sure I'll find her."

"I already told you, wait until you wake up in daylight."

They'd drunk enough to have buried their natural hunger for food, which also resulted in their stumbling walk back to the old building that housed their room. The room was now bone-chillingly cold. In truth, James had never been in an environment that felt like this. It was obvious that none of them would dream of taking one item of clothing off other than their shoes and boots. They threw their coats on top of the single thick blue and red Indian blanket that covered the single sheet, and crawled in: James on the side towards the far wall, Belu in the middle, and Aurial curled instantly facing outwards on the side nearest the arched wooden door. He could faintly hear music in the distance. They drifted off, or perhaps more accurately, passed out. The chill prevented true sleep from ever descending, though.

CHAPTER 28
JACQUELINE HARPER

Jacqueline Harper woke up about a hundred and fifty yards away, near the remnants of a wood fire whose embers still flickered as the morning sunlight crept in. She felt better than she had in a long time—the feelings of guilt about leaving her family in a scared panic were subsiding. She knew Terry would handle things. It truly had been time for her to take care of herself and maybe that threatening bitch had done her a favor in a way—here in Real de Catorce finally. Still, the past had to be sorted out now. Fucking James's shadow still cast over things. She was sure the call she'd made before she left Monterrey would put an end to it, though.

CHAPTER 29

The morning sunlight poured through the arched wooden shutters, but barely touched the chill in the room. No one moved for a while, grateful for whatever warmth they had, until Belu took the lead—got up and pushed open the half shutters. No one spoke, so she gradually ushered them down the stone staircase.

During the walk into the main plaza with its giant rose-covered cast-iron gazebo and the five-minute walk back to the double-sided street market, it finally sank into James that you would eventually run into anyone who was here during the course of a day. They turned on to the base of one of the two streets that gradually sloped up towards the mountainside. The narrow street had pale blue canopied stands on either side. There were two-story white stone-walled buildings for the first forty feet or so, but they petered out as the market stretched upwards towards the mountains. Two guys in their mid-twenties worked a large cast-iron grill fueled by logs of wood underneath. The smells of chicken, pork, and fish drew them over. The one in the red peaked cap and blue dungarees was almost showing off as his partner in a blue corduroy jacket, washed-out green T-shirt, and jeans kept an eye on a steady flow of green cactus tortillas that flew off the grill onto white paper plates. He dug into a tomato, garlic, chili, onion, and cilantro-laden bowl to adorn the various foods as they came off the sizzling grill.

As they passed the cemetery, James glanced across to the far side and saw the Alcazaba. "Maybe she's there," he wondered aloud, feeling fortified by the food.

The place had four bright casitas, all with panoramic views, and might have fit Jacquie's bill, but once Belu and Aurial caught up and asked the woman who was working in the enormous desert flower-laden garden, it was clear his guess was wrong.

Belu pointed up the slightly sloped streets. "Walk up there and you will pass the other places people can stay at. Ask for a *gringa*." She grinned. "I need a few minutes to arrange the peyote. I'll come and find you." They did as they were told.

The sun came up and warmed things a little, but the memories of the freezing night before haunted him, leaving his self-confidence strangely dented. He mumbled his few words of Spanish as taught by Belu, and struck out twice, but then his gaze strayed upwards and in slight profile on an iron second-floor balcony, he saw her—older, more worn than he would have imagined, but there nonetheless, sporting a dusky tan, sat Jacqueline.

He stood for a moment, taking in how suddenly easy it had all become. He walked not too swiftly, enjoyed the moment and forgot all the shit between them; perhaps she'd be relieved to be almost rescued. He turned to Aurial. "Let me go up on my own. You stay down here and grab her if she bolts, eh?"

The small hotel had blue and red shutters, covered by the revolutionary period wrought-iron bars that protected most window balconies in Real. The sun-shadowed adobe daytime noir-feeling entry area was deserted, so he took the curving stone steps upward, which he figured must lead to her room. There were two choices down a short corridor as it cut back to the left. Despite his lousy sense of direction, he was sure the first door would correspond with her balcony. He knocked on the heavy arched wooden door—a more elegantly carved version, but similar to the door for the room they'd stayed in last night.

Twenty seconds later, he knocked again. The heavy door opened inwards, but oddly, Jacqueline still sat in the wrought-iron chair on the balcony, which was now directly in his line of vision. He sensed how wrong that felt but stepped into the room anyway. A heavy-shoed foot kicked the door shut again, and to his horror he looked into a set of eyes and the barrel of a gun, both of which belonged to Ron Deutch. He could hear a Bernard Herrmann score play in his mind as everything seemed to slow down. He realized abstractedly that it was from *Beneath the Twelve Mile Reef*—haunting, ominous.

The frozen moment lasted part of a minute before disparate hells broke loose. Jacqueline turned to let loose on him. "You of all people would be the one to show up. You caused all this hell to start with!"

Meanwhile, Deutch gently waved a hefty-looking pistol back and forth and ushered him into a chair across from Jacqueline. It seemed he changed what he was about to say when he saw James's Stax Records T-shirt. "The fuck you wearing that for, Dual?" He poked his finger in the direction of James's chest, which bore the logo of the mythic Memphis label.

"Yeah, I know. Unusual to see me wearing any advertising," said James, going along with things as best he could.

"I don't know what you wear usually, asshole. You have any idea what that is?"

"That it's the greatest independent label ever. So many soul-drenched classics you don't even know how to begin?" said James.

Deutch relaxed, surprised but momentarily satisfied until a further thought crossed his mind. "It was a good label, a bit slow on the payment front from what I gather, but, you dumb fuck, the greatest independent label was Philly Soul." The gun rose ominously towards a spot between James's eyes.

James frowned. "Well, much respect to Kenny and Leon, but you are an even bigger idiot than I thought if you'd even speak those names in the same sentence. I mean, come on—William Bell, Judy Clay, Otis *fucking* Redding, Margie Joseph, David Porter, Isaac Hayes, The Memphis Horns, the best horn section in history behind all those singers—the fuck the best you got to offer, the *Back Stabbers*?"

Pure reflex clicked the hammer back on Deutch's gun before he talked himself out of the burning impulse. Jacqueline watched this exchange incredulously, speechless with fear and rage. Ron collected himself, snorted deeply, and seated himself in a very solid wicker chair across from them. He tilted it onto its back legs while he cradled the heavy gun across his lap.

"So here's how it's going to go. Girlie here is going to go the last part to all the way out of her mind." He gently pulled out a worn newspaper and unfolded it to display a sizable pile of the cactus that was peyote. "Now if that was a Philly Soul T-shirt, you might walk out of Mexico alive, but as it is, you'll take that long last walk into the desert. Maybe they'll find the two of you and figure it was a pair of aging rockers trying to relive their youth."

Jacqueline glared at them. If she had been force-fed the peyote buttons, clearly it hadn't started to take effect yet. "You're a pair of dinosaurs. No one cares about old soul music. What the hell are you doing here anyway, James? Don't tell me you're working for Denny."

James's head spun, serious fear mixed with confusion. "Are you nuts? Much as I'm regretting it now, I've been trying to find you for Terry. Remember the husband you ran out on?" The insanity kicked in a notch more. Suddenly the sense that there was always time to heal old wounds was shattered. He hated her indignant, entitled attitude. Trying to center himself, he asked Deutch, "Talking of which, what the fuck brings you here, Ron?"

His finger was still on the trigger. "Ask girlie."

"Oh, fuck me, Jacquie, tell me you didn't."

He saw the fear and uncertainty in her face, too, now. "Well, I wanted to get a blackmailer off my back before I came home, so I called Denny from Monterrey. I thought he might have been contacted, too, and he always knows what to do." It was disturbing to see her instant shift from angry to confused little girl lost.

"Well, you got that right, honey," said Deutch. "He does, and I'm here to clean up some old loose ends. I can't believe how good your timing is for once, Dual. It's going to make everything so much simpler. Here's how it's going to go. You two are going to share a nice large cactus breakfast and then we are all going to take a lovely long walk from which only one of us, namely me, will return."

"Sorry, Ronny, I gave up hallucinogenics when I was eighteen." James tried to sound way tougher than he felt.

"Suit yourself, you limey fuck. If you'd rather die of lead poisoning right here, I can do that too. Don't know if you've noticed but there's no law in this godforsaken spot. I'll shoot the pair of you and walk out. No one will even figure out who you are, let alone what happened."

Jacqueline had a whiney, pleading tone now. "Ron, you've got it all wrong. I can see why you and Denny are still angry at James, but I was always loyal. Even when I found out the plane had been sabotaged, I never told anyone. Why would I talk after all these years?"

Deutch almost smiled. He tipped a pile of peyote buttons

onto her lap and deposited the still laden newspaper onto James.

"Please, I can't. I just can't." She cried; sad, confused tears ran down her face.

Deutch pointed the gun right between her eyes and she started on the first one.

James wordlessly did the same. Two minutes and several buttons later, a pair of knee-length black biker boots flew over the balcony. Deutch fired wildly as the rest of Aurial hove into view. She'd hung onto the base of the balcony and had the strength to swing until her motion brought her high enough. Her left foot caught Deutch's right shoulder and sent the weapon flying into the air. Deutch caught the other leg before it connected with his jaw, and on his feet now, swung her and let go. The girl crashed into the wall on the far side of the room across from the balcony.

James sprang up, grabbed the floor lamp to his right, and smashed the base against the back of Deutch's head. As the big man almost buckled at the knees, James yelled, "Jacqueline, get out of here now—run!" Getting no response, he turned to see dead, vacant eyes that stared into forever. There was a gaping red hole in her forehead where at least one of the bullets must be.

He gagged and stood frozen in horror. Two enormous hands grabbed James's neck and started to squeeze the life out of him. He kneed Deutch in the crotch but was lifted off the ground, the effect almost the same as if he were strung up on a noose. His eyes bulged as a red mist clouded his vision. He still tried to kick Deutch but he was losing any sense of the physical below his neck. The only sound besides the pounding in his head was Deutch's almost whispered death wishes.

"Die slowly now, you little fuck. You've had this coming for a long, long time. Let's enjoy this, and as you go know that the first thing I'm going to do is wake up that trash you brought with you and fuck her up something awful."

James thought if he could gouge a finger into Deutch's eye that he would get loose still, but there was no strength or control left in him.

There was one last boom…

CHAPTER 30

Belu came back up the street after enacting her peyote transaction with the cool guy who'd been tossing the tortillas. She was discreet enough to know she shouldn't allow James and Aurial to be there, not because she remotely distrusted them but completely out of respect for the fact that the peyote purveyor couldn't know that.

She heard the first gunshots and, like the rest of the people on the block, just kept walking. She'd never noticed a policeman in Real and saw no sign of one now. She saw Aurial and James's overnight bags on the street. Blind instinct led her up the stairs to a quickly pushed open door, across from which sat a motionless woman in a wicker chair. She wore a round, red hole in the center of her forehead. James was prone on his back, with a hulk of a man draped across him. Aurial stood across the room, a large revolver's trigger guard hanging by the third finger on her left hand. Sudden violent, needless death was ingrained in Belu's DNA and she feared the worst.

Aurial's expression was tough and emotionless as usual, but she still couldn't hide the shock in her eyes.

Belu dropped to her knees and picked James's head up off the stone floor. She bent her head to his heart and glanced back up at Aurial. "He's alive. We need to leave swiftly."

Aurial nodded and between them, they rolled the bleeding Deutch over and leveraged James up. Each took one arm and shoulder, both seeing but not acknowledging the stark horror of a dead Jacqueline's blank brown eyes, her clearly admonishing mouth frozen, forever accusing.

CHAPTER 31

James came to. He leaned back against an eight-foot high, half-brown-leafed palm tree with a blue and red blanket wrapped across his shoulders. His point of view looked out across a bare desert horizon, broken only by the occasional eight-foot cactus. As he raised his arm to brush dust from his eye, it left a series of delayed images—trails, as they used to call them in his LSD days—and he got a staccato series of violent reminders of his immediate past. He half-bit his lip in fear at what he knew was kicking into his system.

He slowly became aware that Belu sat cross-legged to his left and Aurial to his right. "Jacquie?" he asked.

Belu shook her head. "Okay, James, we are going to take this journey together. You can choose the music. Can I help you find something?"

His tongue was completely dry as he tried to speak. Everything in his neck hurt as if it had all been shrunken. He rasped, "Yeah. Better grab that reggae mix. I think it says Big Youth, Alton Ellis, Joe Gibbs, Clint Eastwood and General Saint, Mad Professor and Lee Perry. Grab The Clash, too. Fuck, I can feel this shit coming on—it don't agree with me, ya know. I haven't done this since I was eighteen and that last time, it didn't go so well."

A worn-looking Aurial forced a grin. "Kiddo, you're going to have to live up to your punk rep about now, you know that, right?"

Belu took his left hand. "James, we will go together, okay?"

And so they did, as the peyote took over.

A stark, frozen moment interwoven with a collage of chapters. He'd never bought into all that Carlos Castenada shit, but he'd been dosed so heavily he was definitely having his own version.

Things melted.

Sue Ann suddenly covered the whole horizon and his tears fell at last, twenty years late, and blurred everything as "Armagideon Time" by The Clash pulsed through all the pain.

CHAPTER 32

Eventually, maybe ten hours later, Belu had experienced what she wanted or needed to, and was ready to pull the exit plan together. They shuffled down the dirt road, avoided the death block and mingled into a line of people who boarded the bus back down the mountainside, but this time, they got on a bus to Mexico City, a few hours closer. They finally had to part at Air Mexicana as James—who knew how much he owed her and appreciated her safety measure detour along with everything else—had paid for all their tickets.

He hugged her as though his life depended on it, wondering whether he'd ever understand their connection. "Thank you." She nodded and smiled.

Reality kicked in as he and Aurial boarded their three-hour direct flight back to Los Angeles. How the hell was he going to tell Terry that Jacqueline was gone? He'd briefly thought to call him but decided news like this had to be delivered in person and besides, a record of a call from Mexico might not be smart. Aurial had nudged him out of the way and grabbed the window seat. They'd barely spoken to each other since they left the bus, but as they flew back along the Pacific, hugging the coastline, it didn't seem to matter somehow. His mind and body depleted, still speechless, he fell asleep against her shoulder wondering what she was thinking, this out-of-the-blue girl who'd brought out all the havoc and then saved his life.

CHAPTER 33

Davey and Katrina lay on top of their slightly raised cast-iron bed, the Wolfhounds on either side of them, when James had shown up, looking destroyed, and given them the bare bones of what had happened in Mexico. Almost as if he was rehearsing his story—and getting ready to go tell Terry—which he, of course, was. He hadn't told the rockers he'd finally heard for sure Denny had sabotaged the Confederacy plane, though. Aurial had stayed in the Town Car while he'd gone in. He returned and she directed the driver to her carriage house in the Hills. He leaned into her, weary as hell. They had zero repartee, but it didn't matter. Somehow they were both comfortable with each other's tough but transparent façade and parted on an ambiguous kiss.

Finally, the black sedan pulled up to the carriage sweep driveway. He had the driver stop so he could walk the last ten yards to Terry's front door.

They sat in exactly the same spot in Terry's den as the first night while James told him everything. Terry's head was in his hands and his voice was thick, but no tears fell.

"Oh God help me, James. I should have realized she knew the truth."

"You can't blame yourself for that."

"I think she came close to telling me at least once."

"How so?"

"During one of her bad bouts of depression, she was semi-hysterical. Said she'd gone to Denny and told him you were serious about killing the band, so it was partly her fault, too. She just kept sobbing, 'Out of the mouths of babes.'"

"What does that mean?"

"I don't know. She said a lot of crazy things when she was in those states and I was always trying to calm her down: shut her up, in truth. It was so hard trying to manage her, the kids, and job. I should have been stronger… Maybe she'd still be here."

"Only you can decide how much you want to torture yourself."

CHAPTER 34
GARY KALUSIAN

Gary Kalusian looked out his office window as the Tower Records clerk changed the window displays, mostly still in the LP shape that encouraged reflection. Ron's petite, auburn-haired assistant had put a half-filled message spike on his desk, figuring calls shouldn't go unanswered during her boss's extended business trip. On top was one from Elmore Leonard, asking for follow-up questions which Gary glared at before he crumpled and adroitly tossed it into the adjacent wastebasket.

When a highly agitated Denny Golden called, Gary reached for a bunch of faxed reports from his locals, figuring he could get some analysis work done while he listened to Denny demand to know where the fuck Deutch was. Neither of them had heard from him in three days. Gary eventually managed to stop the demanding diatribe and shift the conversation in a somewhat more positive direction, which he did by bringing up Damaged.

"We got reports back from the field that I think you're gonna like. If you can get the band to change 'Cool As Fuck' to something more acceptable, you'll definitely get rock radio and maybe do a Van Halen and really cross over. The core rock guys would definitely support the Humble Pie cover. You could use that to keep the base if 'Cool As Fuck' breaks out."

An assuaged Denny lowered his agitation a notch. "Thanks, that'll help me calibrate a deal. Have him get in touch the minute you hear from him."

Gary felt a vague sense of foreboding but decided to distance himself from it and Denny as best he could. *And there's always that shitty Limp Bizkit record to cash in on in the meantime*, he thought.

CHAPTER 35

James woke up fitfully. He heard Rod Stewart's cover of "I'd Rather Go Blind" and Highsmith lay with his back parallel to James's stomach, probably the only reason the desolate Englishman had slept at all. Traces of the heavy dose of peyote lingered and gave everything a slightly unreal air. Being close by the Springer Spaniel had kept him on the right side of sane, but not enough to face the real world the past three days.

He made one drive with Highsmith to Malibu Seafood, grabbed two of their printed recipes and fish to match. Bonnie patiently gave him some encouraging advice and, smiling, sent them on their way. He knew he had to challenge himself if he wanted to get past this nightmare and learning to cook had been on his mind. "Have You Ever Seen the Rain" by Creedence Clearwater Revival came out of the TV and he saw Nick Nolte with a pile of drugs. He wondered why these songs felt pertinent when in truth Bowie and the Spiders From Mars had been his teenage salvation and inspiration before The Clash made the final shove.

He poured some mesquite charcoal into the metal cylinder that sat on the Weber kettle grill he'd bought and wheeled onto his small deck. He put newspaper in the funnel and lit the paper, only then realizing he might torch the wooden balcony too, but he got lucky. He rubbed the whole butterflied trout with extra-virgin olive oil and ground some black peppercorns (the one thing he'd already had on hand) when the phone rang. He was fifty/fifty on answering it, but old habits ruled and he heard Charlie's voice.

"Bubba, you all right, boy?"

"Well, I'm not rightly sure," James threw back, mimicking the Southern man's exaggeration of his own accent.

"How about a drink?" asked Charlie.

"Wanna come over and have some fish? I'm cooking."

"Well, son, that sounds tempting, but I'm a little incapacitated."

James didn't quite know what to make of that or anything else for that matter, but his gut told him that he should go. "Alright, I'm gonna eat first, though. What's your address? All right if I bring Highsmith? Yes?"

Over-carefully, he put the whole fish on the now ashed-over coals and watched, childlike, as the skin sizzled. He carefully turned it over four minutes later and lost only a tiny amount of crispy skin as he did so. He got some Italian flat leaf parsley and garlic. He'd been drawn to this from a distant memory of the elegant, dignified, and soulful owner of Marino's Restaurant on Melrose, who would bring a whole sea bass and butterfly it at the table with a perfect small bowl of roasted garlic, parsley, and extra-virgin olive oil, the only adornment needed on a perfect fresh fish.

He still felt unhinged and removed from the idea of engaging back into the tough business of closing Damaged's deal, but some of these random memories somehow connected him back in a bit of a new way. He probably watched the fish sizzle slightly too long for most people's taste but as he sat on the deck and washed it down with a couple glasses of Cote du Rhone, he lost some of the nightmarish half-seen echoes. He found himself eating some of the actually crispy bones; he'd combined Tuscany and Jamaica, which felt very right. Fortified, he and Highsmith drove back down PCH for ten minutes, passed Malibu Pier, continued on for maybe another two, and barely avoided overshooting the vertical white wooden number sign at the corner of the classic Malibu wooden fence. Man and dog walked through the outside latched gate and down the seven sharply descending steps towards the oblong, slightly lit beachfront joint. A yellow-flamed lantern burned just bright enough to show that the wooden door was open an inch or two.

"Oy oy, Charlie, you about?" called James.

"Down here."

They walked down the further five steps into a bleached wooden living room that was probably called a "conversation pit" when it was built. Charlie was propped up on a once-expensive leather couch angled towards the ocean-facing, house-spanning picture window. The Stones' "Silver Train Coming" played.

Fuck me, thought James. *Who listens to Goats Head Soup?*

The older man wore a handmade denim shirt, but it was his heavily bandaged upper left leg that caught James's attention, along with the very chunky cut glass of whiskey in his hand. "Help yourself to a drink, boy." He waved his free hand towards a fully stocked bar that sat against the adjacent bleached white wooden wall. Highsmith, instead of his usual foraging, flopped on a fuzzy throw rug, half disappearing into the shag. James turned quickly away, fearing he was hallucinating again.

"A beer?" he asked, not seeing one.

"Down the hall. Kitchen's on the left."

He walked past what he guessed must be the master bedroom, glanced in, but then did a double take, seeing *Collage for Seductive Girl*, Roy Lichtenstein's genius recent comment on gender stereotypes. He shook his head, wondering whether there was intentional irony in it being placed over the aging Lothario's bed. He found a Stella in the fridge, returned and flopped on the chair across from Charlie.

"So, what happened, Charlie?" He nodded towards the bandage.

"Well, after I left you the other night, I had a notion to get my gun out of its safe hiding place in case we were right and that perhaps a representative of Denny's would be paying me a visit. Shortly thereafter, my luscious Brittany arrived and suggested we go for dinner. Well, of course I'd just eaten and had more carnal matters on my mind by then. Since I didn't think it prudent to tell her you and I had met, she started to get it in her pretty head that I'd been out with another woman. Not being one to overly explain anything, I just let her get up a head of angry steam. Her eyes lit on the .38 that was on the bedside table. She grabs it and announces that she's going to shoot my dick off. Being somewhat inebriated, I laughed at this, which in hindsight may not have been the right response. She puts both hands on the handle and aims like she's in some dumb audition for a cop show, and fuck me if she doesn't pull the trigger. I don't know if she was slightly off or I moved just enough, but the bullet went right through my damn leg and I swear, exactly in line with my most treasured possession."

James bit his lip and stifled a laugh. "Jesus Christ, you are lucky. What did you do? You going to be okay?"

"Well, fortunately she dropped the gun when she saw the blood spurting and went into a little bit of hellcat shock. I didn't need the cops involved, so I convinced her to get the hell out while I put in an emergency call to Dr. Arkoff. I've known him twenty years or more and convinced him to come and take a look. Fortunately, the bullet had gone right through, so he cleaned me up, bandaged it, gave me a morphine shot, and here I still sit. How's your week been?" He chuckled.

James gave him the uncensored version. Charlie didn't interrupt once, and even when he'd finished, sipped meditatively on the whiskey. Finally, he spoke. "Well, at least getting my gun out wasn't a mistake. If he's in that frame of mind, I really, and of course, you would be the logical next ones to fall."

"Yeah, maybe. Thing is, he can't know what happened there yet, so we have some time."

"How did Terry take the news? You don't think he will go after Denny?"

"Shit. I hadn't thought of that. He's in shock. I think you might say he's being stoic, but honestly I don't think he's taken it in yet. Fuck me, I haven't, and I was there."

"What about the police down there? Would they have found her ID? Reported it back to the authorities here?" asked Charlie.

"How is it you're shot up, drunk, and thinking of things that I hadn't thought of?" James put his head in his hands. Highsmith felt the stress, wandered over, and flopped on his feet. "We got out of there quickly and I don't think Aurial thought about ID, but honestly I'm not sure. The drugs were creeping up on me, and Deutch had come close to choking my lights out. You'd have to have been there to understand, but it still felt like a ghost town in many ways. I didn't see any local police or *federales* the way you do in other parts of Mexico."

"Yeah, anyway, would they give a shit?"

James brightened as, *come to think of it, why would they?*

"More to the point, Ji—" Charlie stopped himself from saying Jimmy, "James—do you?"

"What do you mean?" James asked, dodging the obvious.

"I mean, are you losing sleep or feeling guilty over Jacqueline's death?" asked Charlie. The steady flow of Scotch he'd consumed added a certain directness to his point.

"Not sure. I mean, one minute Deutch and I are giving each other shit about old soul records and the next thing there's a hole in her head. So I replay what I remember, but who knows if anything I did or didn't do would have changed what happened? I do wonder if I should have gone in the first place. What do I know really about detective work except what I've read all my life, ya know?"

Charlie raised his bushy eyebrows up and to the right, his equivalent of rolling his eyes. "I'm betting deep down Terry's relieved, but he sure won't let you see it. I mean no offense, but if he'd really wanted her back, wouldn't he have hired someone with some experience in the first place?"

James glanced at Charlie's leg. "You've got experience and look how far that got you."

"Fair enough, but despite our shortcomings, I'm convinced we need to see this thing through together. This is as close as I care to come." He gently rested the glass on his busted-up leg. "More importantly, my launch party's getting closer and we need to make sure it's a stellar affair."

"Me and we? Classic you, Charlie. I told you I'd help you and I'll stick to that, but I think meantime *we* have to see what harm Denny might try to bring *our* way and if Ron was his only helper— I'd like to know how much I have to watch my back."

"Well, I told you most of what I know back at the Sandcastle. My gut says he had mob help setting up the crash, but what that led to, who knows? My hunch is whatever he's been up to since is limited and very compartmentalized. I mean, whatever you say about that cocksucker, he is totally involved in Olympian. Can't you pry what you need to know from that broad? Seems like you've been through enough together."

"Even though I don't like your turn of phrase, point taken, Charlie. By the way, you're sure the dame who shot you isn't working for Denny?"

Charlie snorted. "Touché. You're not suggesting I'm getting too old for anyone to get that riled up about, are you?"

"Perish the thought," replied James. "However, you don't want your peccadilloes to derail your inspired venture, right?"

"So we're in this together, Mr. Dual? Because I can see our success and salvation joined at the hip."

"Yeah, I think we are. For better or worse, it's time to lay some ghosts. We are going to have to go after Denny before he regroups. I'll go see Aurial and try to get her to give me the whole picture. I need to talk to Ann Landry again, too. Somehow I think that all the Confederacy deals could still open up a can of worms. Maybe if we can give the family a helping hand, it will help us too."

Charlie looked a bit skeptical. "Why do you think we could do anything they probably haven't already tried? It's been a long time."

"I have an idea about licensing income they are likely owed from some TV commercials that used their songs but whether any lawsuit would be winnable or not doesn't completely matter. Point is to make Denny feel like the walls are closing in around him, right? Even though he can't know about Deutch, he has to be worried."

Charlie mustered up the strength to reach his bottle of Glenlivet, top up his glass and nod.

"Maybe. What about your band? How does that situation play out?"

James tipped his beer bottle up and suddenly grinned with

inspiration.

"Why don't we drag out the deal and have them play on your boat? Make it one more element of the courtship? Maybe if I can string things out that long…"

"How do you see Terry fitting into this?" asked Charlie.

"My bet is being the sort of English guy he is means he'll repress all his real feelings and stoically focus on signing the band. Of course, they'll almost certainly want to do that in the end, too, but Denny's megalomaniacal mindset won't allow for that likely inevitability, will it? We can muddy the waters by being nice to John Van Put. Get all that lot out, too."

"You plan on letting Terry on to your game, boy?"

"Nah, somehow I don't think so. Let's see how he does for a week or two. Gonna have to play this tight." Highsmith lay with his chin between his two outstretched front legs, feeling the gravity of the moment. "You got 'All or Nothing' by the Small Faces? Feel like hearing that."

CHAPTER 36

He showered and enjoyed the warmth of the late morning sun as it came through the small skylight he'd had built into the bathroom ceiling. He realized he wasn't feeling pain in his ribs any longer. He continued his morning ritual of coffee and toast with Highsmith before he picked up the phone to call Aurial. She picked up on the fourth ring and sounded like the call had woken her.

"You doing all right, girl?" he inquired.

"Uh huh," she replied noncommittally.

"Can I come over? Thinking we should plot our next moves."

"Mine need to translate into making money, kiddo. I've gone with your ride and all I see racking up is dead bodies," she said somberly, little of her usual mocking tone present.

"Fair enough. I'll keep that uppermost in my mind. I'll be there at two."

He walked onto the deck where Highsmith sat meditatively, flopped down and put his arm around the spaniel's shoulders. "Sorry to have been away so much, old boy. I'm going to try to stick close from here on out." The Springer leant into him understandingly and laid his head over James's shoulder, looking out to his beloved beach. A few minutes later, James took the hint and they padded down the steps to the ocean. The Jamaica-like catamaran was still there, the low winter tides not interfering with its location. Highsmith engaged him in a toss and throw game after choosing a suitably oversized piece of driftwood.

A few minutes later as they drove to Aurial's, he called Lainey to ask her to try to get Ann Landry to meet at his office later. She gave him messages, including five from Eric and worryingly, one from Detective Perkins. He wasn't sure whether he was glad or scared it was from only a day ago. On one hand, it wouldn't hopefully piss that asshole off if he called today. On the other hand, what if somehow he knew about Mexico? James realized his hands were tightly clenched on the small leather-covered steering wheel.

Stop. Don't let that kind of paranoia creep up on you. There's no way he could put all this together, right? He relaxed a little. Then another thought occurred. The only logical way the cop could know would be if he'd found out who—if indeed there was a who—had murdered Jeff Stanley. Then it was just possible he'd find out more from the assassin. He knew he'd best get his head straight this time before he talked to the cop. He couldn't let himself get needled again and decided to call once he got to the office later, but called Eric meantime on the speaker as he drove. The secretary put him through to the clearly irritated lawyer.

"Jesus, James, why the hell am I having to chase you?"

"I'm sorry. What's going on?" He tried to placate the guy.

"I've got a proper, old-fashioned bidding war going on. I've had improved offers from Barry at Pacific Records for Van Put's imprint."

"Better than their preemptive one?" laughed James.

"Exactly, but that's not all. I got a better one from Margery Cunningham, too."

James felt the weird mix of elation and tension as he realized Denny was still on the hook. He waited while the lawyer ran some of the basic numbers past him, hearing that for all his suspicions,

Eric seemed to be fully committed to squeezing every concession he could get out of his label adversaries. Particularly impressive were the reversions, the year when the band would get ownership of the masters back at which point all future revenues would go directly to Damaged.

"When I couldn't get you for the last few days, I had to let Katrina and Davey know the latest."

"And?"

"As I think you'll agree, I told them Denny's offer looks a little better."

"Maybe. I'll get with the band."

CHAPTER 37

He was on La Brea Avenue, headed north. He turned right onto the always seedy Hollywood Boulevard and made a quick left at Orange Drive, which within a few blocks took him away from the din upwards into the Hollywood Hills. He passed the magicians' hangout, the Magic Castle, and Yamashiro's restaurant. Highsmith sat up and sniffed at the earthy, warm smells that wafted through the early afternoon air. A few curling canyon minutes later, he crunched over the loose gravel in front of Aurial's rented carriage house, which stood on the grounds of a Deco estate. He felt a shiver of anticipation, and wondered whether he'd gain any insight into this guarded, secretive woman from seeing inside her living space.

She opened the barred window set in the heavy old Spanish-style wooden door and smiled out at him before she flung it back in place to let man and dog in. Highsmith jumped up at her; his short, docked tail clearly suggested he'd decided at some point she was okay by him. She leaned down, kissed the dog's ears, while she deftly unhooked his leash and implicitly gave him the run of the joint. Highsmith took immediate advantage, his nose making snuffling sounds as he bounded off through the small living area, nudging open the one half-closed door (the bedroom?).

James took in the rest of her space with a quick glance over her shoulder while they hugged. A narrow blue tiled kitchen was so spotless it suggested a complete lack of use. Her coarse hair was damp. That and a still steamy mirror in the bathroom next to the kitchen confirmed that he probably had woken her earlier.

"Mi Buenos Aires querido," a beautiful, mournful Carlos Gardel tango song, emanated from a boom box that stood on a small round wooden stand. An overstuffed, saggy couch and matching chair were the only other furniture. The whole space was dominated by floor-to-ceiling bookshelves that were packed to the point of overflowing. He was immediately curious to peruse, believing book collections are the best window into the soul.

The fingers of his left hand were lost in her long hair and their upper bodies rested against each other, almost as if the tango positioned them. It wasn't until the song ended that the spell was broken but the music allowed him to express simply, "Thank you for saving my life."

She pulled back slightly and put her long fingers in a V, holding his chin to cheekbones and nodded her acknowledgement of the gratitude.

"Now what?" she asked.

"I—or we—have to take Denny down. There's no other choice. It's all gone too far to walk away. At least for me. I tried twenty years ago but that clearly wasn't my fate. The only questions are how and whether to try to do it legally."

"I'm in as long as you'll do everything to help me cash in, and of course to make sure I'm not looking at a murder rap."

He realized that while he worried about Terry's shattered life and maintained his own, he'd neglected to include how the girl who had pulled the trigger might actually be feeling. He was still close enough to take her hand without making a big deal of it.

"Are you sleeping okay with that?" he asked.

"More or less. I'm not second-guessing the decision, let's

put it that way," she said steadily, not pulling her hand away as he suspected she might.

"Okay, I'm going to lay all my cards out this time and hope at the end, you'll let me see yours," he said.

She was expressionless and didn't speak as he let go of her hand and sat on the couch, where momentarily she joined him.

"When Terry asked me to find Jacquie we decided, as a starting point, on needling Denny to see if he was involved in her disappearance. I really started managing the band to do the same thing, hoping if we got him going enough he'd show his hand, which he obviously has, but all that's resulted is violence and Jacquie's death. Right now, going to the law and telling them what we know would be more likely to get us arrested than him, without more proof he's behind all this. As disastrous as it's been so far, I still think the only hope is to increase the pressure on him and hope he makes a mistake.

"I'll meet Ann Landry later and I hope I can convince her to let me talk to the Confederacy heirs. I keep thinking with a deal as dirty as he got them to sign back then, there must be something that could be done to at least try to get them some money now. It may be a long shot, but at least it would put more pressure on him. A proper audit might turn up something. Meanwhile, Charlie Major's got this mad, brilliant idea to start a floating club outside the three-mile limit the way Tony Cornero did back in the 30s and 40s. I'm thinking if all else fails, we lure him out there where he would be isolated and somehow corner him…"

She looked a bit skeptical. "That's it? Seems a bit vague. How will you lure him?"

"I'm going to ask Damaged to play the opening night. Let him think they're close to signing with him instead of Terry or anyone else," he said hopefully. "His offer right now is good enough, actually, and he's probably hoping Eric will trump me with the band. I know it's all flimsy, but what I'm betting on is that when you add Deutch's disappearance to the pressure on him, maybe, just maybe, he'll crack."

"Well, that would depend on whether there are more Deutchs where he came from, boy, wouldn't it?"

"Yeah, I wondered a bit about that, so I guess this would be as good a moment as any to ask to see your cards. I know you've got more tapes. Is there anything you can share that would help?" he pleaded. "Charlie had a hunch Denny got mob money to help him start Olympian, but somehow it doesn't quite add up to me. It might be the only way someone with a giant ego like Charlie could accept why he wouldn't be anyone's number-one choice of promotion head..." He trailed off.

She rose solemnly. "I never thought I'd say this to anyone, but I am going to trust you. One condition. I want to extort a lot of money from Mr. Denny Golden, and you have to go along with that and help."

He reflected on that for a few seconds before he nodded his acquiescence. "Where have you stashed the tapes? Are they close?" He figured she wouldn't have risked keeping them in an easily searched place like this.

"Very close." She smiled and walked over to the wall of books. "The main house and this whole estate were owned by Dick Powell and Joan Blondell in the 1940s, who left things pretty much intact from the previous owner, who'd built it during the Prohibition era."

She turned her back to him and pulled out an old book, *In A Lonely Place*, written by Dorothy B. Hughes, in fact. She then pushed her middle two fingers against the wood panel she'd uncovered, and a four-foot area of books swiveled into the wall to expose a full bar, replete with an array of vintage bottles. The centerpiece, though, was a battered metal box that she lifted off and placed on the wooden table that held the boom box.

"There's two in particular that you should hear, but I could play you Jeff Stanley's, too, if you'd like," she said.

"Want to fill me in?"

"Well, dear departed Jeff was clearly wired, probably a bit drunk too. He blathered on enough to implicate himself in their piracy, but nothing to suggest he knew anything untoward about the crash."

"So he lied to me." James was not particularly surprised.

"Maybe, but who knows? I never actually played him the tape and from what you've told me, he may have been so high most of the time, his memory of the era probably had huge holes in it," she suggested.

"And Jacqueline?"

"Well, Miss Goody-Two-Shoes knew plenty, certainly enough to implicate her in big-time piracy and she clearly found out about the plane's sabotage at some point."

"Is Denny on these tapes too?" he asked.

"Yeah. I couldn't understand at first why he would keep evidence that implicated himself, too, but I think I figured it out," she said.

"Let's hear it," he said.

"Well, clearly, he got away with everything scot-free, so no one was investigating him at any point, as far as we know. The only threat in his mind would be blackmail from the handful of people who knew what he'd done."

"That makes sense," he said. "Come to think of it, how come you haven't kept me as a suspect yourself?"

"Well, other than my being an impeccable judge of character, there'd be these two tapes."

She ejected the tango cassette and replaced it with one from the box. "This one is dated ten days after your boardroom speech."

Jacqueline's quavering young voice: "Denny, Ron Deutch is in reception for your meeting but I have to talk to you first. Terry, Ann, and I ran into James Dual at the Cock and Bull Saturday. He was really high and started in again about how easy it would be to do the world a favor and send the Confederacy to a fiery death. I'm scared he really means it."

"Come now, Jacqueline."

"Honestly, Denny. I thought he was okay when I met him, a little wild but okay. Now he's so dark and those awful girls he hangs out with scare me, especially that one Drea. They could be the next Manson girls for all we know; they certainly admire them."

"Thank you for telling me. Now run along and fetch Ron."

There was a brief silence until a door opened and the sound of REO Speedwagon's "Roll With The Changes" drifted in. The door closed again.

"Hi, Ron. I have one additional thing to add to our business today," said Denny.

"Oh yeah, what's that?"

"In a beautiful case of 'out of the mouths of babes,' my tearful assistant just reminded me of young A&R kid James Dual's punk rock fantasy of murdering the Confederacy. I think we should make his dreams come true."

"If it makes sense, Denny, sure," said Deutch casually.

"The Confederacy record's not selling, which is making

me look bad. If Dual's crazy theory that tragic rock death equals immortality and instant sales, great. If he's wrong, they're still dead, so I won't have to pay out the exorbitant advance on their next record and the industry will understand this record flopping. It would be a disaster if my credibility takes a hit while I'm setting up my own label. The band is playing The Roxy in three weeks. They're traveling on a private plane and will land at Burbank."

"Okay, Denny. I'll scope things out. Let's make sure everyone's well liquored up before they leave. I'll barely need to lend a hand." He snorted.

Denny chuckled. "To add to the perfection, if anyone does get suspicious, we can point them to Dual and his big mouth. I tell you what, Ron, if you pull this off smoothly I'll put all my new label's radio promotion business through you and Gary's new company."

"What about Charlie Major? He's not going to like that," said Deutch.

"I'll string him along for now and then we'll see where and if he still fits in. Don't tell Gary about the Confederacy plan, though. I'm not sure he still has the stomach for this kind of action," said Denny coldly.

Aurial pressed the fat stop button, ejected and then popped in another cassette.

"This next one's from several months after the crash," she said.

The vintage hiss lasted twenty seconds or so, as if recording a lull in the conversation before Ron Deutch spoke.

"So it would be a very high-priced service to rid a label of a particularly troublesome or no longer performing act? Well, yeah, back in the day when labels were a bit more integrated with the mob, things got handled. Ask Bobby Fuller. You know, 'I Fought the

Law.' Turned up dead in his car in Hollywood in '66, and even now no one's any the wiser exactly how he got there. I understand why you're asking me, as my day-to-day with my label clients would allow me to, uh, sense their needs. But my only question is why? We're in the clear—why push our luck?"

"Because we can, Ron. Because we should. Because it will forestall taking on any undesirable equity partners. I don't want to take mob investment money," said Denny.

"Out of the mouths of babes still, eh, Denny? It cracks me up that Dual and that dumb broad assistant inspired you. How are things going with the Olympian setup?"

"I just got back from the manufacturing plant in Indianapolis I've set up for the new label and the crew are cranking out counterfeit Confederacy records like there's no tomorrow. Neither Real Records nor the band's estate will see a penny but funding Olympian is costing a fortune and I need more. Come on, Ron. 'Out of the mouths of babes'? Dual was right about the Confederacy, so why wouldn't it work over and over again?"

She stopped the tape. "There's more, but you get the gist, right?"

He wondered aloud, "Given that Deutch had a mob history and if Charlie's right, they could have been a possible funder for Olympian. When Denny managed to rake off almost enough from the Confederacy crash, sounds like he cooled on their investment and Charlie's, for that matter."

"And what if having this on Deutch gave him insurance from a mob retaliation?"

James grinned. "You're smart, huh? Now it's easy to see why he would agree to go and take care of Jacqueline. So, tough girl, how come you didn't, er, put the frighteners on Denny?"

"Because when I really absorbed everything, I decided you'd be the man for that job."

"Oh yeah? How's that?" he challenged.

"Well, he took the worst of you and turned it into a gold mine. Doesn't that piss you off a bit?"

James was speechless. There had been a glam moment just before punk when fame and money had seemed the most fuck-you, Clockwork-Orange fun you could have. Could those Performance gangster fantasies have allowed him to get rid of bands he despised? On some level, did he lack Denny's nerve or bottle as he would have called it then? Or was it that punk and The Clash forever changed his point of view? He got a quick flash of being in his east London living room: With the arm off the turntable, 1977, the B side of The Clash's first single, endlessly repeated. He watched Bert, the old shirt sleeved-and-braced man across the street, usher a string of expensive-suited East End gangsters laden with boxes of TVs and stereo systems down the side of his place, where no doubt the stolen goods would be safely stored. One of the men had glanced across, alert, and looked at the teenage James lying in the bay window, but the old man had mouthed something reassuring and whatever danger might have existed passed. If that was the meeting point of two philosophies, had he ever really committed to either one?

"Maybe I am." He smiled finally. "It has to come at him from all angles to give us a real chance, though." He was on his feet, inspired. "I'm starting to see how to time this. Give me a few days. Maybe we can get you paid and push him over the edge at the same time."

A heavy sigh came from the open door. They walked through to see Highsmith on his back, paws curled, situated in the middle of her bed.

"Someone's got the right idea," she noted.

They left it at that.

CHAPTER 38

James and Highsmith climbed the wooden steps up to the office, both smiling in their own way as they saw Lainey animatedly talking on the phone amid the roar of Primal Scream's "Come Together." As they pushed open the white wooden door, she spun around.

"Finally, boss man. It's all action. Where've you been? Lots to go over. Ann Landry will be here at four, but meantime, you've got visitors." Her thumb pointed to the ocean-facing meeting room.

With a glance at a renewed pile of music that spilled out of his office on the left, he walked in while he half looked back at her for a clue. Katrina sat on the couch, half turned to the ocean, legs akimbo; Davey draped, stretched out, and propped her up. A possible view of rock's immediate future, he thought distractedly, before he focused on their current reality. "You're up early, aren't you?" he queried by way of greeting.

Katrina half snorted. "Like you're one to talk." He leaned down and hugged her. Davey sat up, clearly trying to be as businesslike as possible. She dived in, though. "Things are getting confusing, James. There's so many offers. Eric's actually making us think about Denny again and that's doing my head in."

James nodded. "What are you feeling, Davey?" he asked.

"Well, Terry came over and seemed normal, but somehow too normal, considering his wife's death, you know? He said he'd had a loss but it wouldn't affect his attention to us. We just worried that he hadn't felt comfortable telling us somehow. If we are going to sign based on a relationship more than money, then we've got to have total honesty and commitment, right?"

James felt all his concerns about Davey from right before the Viper Room resurface, but there was some logic in there too. His turn to decide how honest to be.

"I get how you feel. Truth is, I'm sure he thinks he's doing the right thing, keeping things to himself. So fucking English, right?"

Katrina nodded ruefully and glanced across at Lainey, who had wandered in and perched on the arm of the couch. James continued.

"I know who I'd trust to have your back in the long run, but you're only getting one shot and it's rushing at you right now, so I think we have to pay close attention to every offer. Play the game a bit. Let Eric wring the best deal he can for you. I hate to say it but a bit of careful flirting wouldn't be the worst idea, if you can stomach it. Like I said before, be taken to some dinners."

"Uh, we did one while you were gone. John Van Put and Barry Gordon took us to the Palm for lobster and shit," admitted Davey.

"Classic," laughed James. "They didn't try to be trendy, just old-school expensive." The tab at the classic Santa Monica Boulevard restaurant was always exorbitant, but fit the profile. "Glad to hear you are taking it all in. Given that, I'm going to ask that you keep in that mode. Here's what I think. Let's put a deadline on it all. I don't know if you've ever heard about Charlie Major, a legendary radio promo man. He's about to launch an offshore boat. There's something about the outlaw way he wants to do it that made me tell him I'd suggest you play the opening night."

Katrina raised an eyebrow at this, not suspicious but definitely surprised. "What gives? This doesn't seem like your style."

He looked right at her. "I know what you mean, but it's actually an inspired idea for a club. It brings the noir sensibility of 40s LA and mixes it up with the debauched 70s that Charlie clearly misses, and if he pulls it off, it'll provide a rare chance to do it all out of the media's harsh gaze."

"Sounds like fun to go to, but do we need to play?" she said.

"Honestly, there's layers to this. We can make it a brilliant coming out party and for dramatic effect, the three labels will only find out who you've chosen to sign with that night."

"Just promise me…us…that you don't complicate things too much," said Katrina.

He nodded solemnly. Lainey looked at Katrina. "What are we going to do with him?" Clearly they'd become allies when he wasn't watching.

He answered for her. "Obviously I'm a hopeless case. Why don't you all go down to JiRaffe or someplace and have a drink or a late lunch, whatever, while I wait for Ann Landry?"

"We're only going to JiRaffe if you hand over your credit card. That place ain't cheap," Lainey pointed out.

Appreciating the relative normalcy, James acquiesced.

CHAPTER 39

Ann entered right on time. He liked how she'd kept her original style intact, even though the post-hippie clothes now went through an expensive designer filter. She glanced around the office with an appraising eye.

He pointed the way through to the ocean-facing meeting room. He was happy to note, Hollywood-based as she was, that she couldn't hide her appreciation of the surroundings. Highsmith enjoyed the home turf, too, not intimidated this time, and bustled around her ankles in a happy fashion.

"Such a surprise, James," she admitted out loud.

"Yeah, thanks, I think," he said. "So I've thought a lot about what you said to me. I know a lot of it, at least from your point of view, is true. I can't change that but I want to try to get the heirs some money. There's clearly a lot of dirty money that's been made. Especially with Denny's scam to trick them into signing over their publishing before The Roxy gig."

"All right," she said. "Supposing that I take you seriously. Why and how can you help?"

"Well, the Confederacy now seem timeless and authentic, as much as I would never have imagined that could happen. It means there's licensing money to be made from film, TV shows, and commercials. I'm guessing, given that's largely a new revenue stream, that their contracts don't cover it adequately. I'm sorry, but if they have out-of-state lawyers trying to deal with Hollywood's finest scum, they are clearly out of their depth."

"And you're scummy enough to make a difference?" she asked. Thick-skinned as he was, that still pissed him off.

"Look, if you've supposedly been a friend to the families all these years, how come you couldn't help? Taking the moral high ground and achieving nothing isn't doing anyone any favors."

She glared at him. "But what's in it for you?"

"I'll admit I want to take Denny down."

"But he's long gone from Real. How would this affect him?" she asked.

"In essence, he stole their publishing. That income must still flow to him. It will build pressure on him. Any contracts from then will bear his signature. If his carefully cultivated lover-and-protector-of-artists image can be destroyed, it'll open him up in other ways."

"He sends quite a bit of business my way," she reflected.

"Fuck me, did you really just say that, Ann? He's everything that's dirty, hypocritical, phony. I mean, honestly, at least Walter Yetnikoff, Azoff, maybe even Geffen, to a degree, don't pretend to be someone else."

She glanced at the ocean, perhaps slightly chastened. "Okay, maybe your obnoxious way of going about things might stir things up in a way that could help."

For a moment, inexplicably, he could hear Boz Scaggs singing "Lido Shuffle" on KMET as he walked into the Real offices and saw this woman for the first time. She spoke and ended that reverie. "I'll get you copies of the contracts. If you've got any real ideas after, I'll introduce you to the trustees of the estate."

"Oh yeah, and who might they be when they're at home?" he asked.

"All the families are represented but Sue Anne's sister has been the most involved."

He inwardly reeled, not having known there was a sister. Truth be told, he could have found out years ago, but had never reached out to the family. Too damaged and emotionally repressed at the time for the thought even to have occurred to him. Determined not to reveal the effect her words had upon him, he just nodded. "Look, just for the record, I haven't changed my opinion of how their music felt at the time, but I fucking hate artists being stolen from, no matter who they are to me, so I will try to improve the Confederacy situation, okay?"

Highsmith had positioned himself upright in front of James. She studied the pair of them for a moment. "Okay, James. Unlike you, I'm prepared to reconsider my position...if you earn that choice." She got up. "I need to get going."

"Thanks for coming here." They shook hands, which almost felt momentous. He didn't return to his office, but flopped back against the couch. He dialed Dwayne Perkins' 615 number.

The weather was a little better in Nashville as the phone rang. The faint sunlight that hit his blinds just stopped him growling at James.

"Thanks for checking in, Dual."

"Yeah, of course. What's the latest?" James said, relaxing slightly.

"Here's the thing. I got nothing in general or on you specifically, but I know it's dirty. My gut says you're connected, but I've got nothing and this case will get closed and all I'll be left with is a gnawing in my gut. So I'm going to tell you something and see how you react."

"Fair enough." James raised an eyebrow, not quite knowing

what to make of this switch from bad cop to good cop.

"I would have figured a lifelong partier lost his reaction time and wiped out. There's just one thing. His busted-in skull injury isn't consistent with what would have happened to the rest of his body. His ribs are completely undamaged. There's no way if his seat belt was off that they wouldn't have smashed into the steering wheel along with his head."

"Meaning what?" asked James.

Perkins, quelling his irritation, offered, "It could be someone removed the seat belt after the crash and caved his skull in."

James's heart sank. He handled things smarter this time, though. "God, do you think so?" Let this cop figure he's an idiot while he thought this through.

Dwayne continued amicably. "Way I figure it is if persons unknown took him out the same night you showed up, there's some kind of connection. Which means, odds are you either had something to do with hitting him or, maybe slightly more likely, you are under the threat of ending up the same way, which would mean you'd be smart to come clean with me."

James thought furiously. Was there any percentage in wondering aloud about Denny? Let the heat rain down on him from one more direction? Trouble was, he would be buried up to his own neck in the cop's mind. Fuck it, no. He took a breath. "I promise to give a great deal of thought to everything Jeff said at dinner, but there's nothing I can think of right now that might help you."

"All right, limey, don't say I didn't give you fair warning."

"You may be all right, Detective," said James placatingly before he hung up.

So Stanley had been murdered, in all likelihood. Not a huge shock, but he wondered who'd done it. Deutch? Maybe. His big relief was that nothing seemed to be known about Jacqueline. If this guy ever heard about her death, he'd be one of the common denominators with entry and exits into Nashville and Mexico when the deaths occurred. He realized he could only leave Terry to his grief for so long before they had to talk all this through.

Highsmith joined him on the couch as they looked at the big Pacific undisturbed until the Damaged/Lainey axis returned, clearly having added some cocktails to the credit card he'd foolishly let go of.

Katrina proved the notion as she announced, "That was such a good lunch that we decided to play the boat launch if you want."

"Yeah, I want." He grinned and hoped there was more to their trust than ill-advised cocktails.

CHAPTER 40

Unannounced, he drove to Terry's place, feeling good about Davey and Katrina, at least. He wasn't worried about what wagons they were on or falling off. No matter what, they seemed ready.

A gaunt-looking Terry opened the door and let them in.

"The kids are in their rooms. I brought them back. Why don't you let Highsmith off his lead so they can all play while we go and talk? That is why you're here, I imagine?"

"Pretty much," said James. Dog looked at man and acquiesced, bounding down the hall to look for his young friends.

"You been into the office?" James thought that Terry's fairly smart attire of an open collared gray shirt, black pants, and Paul Smith shoes suggested as much.

"No. Working from home for the time being."

James sensed the pain and barriers that had obviously been erected to retain some normalcy, but knew he had to get to the point and slip the repressed ways they'd both been brought up with.

"Go get us a drink, Terry."

"What would you like?"

"A beer."

Terry pulled a Red Stripe out of the fridge, handed it to James and pulled a cork from a half-full bottle of Chianti for himself. They sat opposite sides of the simple white kitchen table, where likely numerous breakfasts involving Jacqueline had taken place with and before the kids.

"Mate," began James, "I'm not sure if I know how to do this sensitively…"

Terry smiled at him wanly. "I'm so numb I doubt that anything you say is going to matter too much, James."

"All right then. I'll have at it. Have you told the kids anything?"

"No."

"Good. Look, I've been doing a lot of thinking. I'm not going to pretend some of this isn't self-preservation, but if anyone knows what really happened, it's going to be bad for all of us, especially the children.

"First off, Aurial played me the tapes where Denny plotted the Confederacy murders with Deutch. He joked more than once that the idea came 'out of the mouths of babes,' referring to Jacquie and me. She'd gone to him, saying she was scared I was really going to murder the band, which seems to have inspired him to do it. At some point, presumably after the crash, she must have heard him make that joke or discuss it with Deutch and that's why she was so permanently damaged. She hated me, but she felt deep, unbearable responsibility too.

"You're going to have to file a missing persons report. Don't say anything about me. I have flights in and out of Mexico and Nashville, for that matter, at just the wrong times. There's the girl, too. She saved my life and I won't see her go down for that."

Terry hadn't drunk or moved while James spoke, but did now. "So you think I should bury everything except, of course, my wife's body?"

James felt the bitterness but didn't allow it to affect his tone. "It's what happened, Terry. I've wracked my brain but I can't see doing anything different that would have saved her life."

"Other than not giving Denny a new business plan in the first place?" Terry asked.

"Fuck you, mate. Maybe you shouldn't have dragged me into this flashback in the beginning," snarled James.

Terry's head dipped. "You're right. That was unfair."

Highsmith had returned without the children and laid on the kitchen floor, not looking for attention from either of them, but now raised his head and gave a mournful howl a hound dog would have been proud of.

Terry acknowledged both James and Highsmith with a gentle nod. "It's just hard being in this limbo, pretending to the kids everything's okay. I can't keep it up forever. What the hell am I going to tell them?"

James relaxed a little. "You'll figure it out when the time's right. No one can tell you how, but if you want my opinion, you'll involve Martha. Meantime, you need to tell me if you're up for seeing things through with Damaged. I'm setting up one more show and by the time it happens, they'll use it to announce a deal."

Terry didn't react as indignantly as he might have, but asked, "That doesn't seem like your style. What are you up to? And where is the venue for this announcement?"

"Charlie Major's opening a floating club outside the three-mile limit. The spirit of it suits the band. It makes me think of the Stones playing on a flatbed truck in New York or the Sex Pistols playing on a boat on the Thames for the Queen's Jubilee. It's an announcement of intent to do things the right, exciting way."

A faint smile crossed Terry's mouth. "Okay, I won't ask more, but no matter what the circumstances, I didn't involve you with the band to see you go make a record with some other fucking label. I'll make sure Real's bid is as good as anyone else's, within reason."

Much like the desert, the kids suddenly raced into the room, whooping, "Where'd you go, Highsmith?" and leaped onto the Springer, who reared up on his back legs and tussled with them as if they were puppies, too. James somehow knew in his heart that the kids' behavior was a happy act to help their father, and that they somehow sensed nothing would ever be the same. He had an urge to do the same unannounced drive-by to Aurial's, whose place was on the way home, but resisted the temptation.

CHAPTER 41

Two weeks later, Charlie Major stood at the end of the pier at Paradise Cove that faced the Sandcastle and the scattered trailer homes that arced back around the beach. A thirty-foot cruiser bobbed in the water somewhat riskily close to land for a boat of its size as James and Highsmith strolled down to meet him.

Charlie wrapped his arm around James's shoulder and led them to a gangplank. "Boy, this is likely a bit more civilized than when the rumrunners and bootleggers used Point Dume as a landing dock, but don't let that detract from what we are doing and what they did."

"Oy, Charlie. Are you getting carried away with the pain medications? Those fucking Percodans are well addictive, you know."

"One of your weaknesses, boy?"

"Absolutely not. All that sort of shit made me sick, fortunately, but I've seen what can happen to strong people, let's put it that way," said James.

"At any rate," Charlie continued, "I'm moving around just fine and a little bourbon for motion is all the immediate medication I need. How are ya' ribs?"

James shook his head carefully. "We can't start talking about our war wounds, all right? Or else we are going to get old fast."

Charlie rubbed his gray stubble and nodded, wordlessly

acknowledging the truth. As they climbed down onto the uncovered back deck, James glanced forward to where the raised covered wheelhouse housed a redheaded dream dressed only in a 60s bikini and a captains hat, as if she'd just arrived from one of John D. MacDonald's early Travis McGee books. How was it he'd have put it? Pneumatic.

He glanced at Charlie and in a semi-whisper asked, "She's not the one who…" He pantomimed a hand cocking a pistol.

"Heaven forbid. I'm moving on from blondes to redheads for the time being."

"Out of the frying pan, mate, if you ask me."

She kicked the engine into motion as Highsmith pulled loose and ran up alongside her. The ocean spray hit the windscreen in front of their dog and girl eyes. James grinned as they bore towards the somewhat surreal image of a boat which, as they got closer, could clearly be seen as something from a different era. The Englishman's jaw dropped as they climbed up a stepladder attached to the deep bowed ship.

"Where on earth did you find this? God, Charlie, it could almost be Tony Cornero's."

"Ole Charlie's always had luck and timing. This could be the most blatant example of that. I'll tell you the whole story one day, but for now we need to live in the present. Opening's a week away and I need your help."

He led them around the upper deck, where a small gang of carpenters worked to put the finishing touches to the Southern man's vision.

"Incredible, Charlie! The craftsmanship is amazing."

"Thanks to your countrymen. They're English carpenters. Met them back when they were builders on the A&M Studios lot," said Charlie.

"Bet they drank you dry too, along the way," said James.

"Of course," demurred Charlie. He led James and the trailing Highsmith down to the club floor a deck below. The girl had disappeared with a grin after they'd boarded. The interior was immaculate smooth light-colored wood for the dance floor, which was surrounded by a series of booths that were interrupted at the starboard by a raised black wood stage. An elaborate bar faced it from the port side.

"Genius, Charlie. I love it," said James with unabashed admiration.

"You need to see the rest," said Charlie, almost reverently, as if he couldn't quite believe it himself.

As they went down the main corridor, James could hear Bryan Ferry's version of "These Foolish Things." Charlie opened each door left and right as they walked along. "Some of these are living rooms with a small bar and couches, some more like opium dens with cots, but as if Keith Richards had created them. There's a David Bowie-inspired room for those who like to move like tigers on Vaseline. Many are noir-era correct, like the staterooms for those who prefer to sleep over. There's kitchens built down one deck so we can create great food for the nighttime and a recuperative breakfast for the morning, if desired."

"Looks like you're all set," said James, again admiringly.

"Maybe. However, I do have my limitations and as I said before, I need you on this."

"Well, I will deliver Damaged, and more importantly to you, I'm sure, I will call everyone I know to help turn this into a memorable opening."

"That's great, Jimmy, but my gut tells me you are the man to run this with me. I haven't changed my mind since the last time we discussed this."

"I did that in another lifetime, and I don't need to relive it. Besides, you can take your pick of whatever slick guys are promoting clubs these days. Shit, a lot of them have investors. Might help you keep this thing afloat for the long haul."

"If I needed them, I'd have done that. Thing is, I'm not totally crazy. I know heat will come from all kinds of places after we get rolling. You had a joint down on Sunset and Silver Lake, which just happened to be in the Rampart Police Division during its notorious heyday. That strongly suggests to me you could navigate any shit storm that might percolate here—from the police department, Santa Monica, or Malibu on through."

James rubbed his face; despite his better instincts, he couldn't deny that Charlie was reminding him of his younger, tougher self. "If I do, you need to let me have the total run of all your staff and definitely have first say on your security crew. There's a lot that could get leery in this environment and some overreacting jackass could push it over the edge."

Charlie smiled, inwardly knowing he'd now be able to enjoy himself with James taking care of the tricky stuff. James spotted the look. "Listen, just for the record, I plan on cornering Denny opening night somehow, so don't think you're flattering me into this. Make sure you have my back, okay?"

"Agreed," said Charlie.

"Have you hired the bar and wait staff?" asked James.

"Well, I've been scouting."

"I can imagine. I think we should talk to Wanda and see if her Rainbow situation would allow her to at least consult the launch staff hiring."

"Brilliant idea." Charlie was even more sure his genial host role would be an uninterrupted one. "You absolutely have my blessing to make the best deal you can for us."

James's eyes rolled inwardly. "Us again," he said. "I think it's time we write down exactly what that means, especially as I have zero interest in being in the nightclub business."

"Of course, Jimmy," said Charlie, his shit-eating grin of yonder days firmly in place.

CHAPTER 42

A day later, James caught Wanda somewhat off guard with a call to make a lunch plan for the following day. They arranged to meet at the Book Soup Bistro a few minutes' walk east on Sunset from the Rainbow, and less than a minute down the hill from her north of Sunset apartment. He'd parked on Palm slightly south of Sunset and as he walked up the steep hill, realized he'd had sex in America for the first time in a Hollywood bungalow exactly on his right with a dissolute rock and roll clothes designer, except that it was now an uninspiring condo complex.

He was a few minutes early, so he stopped at the alley newsstand that flanked the perfect bookstore and its recently added adjoining bistro. He flicked through the *New Musical Express* but the old geography was still in control as he remembered coming to back then, a hulking brown wood TV with that beautiful washed-out American Technicolor beaming out a cheesy Star Trek episode as the woman's lover came in through the bungalow door, letting in intense August sunlight. Seeing the girl passed out face down, the surly long-haired man who James dimly thought was a hard-drugging Vietnam vet, had just said, "Aw, Ro," turned on his heel and left.

James leaned against the wooden stand to steady himself as the almost too-vivid memory hit him. Was it the peyote after effect offering up these vivid compartments in his mind? He put the

English music paper down and made his way into the minimally lit restaurant. It was just past noon and the place was almost empty. He was taken to a two-seater table—thin wrought-iron topped by a white marble top that faced out to Tower Records across the street. He saw Wanda walk down past the Tower window displays. She glanced, perhaps disapprovingly, at an air-brushed Stevie Nicks record and walked across the curve of Sunset without waiting for the light to turn green. He could see that her body had thickened somehow, but she was a beautiful, timeless force of nature to him as the fast-moving traffic paused for her.

She saw him and gently shook her head, resisting any verbal shock at seeing him at this time of day for the first time. Allen Toussaint's "Southern Nights" played almost too low on the sound system. They hugged and sat quietly appraising one another while they looked at the simple but appealing menu. The black-aproned waitress heard them both ask for the salami chopped salad and water. They shook their heads at each other, amused.

James, still feeling Palm Avenue, asked her, "Do you remember what this space used to be?"

"The Corner Pocket," she answered without missing a beat. "And next door was that recording studio, right? Forget what that was called, but I remember seeing Billy Preston and Sly Stone coming out."

She'd kick-started his memory and he saw himself walking into that studio with Ro, where Tom Petty and the Heartbreakers were mixing. He'd resisted an invitation to partake of the large pile of hullucinogens that nestled in an open folded section of the *Los Angeles Times*, no more keen then than he had been a few weeks ago at Ron Deutch's behest. The band, though, were another matter entirely, the one mainstream American band that had then and now felt truly authentic.

"You here, James?" Wanda asked pointedly, seeing his distraction.

"Yeah, sorry. My mind wandered and we hadn't even got to the Corner Pocket."

"Well, I never did go in that dive of a pool joint, while some people used to find it irresistible from what I heard." She chuckled.

"They had a good jukebox. Pretty sure that's where I first heard Dwight Twilley. It's definitely where I heard Elvis Presley had died one afternoon."

Not knowing how to react to that, she just looked at him.

"Sorry, Wanda, I rarely go to the past."

"I understand, honey. It must be a bit strange sitting in this semi chi-chi joint feeling what lies buried in time underneath it."

"Funny thing is, I'd seen the place in London on TV. It was Huggy Bear's bar on *Starsky and Hutch*, not that I realized that when I stumbled in." Suddenly annoyed with himself, he snapped out of the semi-suppressed memories. "So, Wanda, here we are. I was thinking the only way we will ever have more than this nostalgic lunch is if there's something new to focus on." He looked at her and wondered whether she was happy, before he launched into a description of how fun and lucrative her involvement in the Cornero adventure might be.

She listened impassively and finally said, incredulous, "You and Charlie? Tall, dark, strange bedfellows! I don't know what to make of it."

"Honestly, me neither," he said. "But after all this time, I wouldn't try to rope you in if I didn't think it could work."

"What's going on with you, James? The boat idea might just work and God knows I have the Rainbow down pat, so a bit of moonlighting isn't out of the question, but more to the point—why are you in this? You show up after all these years, presumably with a career, and your act maybe together. So what drew you in? This club with a guy you had no regard for? How many distractions do you need? Are you still playing private eye, looking for Jacqueline?"

He thought he kept it together in that moment, but she must have spotted something in his expression.

"That bad, huh?" she wondered out loud.

"I hate to tell you, Wanda, but you sound like Charlie lecturing me. Look, why don't you go talk to him about this? I'm going to help with the opening for my own reasons. You can make up your own mind, okay?"

They both picked at the salads as the sun gradually came through the shuttered windows, softening the age lines on their wondering faces so they weren't nudged to focus on the intervening years. A lot was left unsaid by the time they parted forty-five minutes later, neither quite sure how to bridge the time gap, but pretty much okay with each other nonetheless.

CHAPTER 43

He was lost in his thoughts and only became re-aware of his surroundings as he walked from the parking lot up the alley that ran parallel with Ocean Avenue. He walked through the back way, past the pool that looked murky, covered in now-soggy leaves the Santa Anas had blown in. He could hear a producer talking big-time casting from his two-office bungalow before Highsmith's bark from above drowned him out. He climbed the open stairs that led to his upstairs office, seeing the dog's spring as he opened the door.

"What are you barking at me for?" He laughed, and had a brief tussle with the dog, who was clearly remonstrating over James's frequent absences from his presence. Lainey's expression suggested she might well feel the same way.

"Okay, Lainey." He raised his hands, flat-palmed on either side of his head in surrender. "Let's go sit down and we can go over everything you want to, okay?"

This did the trick of stemming her potential indignant outburst, but certainly wasn't getting him off the hook of a proper update. They went and sat in his office where the 50s turquoise desk was again obscured by the piles of recently arrived music. She handed him a thick manila envelope.

"This came by messenger from Ann's office," she said flatly. "Thought you might want it first."

"Yeah, thanks." He opened it and pulled out the fat package

of Confederacy contracts he'd have to plow through.

"There's the show arrangements to discuss too, if you really plan to have Damaged play on a boat?"

He looked at her pensively. "You don't like that idea?"

"Well, I think they are a bit nervous about the sound," she said.

He rubbed his face. "Yeah, I know, but the environment and atmosphere will transcend any sound issues. Make sure we get Charlie to put down a card at SIR and we'll get the best gear possible, okay?"

"Yep. Can I ask, though, is the only reason you're doing this is to be cool? I mean you have all the offers to get them a great deal, right?"

"Yeah. Look, in a way it's about momentum, but you're right, there's more to it than that," he admitted.

She looked right through him and he suddenly realized she must know. "Jacqueline's dead. I'm so sorry not to tell you when I got back. I guess I'm still trying to keep you out of the worst of this," he fumbled.

"I could almost accept that, as misguided as it would be, if you kept it a total secret, but you didn't, did you?" she said accusingly. He cursed himself for his lack of forethought. "Why would you tell the band and not me? I thought we'd come to an understanding," she said, clearly hurt.

"You're right. It'll be the last time," he promised. "I was in shock when I got back. I guess I told them out of loyalty to Terry, so they would understand if he lost focus on them. I know that sounds crazy with hindsight. I'm sorry you found out from them and not me."

She looked as if she fought back an angry tear. "Just tell me what's happening now and what's next," she implored.

He noticed Highsmith had gone and sat upright next to Lainey, clearly presenting a united front. "I hope next I put enough pressure on Denny Golden to finally reveal himself. I tried to walk away from this, which I know now was a mistake."

"Boss, he revealed himself pretty good back at the Viper Room. Are you sure you can win this one? I know I said I was bored, but this job's not that bad and you have a pretty good setup here, not to mention this one." She rubbed her long fingers down the side of Highsmith's black-and-white face.

After a pause, she continued, "You said you got into this to find Terry's wife. As tragic as it is, she's dead. There's nothing you can do to change that. Maybe you should go back to your day job."

He sighed. "I know you're probably right, and that would be the smart and likely safest way, but I could never be sure Denny won't look at me as another loose end to take care of at some point."

"It could get that bad, huh?" she speculated. He nodded. "Okay then, I'll help you in any way you want, but don't hide anything from me."

He smiled wanly. "I promise."

He spent the rest of the day with the contracts and continued later with a bottle of wine back at his place. Those Southern boys had indeed been stitched up something awful, but as far as he could see, it was all legal. Impossible to say, of course, what a thorough audit might turn up, but getting it would be expensive. The manufacturing of the "cleans" that were the core of Denny's illegal manufacturing operation, of course, wouldn't show up in any audit at Real. He had been right about one thing, though. There was no language that adequately covered synchronization rights for commercials and TV shows. He knew he'd heard their songs on at least two national commercial spots, meaning the heirs could be looking at hundreds of thousands, even if they settled at the traditional fifty percent split between label and artist.

He put the contracts back in the envelope and deep in thought, led the way down to the beach. Highsmith padded quietly alongside as they walked down to the Sandcastle. James got a beer for himself and a beef bone for the springer just as the bar closed up for the night. They took their respective treats to the end of the pier and by the time they finished, James had the beginnings of a plan.

CHAPTER 44

He was in the office early, within earshot of Lainey, when he started to make calls. First he talked to Eric, ascertaining the deals were so close to one another that there was little to choose from with regard to royalty points, reversions, marketing commitments, etc. The lawyer didn't bother to argue too much about the boat signing idea, other than grumbling about having to draw up multiple long form deal memos, which, of course, he would bill full rate for even though the work would be done by his paralegal.

The next call was to Pete Davis, Denny's A&R guy. "So, Pete, here's the thing. Clearly it's no secret Denny and I can't stand each other, but the band does like you and the Olympian offer has our attention. I expect you've heard about Charlie Major's floating club, right?" The excited young guy acknowledged he and everyone else in the business had by now. "So the band is going to play the opening and announce and sign the deal on the spot," announced James.

"Are you serious? That's a pretty fucking cool idea," said the excited kid.

James was feeling shitty at this point, but pressed on. "Obviously, you are invited, but I think if we are maybe going to all work together, Denny and I need to sit down and put our differences aside."

"Yes, of course," said Pete, who would have agreed with

pretty much anything he needed to right now.

"Well, see what you can do. I'd suggest Denny and I sit and talk on the boat before the band plays. I'm telling you instead of Eric because I think you actually may be in this for the right reasons—not that that will necessarily do you any good," he chuckled gruffly, "but I expect it will motivate you."

He called John Van Put and sleepwalked through the conversation, already bored with the idea of even potentially talking to this wanker every day for the next year. Then he moved into invite mode, asking everyone he thought would appreciate the idea behind the boat. He rang Aurial mid-afternoon when he felt things were shaping up well, and suggested dinner. Deciding to meet where they would not likely be seen together, they settled on the Twin Dragon on Pico, which was midway between both their locations and an old-school neighborhood joint where industry people were nonexistent.

The pagoda-style entrance looked early 60s. James didn't know when this joint originated, but it had a mythic US take on a Chinese restaurant with red and gold pillars, beautifully fashioned around dark wood tables, the larger of which had revolving inner trays for family-style serving of meals.

She was already there when he walked in, standing erect and insouciant, dressed in a green thigh-length dress that fit the restaurant's era and style. The sixty-ish tall, thin, formal Chinese maître d' escorted them to a small table for two in an out-of-the-way corner of one of the three expansive dining rooms. He could swear Yma Sumac played quietly on the stereo, but he knew that had to be unlikely.

They ordered a bottle of wine from the choice of three reds and settled on a double order of crispy fried garlic chicken pieces and fried rice. She looked at him, with an almost amused expression, and wrapped the extraordinarily long thumb on her right hand around his long, but nonetheless shorter thumb. She held his tight.

"Crunch time, kiddo, huh?"

"Yep," he acknowledged.

"You got it figured out?" she asked.

"Yeah, I think so."

The food arrived shortly on the heels of the wine. He was convinced he heard "Xtabay (Lure of the Unknown Love)" by Yma Sumac, and asked the old boy who served them to check.

They both took bites of the perfect crispy chicken with not a drop of grease on it and grinned at each other, relishing the garlic kick, happy they'd both ordered the same thing.

"I need you to be there, but out of sight. We're gonna play him some tape and make a deal on the spot. Get him to pay you half a million and make a donation to the Confederacy's trust of five million, and he ain't getting Damaged, of course, which will have to be all the satisfaction I get, at least for now."

"Well, I could live with that, but it doesn't seem enough somehow. Why can't we take him all the way down?" she said emphatically.

"Maybe we could, but I don't see how that would get you paid any more. Plus, we would be just as likely to go down for Deutch's and Jacqueline's death. Denny wasn't in the same country, and I was the last one to see Jeff Stanley alive. We've definitely got him on conspiracy, but this shit is twenty years old. He'll be scared, I hope, but fear may be all we have. The odds of the law reopening the band's demise in real life are probably slim to none."

"And you can live with this end?" she asked.

"I think I may have to. I wouldn't even be here but for you. I never told you, but you looked pretty damned impressive when you and your boots came flying over that balcony. I think that may be enough."

"All right, boy, one suggestion. Threaten him on the phone and have him bring cash to the boat. Why risk him wriggling out? All the controlled environment…being on the boat won't mean shit if the money's not dropped."

"Yeah but the whole setup with maybe signing the band and, of course, the disappointment of not getting them, goes out the window. Plus he might not even show," he said.

"Not if I call him."

"We'd have to bet on him not connecting us yet."

"If he had, he'd have found me by now, right?"

"I dunno. Maybe," he said pensively. "The fact he came after me suggests it was a lot about back then, and if he doesn't figure you for the tape theft, he isn't thinking about you. Thing is, he's met you more than once. The minute you make that call, you'll be under threat," he said emphatically.

"The launch is Friday. I'll call Wednesday, enough time for him to pull cash. But we'll need to house me somewhere other than the carriage house, just to be on the safe side," she said pointedly.

"Aurial, it's too dangerous. Let's keep the element of surprise. I'm gonna get an old lawyer friend, Brian Rohan, to draw up some iron-clad papers. You can pick them up quietly Thursday. I don't want to be seen with him, to be on the safe side."

She looked skeptical, but nodded her acquiescence.

CHAPTER 45
DENNY GOLDEN

Denny Golden hadn't left his Malibu compound for quite some time. Having still no word from Deutch had left him pensive, not to mention, of course, paranoid and angry. He'd been further irritated by spending the last hour reading the purloined minutes and speech by that arrogant French clown who ran rival label Gramo Europa Records. Among other things, he'd opined that the "Internet" would have no material effect on the music business. Denny wasn't quite so sure of that, but he certainly didn't have time to dwell on it now. He already operated on two realities and didn't care to add a third. He still felt somewhat in control of his record label, but somewhat less able to keep at bay the past that had provided its foundation. Ron Deutch's continued absence was disturbing, mostly because of its complete uncertainty.

He'd thought quickly when the combination of Jacqueline's call and Deutch's somewhat irate visit had followed one another. Wondering for a minute if he was being set up, the idea of sending Deutch had felt like a good test of his loyalty. On the surface, questioning the promo man's integrity to him was inconceivable, but Denny had had this nagging thought: *What if Deutch had removed the tapes?* He'd been less than proactive with ideas for their recovery.

On top of that, from the minute Jeff Stanley had called out of the blue, he'd had a nagging feeling there was a conspiracy involved and an extremely limited number of people could be behind it. Why shouldn't he have had enough doubt to close that door forever? Certainly the continuation of Stanley's life didn't have any great value to anyone as far as he could see. Probably done his long-suffering wife a favor, in fact.

When Ron showed up and questioned his handling of James Dual, he'd listened a little more patiently than usual. He loved how he'd ruined the limey's life back then, but the sheer physical joy of putting the boot in had been truly exhilarating. Still, he had to acknowledge it could have been embarrassing if he had been observed. His carefully manufactured liberal philanthropic supporter of arts and artists façade could have crumbled before his eyes. Ron was right, but he'd got away scot-free, so he could only manage so much remorse. Ultimately it had been a lack of conciliatory advice from Deutch that had tipped him towards sending the big man to Mexico, even if it was just to show who was in control.

Reflecting on Deutch again, he was reminded of the Granita dinner. Presumably that must have been when Harper found out his wife was missing. But why was Dual involved? They hadn't been friends for years, as far as he knew. On top of that, why would they accuse him of causing her disappearance? He still couldn't work that out. On the surface, it also suggested they didn't have the tapes if they had been used to threaten Jacqueline but maybe they'd acquired them since.

When Pete called him later that day with the whole stupid sign-the-band-on-an-old-gambling-boat plan, he resisted dismissing the notion out of hand, figuring the old adage "keep your friends close and your enemies closer" may apply here.

CHAPTER 46

When James and Highsmith showed up at Katrina and Davey's joint, the singer was reading aloud from Stanley Booth's perfect book, *The True Adventures of the Rolling Stones,* to her lounging boyfriend. James grinned as he wandered in through the half-open loft door. The Wolfhounds loped over to greet the slightly wary Highsmith. Suitably—and no doubt by design—*Exile on Main Street* was playing; "Ventilator Blues" to be specific.

He looked at them for a moment, getting the clear sense that they were growing ever more comfortable in the roles they'd imagined for themselves. Katrina broke off from a particularly mythic Keith Richards story. "Well, hello, James, it's almost dark. Can I get you a beer?" she asked.

"Yeah, that sounds good." He nodded.

She put the paperback open-face down to ensure not losing her place and wandered through the open area to a large 60s looking fridge. She pulled out a couple of Red Stripes, one for James and one for herself, not asking Davey if he cared for anything. Something about the way the noise of the door closing sounded made James think there was likely little food inside. The familiar sound from his teens and twenties made him smile. He flopped down on some goofy 70s beanbag.

Davey was quiet, obviously lost in the tale he'd been listening to. "So why'd ya give us this particular book?" Katrina parked herself on one of three barstools that sat in front of a breakfast counter that divided the kitchen from the living area. A metal spiral staircase led up to a balcony where their bed was.

"Preparation, of course, plus Mr. Booth's the perfect guy to write your bio," he replied.

"So all kidding aside," she wondered aloud, "what is it about the English that makes the music everything?"

His guard was down, liking these two and feeling somewhat of a kindred spirit. "I never gave it any thought. It was just the driving force in my life since I was about eight or nine years old. You've got to realize in England you didn't talk about or acknowledge any emotion or feeling. Everything was completely repressed. You were still dealing with a post-World War II mentality, but you weren't born until later, so all their 'I fought in the war for the likes of you' was like 'yeah, so fucking what?' When I started hearing songs, it was the only true emotion around."

"But what were you listening to?"

"First off, the obvious Beatles, Stones, Animals, Kinks but especially the Small Faces and Dusty Springfield, then hearing the Stax acts—William Bell, Judy Clay, Otis Redding, and The Memphis Horns, of course. After that, the Jamaican stuff: bluebeat and ska. There wasn't a choice; it was the only escape. I was beyond compelled."

"And now?" she asked appraisingly.

"Not a lot's changed. I'm here because I hear that authenticity in you lot. It's still not really a choice for me," he said.

"Good," she said.

"So leaving everything else aside for the minute, are you ready to decide who to make your record with?" he asked.

The rockers didn't need to look at each other this time. They both said yes simultaneously and then laughed.

"And?" asked James.

"Terry," in unison again.

James felt an inner relief but, still trying to be objective, asked, "You're sure?"

Davey took the lead this time. "Yeah, Terry came over here and we had a really honest conversation. He said he knew it might not be the healthiest thing but wanted nothing more than to bury himself in making the record with us."

"Interesting choice of words. Did you tell him then and there?" he asked.

"No," said Katrina. "We told him we wanted to talk to you first."

"Thanks. I'm glad. Truth is, he will probably 'bury' his emotions and be there for you in every way. I just wanted to make sure you got all the perspective you needed from the other labels."

"Among other things," smiled Katrina.

James could see Davey's puzzlement out of the corner of his eye. He figured she was onto him and that she'd kept her theories to herself. He wondered, but dismissed the idea that Lainey might have talked about the Confederacy crash or his kicking at the Viper Room.

"I wouldn't do anything that wasn't in your best interests, but my life is definitely complex right now. It's truly best I don't tell you everything. I do have an ulterior motive for asking you to do the boat show, but it will help build the buzz on you, okay?"

Davey said, "As long as we get to go make a record soon, I'm okay with anything." Katrina just left her gaze firmly on James.

"Okay, so I want to keep your decision to the three of us for now. I'd feel a lot better if Bill and Steve didn't know either."

"Too late for that," said Katrina.

"Okay," said James. "Sorry for even asking. I want to announce at Charlie's opening. Eric is pissed but I've asked him to draw up papers for the offers from Terry, John Van Put and Denny, but I'm going to let him think you're leaning towards Denny."

Katrina said, "Look, James, you're welcome to fuck with Denny any which way you want. He's an arrogant pig. Have your fun, really; we're fine with it. Right?" She turned to Davey.

"Absolutely. We're into this whole boat idea. Just make sure we get a decent guest list so our friends can be there, okay?"

CHAPTER 47

James and Lainey spent a couple of days following up on invites they'd sent out. The idea had appealed to a lot of the people he'd hoped would understand the LA noir history part of it, meaning they'd had yes from the likes of Quentin Tarantino, Johnny Depp, Larry Clark, Elmore Leonard, and, in what would be the ultimate for James, a maybe from Lauren Bacall, who was due to be in LA promoting her second biography with a book signing at Maxfield on Melrose that week.

Late on Tuesday afternoon, James looked at Lainey and grinned, all the darkness forgotten in the moment. "Fuck, girl, we did pretty good, huh?"

Her usual laconic attitude was missing as she hung up after getting an RSVP from Shirley Manson and Smashing Pumpkins singer Billy Corgan.

They headed for an early dinner and walked south on Third Street through the open-air shopping area which now had a Wolfgang Puck café, a multiplex movie house, along with a couple of halfway decent Italian restaurants, replete with sidewalk patio dining areas. He didn't have a big problem with the Bay City Chandler-era neighborhood getting an upgrading, but was saddened by the imminent loss of the rundown record shop on his left and the sense that lefty bookstore Midnight Special wasn't far behind. In truth, the block had been pretty moribund and depressing, but those two joints didn't deserve to be lost to the rapidly increasing lease prices and overall gentrification.

They turned onto Santa Monica Boulevard and ducked in the front door of JiRaffe right as the venerable French grandmother of one of the chef owners unlocked the glass front door, her smile framed by the classically cut gray hair. They were the first diners. She seated them at a table for two against the glass that looked out to nothing really, except a parking lot on Fifth Street, but they did have the warmth of the slowly setting sun radiating across them.

She ordered a vodka and cranberry juice. He settled for a glass rather than a bottle of Bordeaux, knowing he had to roll up PCH with Highsmith, who was looking after the office meantime.

Raphael, the chef partner, came in, already wearing his white chef's outfit and carried a box of vegetables likely acquired from the twice weekly farmers' market that took place at Second and Arizona.

"Wot we 'aving then, Raphael?" asked James by way of greeting.

"For you, some crispy white fish with asparagus maybe?" said the amiable young chef who, California-raised surfer that he was, displayed none of the attitude or pretentiousness of many French-inspired chefs.

"Yeah, whitefish sounds great, but I'm not much on asparagus." James joshed the chef a little.

"Oh, some nice peas to suit your English habits," said Raphael, coming right back at him. "If you actually show up to one of our monthly cooking classes, you could come with me to the farmers' market and create the meal you want."

Raphael looked across at Lainey. "The steak au poivre for you, perhaps?" he suggested.

She nodded and he headed through the narrow double doors

in the back. He returned a minute later to write up the night's menu on a chalkboard on the back wall just to the left of those doors.

They relaxed into their drinks. "So all diplomacy and job security aside, do you like this whole boat thing?"

She smiled slightly. "Yes, I think it's okay. I wasn't sure, but I think it suits everyone somehow."

The crisply-attired, slightly conservative young waitress carefully placed their drinks in front of them, along with an amuse-bouche, the likes of which he often found pretentious but in this case loved without being able to tell what it was.

He raised his glass to Lainey. "Thank you. You've done a great job keeping on top of everything we've got going on. Do me one favor. On the boat, just keep an eye on the band. Katrina obviously trusts you and it would be best if you aren't around me once I meet with Denny, just to be on the safe side."

She looked worried, but nodded reluctantly. Their food arrived as other diners trickled in, a mix of upscale but low-key types. The fish was so perfect everything else dropped away for a while. Lainey's steak clearly had the same effect on her as they found themselves talking about the surreally fun list of guests they'd conjured up for Charlie, and wondered what debauched rockers the venerable promo man had undoubtedly secured himself.

It was still early when James asked for the check, but the sun was long gone and darkness had descended. The waitress arrived back with the check but also a mad fun-looking dish that she announced as banana cream pie, replete with two spoons. "Raphael said this is his latest attempt to Americanize you."

It was killer, but Lainey was quick to point out this was like no other banana cream pie anyone in America had ever eaten. They floated out into the night, the air still warm as they strolled beachwards down Santa Monica Boulevard and absorbed the sage smells that blew at them. The winds had picked up again and as they walked up to Arizona, they could see fifty-foot palm trees bending almost horizontally. Fronds had fallen and blew along the sidewalk. Some had just dropped and lay helplessly across car roofs. They walked into the alley behind 1333 Ocean Avenue.

"I'm gonna get Highsmith and head home. You need anything from up there?"

About to reply, her mouth suddenly gaped. "James, the back door's open!"

He sprinted in past the pool and raced up the stairs, where the wooden door was open and hung off its hinges. Inside, the reception area was trashed. To the left, his office looked like an earthquake had hit. The piles of CDs and cassettes were smashed and scattered like a thick carpet across the room. The four-drawer filing cabinet was on its side, contents scattered. Then fear suddenly struck him.

"Highsmith!" He raced through into the conference room, which was lit by the almost full moon that shone down on his prone dog. He dropped to his knees. There was a drying trickle of blood on the unconscious Spaniel's slack lip.

Lainey stood silhouetted in the door, frozen, and feared the worst.

He gently cradled Highsmith, not moving him, head to his nose, feeling a very shallow breath. He put his ear to the dog's chest and detected a faint heartbeat. Lainey read the slight relief in his expression as he looked up at her.

"We have to call the police," she said.

"No law," he said.

She didn't argue. He carefully let go and made his way into his office, only now turning on a light as he flipped through the bulky old Rolodex to find Dr. Lisa, the vet's number. Of course he got the service at this time of night. He left both office and car numbers. He got on the floor next to Highsmith. "I'll give her a few minutes."

"What do you think?" she asked. He knew she meant everything. Would Highsmith make it? Who the fuck did this? What's next?

The phone rang and she answered. "Yes, hang on, Dr. Lisa."

"It's hard to know what happened, but Highsmith's been attacked. No, not by a dog, this was human…. You will? Okay, I'm in Santa Monica. It shouldn't take more than twenty minutes this time of night. Thank you, Doctor."

He hung up and turned to Lainey. "All right, I'm going to take him. Can you open the car and lay some pillows in the back seat? You are going to leave when I do. Go stay with a friend if you can. Call the cleaning company and get them in tomorrow. We'll work from elsewhere. Not a word to anyone, all right? This could mean our homes have been hit, you understand?" She nodded. "Do you have someone who can check for you?"

"Uh huh," she replied.

CHAPTER 48

Five minutes later, he carried Highsmith down in his arms. He felt the dog was fading, despite his indomitable spirit. "Please, please, no," he muttered to himself as he fired up the engine and blazed down the California Incline onto Pacific Coast Highway. He made it to Malibu Animal Hospital in eighteen minutes and pulled into the brown gravel driveway that was situated on the highway just after Cross Creek Road in the same slot it had occupied since 1954. The lights were dimmed, meaning she hadn't arrived yet, so he switched off the engine and went to the back seat and sat with his hand on Highsmith's head, fearful to touch much else unnecessarily, not knowing where the damage might be.

Moments later, the gravel crunched. The soulful savior of many an animal's life walked quickly to the car. Her short blonde hair framed a happy, optimistic face. James got out and let her sit beside the still-unconscious dog. She gently ran her hands over him.

"Okay, James, I'm going to open up and put the lights on in the surgery. I'll prop the door open. Carry him as carefully as you can. Walk slowly, okay?"

He was too petrified to ask questions, so he did exactly as he was told. Two minutes later, Highsmith lay on a stainless steel table, surrounded by the instruments of Dr. Lisa's vocation. She took a breath and smiled at him. She could have used an assistant, but made the snap judgment that James would add more tension than he could help, and quietly told him to wait in the lobby.

He sat on a bench under the window in front of her reception counter, head in hands, and second-guessed his every move. Thirty minutes later, she emerged and he looked up expectantly.

"James, I've done all I can, but honestly it's going to be touch and go. He took an awful beating. He must have been fighting for his life. There's bits of human skin in his mouth and several teeth missing. There's some internal bleeding, but his vital signs are steady, if weak. Thank God he's young and I know he's got a strong spirit."

"Can I take him home?"

"Absolutely not. For once we've got no other overnight visitors, so I'll have to page the on-call tech tonight. Go home and I'll let you know in the morning, okay?"

"Lisa, I know that's the smart advice, but I can't leave him."

"James, I know how you feel, but you can't stay here," she said firmly.

"I'm not leaving him. Look, if it's an insurance thing or something, I'll sign a waiver, whatever you like…"

She sighed. An hour later, he was sitting on a blue dog blanket beside the gurney. Dorina, the young Mexican girl, knew and liked Highsmith from when she'd given the flea-bitten rescue his puppy shots. There were no other dogs to keep an eye on, so they'd dragged a couch from the waiting room in to have a comfortable spot to sit through the long night ahead.

The room wasn't much different from a regular hospital, and Highsmith was hooked up to some kind of IV-like contraption. His eyes closed, flickered periodically, and James could see his chest moving slightly but steadily as he breathed. He had a sudden thought and excused himself while he went out to the car and called Aurial.

He got her answering machine.

"Listen, my office was broken into tonight and Highsmith got hurt pretty bad. It could mean they were looking for something by the way the place was torn up. You're probably fine, but I'd suggest you sleep elsewhere for now."

He hung up and wished he had a beer. He went back in and made small talk, trying not to ask much about his dog's odds. She kept an eye on the monitors. About 10:00 pm, he curled up in the blanket and suggested she wake him up if she wanted to sleep. But she shook her head and said she was used to doing the late shift. He lay awake for an hour or so, trying not to let fear and anguish take over.

He woke just before six o'clock, stiff and tense. Dorina was reading a Spanish language paperback. She gave him instructions how to go make them coffee. He gently put his hand on Highsmith's head and felt a small sigh. He came back ten minutes later and they quietly drank.

Dr. Lisa arrived at 7:30 a.m., hugged him, and sent him out to the lobby. She came out twenty minutes later as other staff trickled in. She sat down beside him. "He's going to live, James." He tried to push back tears of relief. "I don't think there's going to be any permanent damage, but he has to stay with us for a couple of days so we can keep a close eye on everything, okay?" She continued, "He's very weak."

"Of course." He nodded.

"You have to go home now, though. I broke all my rules for you. Please don't let anyone know you spent the night or else I'll have every crazy dog owner expecting to do the same."

He smiled wanly. "Thank you for everything."

CHAPTER 49

He found his home unscathed, as had Lainey and Aurial. The next two days leading up to Friday's party were spent taking care of a seemingly never-ending list of details—from getting the band's gear on board and set up, to keeping Eric from sabotaging the pressure on Denny, John Van Put, and Terry by closing a deal.

Charlie had cut a deal with Music Express to exclusively shuttle guests to the embarkation point at Malibu Pier, where speedy launches would take groups out to the boat. He'd also quietly arranged for their key celebrity types to leave from Paradise Cove on a couple of small speedboats.

To keep Charlie's debauched vision intact, they did everything they could to ensure no photographers or TV or print journalists got on board. This was helped by the fact that the two restaurants at Malibu Pier sat closed and empty anyway, so restricting parking lot entrance to Music Express cars only was pretty easy. Lainey would accompany the band, and Aurial and James agreed to leave from his place. Just to add to the list, Lainey informed him their office landlord had happened to come by just before the cleaning crew and wanted to know what the hell had happened.

"Tell the prat I'd like to know, too," he muttered. He took his mind off this by immersing himself in picking the songs to be pumped through the immaculate sound system Charlie had installed. Instead of badly piped-in shit, there were tiny high-end speakers along every square foot, so wherever you were it felt like your own subtle, but crystal-clear, system. The staterooms, private dining areas, and sundry other rooms had their own controls so you could play your own choice or listen to what everyone else was. It was this lovely touch that had inspired James to the exact details of how to handle the denouement with Denny.

Aurial arrived looking poised and lethal, even though she'd yet to change into the outfit that she carried along with her other gear in a Tintin duffel bag. They walked hand in hand as the huge afternoon sun descended on their backs as they arrived at Paradise Cove to board the speedboat that bobbed at the end of the pier.

The sand blew hard grains warmly straight into their eyes.

"I love the Santa Anas. Always feel at the absolute top of my game," he said.

"Yeah, they've had a hand in keeping me here too," she said.

"Really? I'm so used to people looking at me like I'm joking or mad while reminding me they cause fires," he said disgustedly.

She grinned. "But it's people who cause fires, right?"

Maybe because *Exile on Main Street* was the last CD he'd pulled tracks from onto his new blue toast disc maker but he could hear "Casino Boogie" as clear as if it came off the boat.

She looked at him as they clambered on board. "You ready, kiddo?"

"Never more." He meant it. Even though stone-cold sober, there was a calm but intense pulse of adrenaline that he could only compare to the purest amphetamine buzz. He was ready all right. The boat was barely twenty feet long and had two rows of wooden benches. The same girl who'd taken him out the first time gunned the engine hard; they slammed into waves and bounced slightly off their seats as they hit each one. The ocean was a little choppy, which heightened the experience—a hard spray blew across their faces. It definitely felt like all three of them were caught up in the same moment, that rush of something different that everyone with their sensibilities would want to be a part of. The ride was just enough to make you realize you were headed out to sea and possibly adventure without getting boring.

They bumped against the hull of the already brightly lit ship, climbed the metal ladder up, and stepped into a hive of activity, Charlie at its hub. Clearly, his ignorant act about how to run all this was just another one of his consummate manipulative ruses. He spotted James and Aurial, perhaps realized he had been found out and yelled, "Jimmy, you're here at last."

James knew he couldn't lose focus right now. "Listen, Charlie. Aurial and I need to get set up. The launch is going to go great. Just make sure you get word to me when Denny boards." He put his arm around the taller man's shoulder. "You know, if this is handled right, we'll all be better off. And besides," he pointed out, as Wanda strode across the deck with a dozen or so girls in her wake, "you can't go far wrong with this woman in your camp, right?"

Charlie gave him a steely glance. "Make your plays, Jimmy. Ol' Charlie will keep an eye out for you."

James and Aurial went down to the lower deck and walked to the back of the boat. There was a suite that was top to bottom glass—sliding doors opened across half the entire curving rear, maybe ten feet above the lapping ocean. Those English carpenters had stunningly done the entire space in completely authentic 1940s cherrywood. The desk he'd asked for faced out to the sea. A bedroom was through the adjoining door. Aurial went straight in and set up, but handed him a manila folder on her way. He sat behind the desk and could see a glassy half reflection. Abstractedly, he was glad he'd worn the pointed-toe, handmade Jeffrey West black Chelsea boots.

A few minutes later, the sound of the ocean was overwhelmed by the crunching sound of Damaged's sound check.

Aurial changed; her beach walk clothes dropping to the floor to be replaced by the noir-ish black sheath dress he'd seen before. He went through the papers, satisfied everything was primed. He stared out to sea for something like an hour as the sound check eventually dissipated, briefly hearing only the slap of the ocean against the bow before the gradual darkness descended and the slowly building noise of arriving motor boats brought the early party participants. He knew she'd stood behind him for most of the reverie. Nothing needed to be said.

They checked the speakers and the sound system control panel and sat back to wait. The only interruption was in the form of Lainey, who came by and confirmed all was good with the band. He gave her seven hours of music he'd chosen, figuring by 3:00 a.m. no one left standing would notice whether they were replayed.

CHAPTER 50

An hour later, Charlie, awash in his invited guest glory, gently pried himself away from U2 guitarist The Edge as he saw Denny and his A&R guy Pete arrive. He frowned slightly as Gary Kalusian stepped up behind them. He'd consciously not invited him, but of course he could be Denny's plus-one. What the hell, let him see how to expand your horizons. Primal Scream singer Bobby Gillespie half stumbled into Charlie, clearly ahead of most guests' consumption, but was quickly righted by his old friend, Creation Records iconic creator Alan McGee who put an arm on Charlie's shoulder, leaned in and said a few placatory words, or at least the host thought he did. Not for the first time, Alan benefitted from Americans acquiescing to his thick Glaswegian accent for fear of offending him by admitting they didn't know what he was saying. At any rate, a potential altercation was avoided.

It took Charlie a minute to spot Denny again as his party headed to the nearest bar on the top deck. Good, let him drink a little. He realized with a few seconds' delay that Alan had asked after James. "Why don't you head to the bar and I'll let him know you're on board when I see him."

Denny, having taken the Stoli vodka and cranberry he'd requested from Peter, looked out at the gradually thickening crowd that gave the look of a successful launch to the proceedings, and in a rare moment of doubt wondered whether he should have come.

Primal Scream's "Loaded" revved up the proceedings for everyone else. The booze flowed in generous proportions.

Lainey had left the band to prepare by themselves and was startled as she came up to the top deck to see Terry boarding with kids in tow, but on reflection, she liked his decision, as they were clearly enjoying the adventure. She led them to the lower deck and situated them in a booth close to the stage where Damaged would play, exchanged small talk with Terry, but remembered that the last time she'd seen him, they were trying to undress James at her apartment. She suddenly felt uncomfortable, sensing no matter how low-key things were, that sad final danger was in the air for all of them.

CHAPTER 51

Forty-five minutes and two and a half drinks after he'd boarded, Denny Golden was impatient, accustomed as he was to everything revolving around his timetable, when Wanda sidled up.

"James is ready to see you now," she told Denny, using the words James had known would annoy him further, after having deliberately left him cooling his heels. Pete and Gary rose as if to follow. Just as Wanda was going to dissuade them, Denny did the job for her.

"Any settling will be strictly between Dual and I." Denny forced a smile that convinced no one. "Don't worry, Pete, I'll get your band." He put a condescending hand on the kid's shoulder.

He wordlessly allowed Wanda to lead the way and open up a path through the growing crowd. His cocaine and vodka-lubricated mental wheels raced as he wondered whether Dual suspected him of the office break-in. In truth, he hadn't been particularly optimistic about finding the tapes, but fucking up the dog had been an assured outcome and a nice way of venting all his current frustrations.

They walked down the steps to the lower deck and left the crisp night air behind. Denny knew Kraftwerk was the sound that gently pulsed from each speaker they passed, but couldn't recall which song it was. He glanced across when he heard a loud, coarse English accent come from a table situated near the stage to his right. His lip curled in disgust at the sight of John Van Put, Barry Gordon, and sundry silicon-enhanced hangers-on, although cynically amused that they could imagine they were in with a shout at getting Damaged. He was begrudgingly appreciative of the stylized rooms he glimpsed as they passed. T. Rex's "The Slider" was briefly heard as the Bowie-inspired room door closed before he could see its occupants, but its melancholy tones lingered in a manner he was neither accustomed to nor liked.

Finally, they came to the end of the corridor and the closed door that faced them. Wanda knocked lightly and paused briefly before admitting Denny. James sat and faced him from the far side of an immaculate Art Deco desk framed by the night sky and wash of water below that was audible above the low tones of Isaac Hayes's epic twelve-minute version of "Walk On By." Wanda stayed just long enough to fix Denny the identical drink he'd got at the bar, which further disconcerted him somehow. *Time to take control*, he thought.

"So, Dual, I'm happy we can meet amicably and make the right deal to let this great band have the best possible opportunity for the success they deserve," he said magnanimously.

James looked at him implacably, so focused he actually didn't hear anything but the song. He wordlessly pushed the two manila folders from his side of the desk across the two-foot expanse to Denny. The twelve minutes played through with the only voice heard being Isaac Hayes's, at which point a seething Denny looked up, speechless with rage.

"Yeah—so here's the story. You aren't getting the band, which is the least of your worries," began James. "I'm going to let you hear something and if those two contracts aren't signed while you are listening, everyone on this fucking boat will hear it through the immaculate sound system you no doubt noticed already."

Deutch's voice: "So it would be a very high-priced service to rid a label of a particularly troublesome, or no longer performing artist."

Denny's voice: "Because we can, Ron. Because we should," echoed like a waking nightmare, and as the deadly incriminating words continued, he read the fine print on the binding agreements that scorched his hands.

James watched, fascinated, as any façade on Golden's face fell away and revealed pure malevolent hate.

"What is this?"

"Well, dear Denny, I imagine you grasped what it is even without Margery Cunningham's usual help. However, the first is the creation of a five million dollar a year trust to benefit needy artists or their families, to be funded by you. The first beneficiary will be the estate of the Confederacy. The second is a consulting agreement with a dear friend who will choose subsequent artists to benefit. You will pay her an up-front, post-tax fee of $500,000 annually for the next ten years. She will, with my help, form an advisory board of artists who will guide her decisions. You, of course, will not have any input other than writing the checks." Denny snorted derisively. James thought he saw a speck of cocaine drop to the desk. "You can sign it now and make like the David Geffen you wish you could be. I'll get Charlie to bring you up to announce it. Your two-bit legacy sealed. If not, the tapes start playing and you go down in flames."

As Aurial heard the last hiss of that particular tape, she flipped the switch just as Big Audio Dynamite's "E=MC2" pulsed across the boat and her eyes gleamed on the other side of the wall. James almost gasped at the timing as the Nicholas Roeg-inspired song that laid it all bare, *The Man Who Fell To Earth* allusions, and perfect dialogue samples from *Performance* giving him a pure adrenaline shot.

Denny tried to regain his composure meantime. "Twenty-year-old tapes? I'd walk out of any court laughing."

"Maybe, but that was before you started tidying up loose ends. We know how to tie it all together now in a nice tight noose. We know about Jeff Stanley and that you sent Deutch to kill Jacqueline. By the way, your boy Deutch isn't coming back. So last chance to get off lightly."

Golden's mind spun, and through the jangling coke and vodka cocktail, the tumblers fell into place. He picked up the silver pen and signed both contracts.

James rose. "Go and wait upstairs. Charlie will come and get you when it's time. After you have your big moment, we have a nice room arranged where you can stay until the wire transfers you signed go through." Roy Orbison's poignant, "It's Over" played. *A little obvious*, he thought, *but what the hell.*

As Denny planned ahead and reflected on what had been left unsaid, James chimed in. "I hope it goes without saying that if anything remotely untoward happens to me or anyone else connected to this, tapes, testimony, etc. will go to every imaginable law agency and media outlet."

Golden rose shakily, silently, and determined to keep his dignity intact. He nodded his apparent acquiescence, turned on his heel and opened the cabin door to find Wanda waiting outside, ready to lead him to a stage-side table. He thought furiously how to spin the non-signing of Damaged and huge charitable donation to his cohorts while still being in control of the situation. Another cocktail was the only occupant of the large round table. He'd drunk most of it by the time Wanda returned with Pete and Gary in tow. Charlie watched that moment from the top of the stairs, where he could see both the nicely mingling crowd on the open-air upper deck and the downstairs tables that were beginning to fill. James had smartly insisted there be no VIP area. They had quietly made likely suspects aware of the unique overnight accommodations, though, which would mostly be comped tonight.

Aurial came through the bedroom door and found James's chair swiveled facing out to the darkening ocean night. She picked up the signed documents, and put her left hand on his shoulder, her thumb pressing down hard. "Close, boy, close. Sure you're still okay with this solution?" she said.

"Yeah." He sighed. "I need to be. I think he'll realize he's gonna be dangling with no control just the same way he had me twenty years ago. Five million a year will hurt him but not to the point where he'll go out of business."

"You happy enough with that?" She'd come round to face him, now silhouetted by the huge moon that loomed outside. Her hands cupped his face. "The amount's fine, but why did you create the job for me?"

"Figured it might keep you out of trouble for a while," he said.

"Maybe, but not likely," she said.

"At any rate, finding artists to help will give us something to plot," he said.

"Us, huh?" she said. "I'll have to think about that on the way to the shore."

"Yeah, Brian will be waiting up. He's got a guest room you can stay in. Best you two go to the bank together. He's a tough old geezer, but make sure you have his back just in case."

"What's his story? Why him?" she queried.

"Let's put it this way. He started out getting 60s San Francisco bands out of drug busts and marched onward in legal recklessness from then on, punching out, among others, David Geffen along the way."

She smiled. "We should get on well. Just make sure Denny doesn't get off the boat."

"As if," was said over Aurial's shoulder as she left.

CHAPTER 52

Davey and Katrina picked at the fancy deli tray that was set atop a white-clothed table in a large cabin at the opposite end of the boat from where James and Aurial were.

"Say, when will we actually get the advance?" asked Steve.

Davey glared at him. "We're going to make a great record. Why the fuck would you ask that before a show like this?"

"Well, the show's great. It's a wild scene here, but we got a guest list of ten. Without our friends, we're the sideshow, right?"

Katrina paused, about to shoot him down but thought better of it. "We are going to rip this place apart. Who gives a fuck about the rest?" She glared. The message got through. There was a mutual grin, and by the time Lainey showed up, they were ready. Given the boat's realities, they had to walk down the corridor and out into the open ballroom tables before making it to the stage. The four of them instinctively spread out across the room, only coming back together as they reached the stage and vaulted up to where their equipment waited—it had a cool, slow build-up effect that had the crowd applauding.

"Yeah, we are Damaged. We subscribe to the circus but we have to cut to the chase." Here she gave a slight nod across her shoulder. "Damaged is going to sign to Terry Harper and Real tonight, but first..." She stopped and let Davey's loose rhythm guitar start up.

They made their mark. The crowd grinned appreciatively, knowing they would talk about this one over the years, while of course many others would claim to have been here. The beautiful 40s surroundings got a brilliant mash-up with guttersnipe rock and roll while James sat down below, still staring out but feeling the perfect pulse through the wall. Then he went inside, shook hands with Van Put while it was still loud enough not to be forced into an unwanted conversation and sidled up to where Terry and the kids were clearly enjoying themselves, music overriding English repression. He flopped into the booth and put his arm around Terry.

"All right, mate?" he questioned.

"Trying to be. I'm taking these guys down to Palm Springs next week, and Martha and I will decide how to do the best job we can. Thanks for not taking Damaged to another label, although I can't believe you of all people would indulge in such game playing," replied Terry.

Damaged was, of course, compelled to finish with "Cool As Fuck," changing the lyric to "Dark As Noir" in the final choruses, delighting those who understood, Uma Thurman included. James saw Charlie usher Denny up to the stage as Damaged departed triumphantly.

Charlie grabbed the mike Katrina had used. "Welcome to the first sailing of the *Cornero*. Come over here, Denny." He clamped his arm around the mogul's shoulder. "Now you all know what a philanthropist and patron of the arts this man is, but he's about to outdo himself."

Denny extricated himself from his almost partner and seized the moment. "I'm here to announce the formation of a foundation to help support important artists and their survivors who are having difficulties. I'm pledging five million per year from Olympian and

I'm here to challenge my major label competitors to match that."

The crowd, although initially disinterested in the evening's change of tone, mustered up some applause amid vague amusement that label heads were getting called out. Terry looked at James with undisguised surprise. James, half smiling, not unpleased by Denny's braggadocio, figured it was a sign he'd accepted the price and was already trying to turn it to his benefit. Wanda took all this in just before she turned towards James and beckoned one of her protégés over. "I think drinks are called for," she announced.

"Absolutely," said Terry.

"Shirley Temples for the kids," said Wanda to the petite Asian protégé who shadowed her, "and bring a bottle of Bell's Scotch for the table. James and Terry get it, and don't argue."

Wanda's hip-bumped James around into the booth enough to join them. They sat wordlessly, very conscious of how long it had been, and loving how the quickly consumed bottle let them linger and enjoy the moment. Friendship transcended death, at least for now. James was very aware that Charlie kept Denny close—crucial he not slip off the boat until all the bank transactions finalized in the morning.

"Wanna go find the band?" he asked finally.

Wanda cut in before Terry could acquiesce. "Don't break this minute up just yet, limeys. Heaven forbid you're feeling a bit of emotion. I'll send Cindy to go find them. After all, you're the one writing the fat check, Terry. May as well enjoy the last time they'll come running." She chuckled.

Davey and Katrina, along with Bill, Steve, and Lainey, made their way through the throng of the crowd. Katrina put the follow-up bottle of Bell's on the table as everyone rose except the kids. Wanda poured serious measures.

"So, what's the toast? To this band of rockers we hope will keep certain traditions alive?" she wondered aloud.

"To a great record," said Terry.

James nodded. "But just remember, your problems don't end when you sign a record deal. They begin."

Davey wasn't having any of that right now. Glass in hand, he leaned into James. "Me and Kat have been thinking we should take the band to Memphis and get Jim Dickinson to produce it."

James smiled, while realizing Terry's radar had caught every word, but was instantly torn, of course. Go for the mythic or rein the band in and record with the mainstream producers of the day. Not a decision to make tonight, though.

Wanda, seeing the kids' buoyancy fading, then cut the reveries short and put an arm around George and Amy. The room subtly changed atmosphere as couples and groups drifted up to the top deck, likely wondering how easy it would be to get shuttled back to land, while those who remained were served by Wanda's fast-moving, wise-cracking team.

Frankie Miller's " The Rock" started as their leader surveyed the room. "What say we get you three on board the first cruiser out of here?" The kids were too wiped to raise any kind of argument.

"All right, then," said Terry, a little worse for wear. "Let's get home while we're ahead." The band rose and gave Terry hugs and grins while they shook the kids' hands. They followed in Wanda's wake.

James's attention shifted back to where Charlie sat with Denny, Gary, and Pete. It nagged at him that even if they kept Denny on the boat until tomorrow, that Kalusian could still foul things up if Golden tipped him off somehow. Now he was pissed at himself that he'd not taken proper precautions to keep him off the boat. Hard to figure how deep in this the promo man was. He watched as James Woods, with a ludicrously stunning pal in tow, leaned in to Charlie and saw Charlie laugh out loud while the actor swung the ornate brass key to his suite in a wide arc. The Mensa-smart method man then said something to Denny that clearly didn't go down well.

All the rooms had been comped for the launch to the sort of characters who would hopefully become regulars and establish the financial mainstay of this floating debauchery.

James said, "All right, you lot, I'm gonna leave you to it. Enjoy it all. When you recover, come down to the office and we'll suss out our next moves." They grinned at one another, his accent stronger with the booze.

He rose and instantly realized he was somewhat the worse for wear. Last time he'd poured this much Bell's Scotch into himself, he'd balanced it with the best amphetamine sulphate. Funny how logical and acceptable that had been at the time. He put his hand on the table for a second before he pointed himself towards Denny's table. He went to the far wall, and then walked through the tables and in doing so, crossed paths with Alan McGee and Bobby Gillespie.

"Ahh, I'm all right with youse song choices." The singer swayed slightly. McGee instantly lent a hand to his shoulder, allowing a continued vertical position for his old friend.

"Yeah, very heavily 1971, '72, James. What's that all about?" asked Alan.

James rubbed his jaw thoughtfully. "Yeah, I was sort of aware of it. You know how it's mostly accepted 1939 was the best ever year for film? I believe 1972 was that for music. Bowie's *Ziggy Stardust and the Spiders from Mars*. First Roxy Music record. *Exile on Main Street*. Bob Marley's *Catch A Fire* recorded, the *Clockwork Orange* and *Super Fly* soundtracks."

Alan didn't argue the point. "I get it. The eras match very well on the boat. You think people will be into it for a while?"

"Yeah, probably for a while. However long that is these days." James grinned sideways. "Haven't seen you since Oasis, what, two years ago? So, you here long enough to meet up properly?"

"I'm at the Chateau Marmont for a few days yet. Come over."

"All right, I'll find you." James moved back into the throng. The hotel name reminded him of the beginning, and he wondered whether Elmore Leonard was floating around somewhere. He knew he was drunk and losing focus. He spotted the dapper author, who stood alone.

"You made it back, Elmore. So happy about that."

"Me, too. Any excuse to escape the Detroit winter. Actually, I wanted to do some follow-up with Ron Deutch but I haven't been able to connect. He's got a wealth of stories I can mine. I can see Gary over by the bar—maybe Ron's around, too?"

"Nah, Ron couldn't make it." James unconsciously rubbed his still sore neck.

"Pity. I think he would have appreciated this beautiful evocation of the past somehow but not to worry, I think I may have my story." He looked at Denny, Gary, and Charlie.

"Jesus, you really have a soft spot for guys like him, huh?"

"Don't you?" asked Elmore with a knowing look but never got an answer.

Dr. Feelgood's classic "Keep It Out of Sight" started and kicked in some chemistry that revved up the memory of death in Mexico, and James felt a nasty edge descend. He strode the last few yards to where Charlie and Denny stood, flanked by Pete and Gary. Charlie, sensing something was off, got the first word in.

"James, you're just in time to bid Pete and our old friend

Gary goodnight. Denny, inveterate partier that he is, has decided to take me up on the offer of an overnight stay."

James saw the sadness all over Pete's face and felt enough to turn away from the others and say, "Listen, I know you actually probably wanted to make the deal for mostly the right reasons. I'm sorry to have given you false hope. Take my advice and find your way out of Olympian." He didn't wait for a response and turned back to Charlie. "Yeah, why don't you, me, and Denny go and have a nightcap then."

He looked at Gary Kalusian, couldn't read anything, and decided to test the waters.

"Who'd have thought Denny would be generous enough to choose Charlie's launch to announce his news?"

Gary looked at Dual, figured he was drunk and being sarcastic so he played along, especially as in fact he'd had his own head scrambled by the announcement. "Yeah, he sure sprang that one on us all right." He desperately tried to figure out what the story was here.

Charlie chimed in, "Personally, I was so impressed, I've comped my old buddy the last stateroom," cutting off any request by Gary to ask for the same. Anyway, Gary's instincts that had helped extend his life thus far told him there was nothing to be gained by sticking around.

"Yeah, I gotta fly to Atlanta in the morning anyway. How do you get off this floating dump, Charlie?"

"Straight up the stairs and step right off wherever you like," said Charlie acidly.

"I'll head up with you, if that's okay," said Pete.

Denny, knowing he was cornered, nodded goodnight to the pair. Charlie led the way through the smaller but noisier throng back to the corridor James had walked earlier.

Charlie unlocked the cabin door at the end, next door, in fact, to James. The wall had a bar setup next to the French-style doors that had been left open and allowed the smell and sound of the ocean to flood the immaculately carved wood room. The inlaid speakers allowed the Canvey Island classic to compete.

Charlie walked over to the bar. "Let me pour you one before I get back to my hosting duties. Jimmy, for you a little surprise. I had some Kronenbourg flown in for you—the classic original ones, not that 1666 high-octane shit." He poured and handed Denny yet one more vodka and gave himself a Jim Beam. They stood, wordlessly reflective for a few minutes; Denny seethed while James and Charlie enjoyed the quiet control of the moment. Eddie and the Hot Rods were on now: "Do Anything You Wanna Do."

"Well, Jimmy, I should get back to it. Denny, there will be someone outside your door all night to attend to any needs you might have, other than leaving this paradise, of course." He chuckled. James was half through the cabin door when Denny finally spoke.

"A word, Dual."

Charlie's head turned as he entered the corridor. James shook his head. "I got this, mate." He turned back and closed the door. He took a swig from the green bottled Alsace-made beer. "Got something to say?"

"Now it's just between us," Denny sneered. "How does it feel to have inspired so much death? All the way back to the Confederacy. After all the artists I removed from the frame, I took particular pleasure when they happened to be your friends. Not that you mattered enough to have them killed, but it didn't hurt. Like when just to keep in practice, we got rid of Darby Crash. It felt good to eliminate a punk threat. I never liked that shit music and it felt great to prove you wrong as often as possible. And of course much more recently, I couldn't help but enjoy taking out Michael Hutchence a little bit more. You were such good friends, weren't you? And so it continued—Jeff Stanley called me, whining. Why would I worry about him? One phone call later, I wasn't dwelling on that minor nuisance."

Denny walked to the open windows, sniffing the sea air along with whatever coke residue was in his nostrils. Right when he knew he had won, seeing Denny's veneer completely receded, desperately depraved, James let the beer and Scotch concoction override every logic. Even though he knew Denny was more than capable of lying about Michael Hutchence and Darby Crash, it didn't matter somehow.

"This is on behalf of rock and roll, you fucking cunt." His right leg swung back, slightly constricted by drainpipe jeans, but nevertheless picking up a violent momentum as his steel-tipped, pointed-toe, Jeffrey West boot crashed into Denny Golden's crotch. Denny let out a wracking, agonized scream and tottered backwards before he flipped over the low balcony and tumbled into the dark waves below. He struggled, clearly unable to swim in his suit; arms flapped wildly, trying in vain to stay afloat, and then he was gone.

"Man overboard," whispered James. He turned and quietly left the room as Roxy Music's "2HB" began to play.

CHAPTER 53
SIX WEEKS LATER

A pile of newspapers, entertainment trade magazines, and an eviction notice sat piled between Lainey and James on the floor of their Ocean Avenue meeting room. A largely recovered Highsmith gazed reflectively out of the window at the homeless clan on the boardwalk below and the sea beyond.

"So what are we going to do?" she asked.

"Well, looks so far like we ain't going to jail." He picked up and discarded various daily newspapers of recent weeks. "The ill-timed drowning of entrepreneur and humanitarian Denny Golden on the eve of his greatest gift to the music world appears to be accepted as a tragic accident. Perhaps the great man had a little too much to drink in his finest hour and tumbled to an untimely demise."

"Well, I guess that's good," she acknowledged, "but what about this eviction notice? All the damage from the break-in apparently broke all kinds of clauses in our lease."

He sighed. "I love this place, but honestly I don't have the strength to fight this right now. Let's start looking for a new space."

Lainey nodded.

"Did we hear back from Jim Dickinson about the Damaged demos?"

"Yes, he's interested and asked you to call him," she said.

"Brilliant. Memphis sounds so good. Terry still in the desert with the kids and Martha?"

"Yep, far as I know. Are you going to go with Aurial to see the Grammy people to talk about partnering in the trust?"

That whole trust thing didn't seem real to him yet. The fact that all that Olympian money now flowed into a musicians' trust due to Margery Cunningham's lack of interference didn't shock him. He'd always hoped her moral core might work in his favor, but still…. it was more Aurial's embracing the role that caught him off guard.

"Yeah, of course. When do I have to be there?"

"Three o'clock. Ann Landry will be there, along with Sue Ann's sister."

He idly flipped open *Daily Variety*, where on page three the headline read "Miramax Grabs Crime Scribe Leonard's Rock 'n Roll Murder Pitch. One-time Oater Author to Pen 70s Music Biz Tale."

"Oh yeah, and Charlie called. He said the Coast Guard is trying to impound the ship and can you help, please?"

find the soundtrack to this book
by going to bit.ly/oncesnd

PLAY LOUD

THANK YOU

I would never have gotten to the end without you

Denise Hamilton
Sonja Bolle
Mary Bergstrom
Ophelia Chong
Carol Cavella
Thea Constantine
Mona Kuhn
Faith Williams

Norman Lynas for the title and for helping me get out of the 70s in one piece

Susan Montford
Don Murphy
Lexi Alexander
Steve Erickson
Patrick Goldstein
Lauren Harman
Miki Warner
Christiana D'Amore
Denise Prince
Jaymes Bullet
Andrea Suarez
Adam Bennati
Mitch Schneider
Robert Wallace
Patricia Lynas
Betty Lourie
Amanda & Britt Brown
Lily J. Noonan
Tara Moross
Wolfgang Frank
The International Set

Front and back cover photographs © Mona Kuhn

Photograph of the author courtesy of Christiana D'Amore

*Cover and record photograph of "Private Number" courtesy of Stax Records
by arrangement with Concord Music Group, Inc.*

ONCE UPON A TIME IN LA

A ROCK AND ROLL NOIR NOVEL

HOWARD PAAR

Printed in Great Britain
by Amazon

44316384R00169